The Great

Ted

In 1932 Ted Wainwright broke his hay baler. Ted was not a patient man, he had no respect or sympathy for the aging baler which his meticulous not to say neurotic father had left in perfect working order. Ted inflicted certain indignities upon the humble baler resulting in a bruised foot, grazed knuckles and a broken pitchfork. Ted greatly desired a New Holland, tractor-drawn, automatic pickup baler, but that particular marvel of agricultural engineering wouldn't be invented until 1942 and the Australian Sunshine model wouldn't arrive until 1944. Ted always thought he was a man born before his time. So there it was – a stationary piece of junk surrounded by much of its once internal workings.

Life had its problems in the wheat country of Western Australia. Ted's farm was closer to Java than it was to Australia's capital. The West had no industry to speak of and while it had started its colonial history as a free colony in 1829, lack of labour and the minuscule local economy saw it succumb to the seemingly endless export of the British criminal classes. The first convict ships hulked into view in 1850 and continued their effluent discharge until 1868. Even if the colonists had opposed the creation of a penal colony, their puny numbers would have been overruled by their British masters who were fast running out of export opportunities for their least popular commodity. Western Australia had problems and Ted had problems - they were pretty much the same problems. The far away eastern states had the numbers and had instituted high tariffs to protect their fledgling industries which in turn inflated the price of imported manufactured goods; manufactured goods

1

that Ted wanted.

"Bloody mongrel, weak gutted, no brain Canberra politicians couldn't find their bums with a funnel."

Ted was given to expressing his frustrations with flawed aphorisms, mixed metaphors and meaningless maxims. He had an unpleasant knack of holding his audience captive and the reputation that preceded him now became a demonstrable fact as he assailed the local machinery dealer.

"And that's not all, Col. Bloody drifters'll rob you blind, bloody Abos won't work, bloody banks won't lend, bloody unions sucking the blood out of hard working people, bloody government's supposed to be on our side but they go and nationalise the wheat board. And this baler is how much?"

"But..."

"It's an outrage. Should be half that!"

"I..."

"Don't try and tell me the grass is greener over the rainbow."

"No."

"Sooner we get out of this bloody Federation the better for all concerned, I'm off to the bank, see if they can make a silk purse out of an iron glove."

"Nice talking with you Ted..."

Col walked back inside to the comfort of his workshop and gently let his hand run over the work smooth surface of his ancient lathe. He thought the faithful machine demonstrated more intelligence than some of his customers. At least it had the good sense not to comment on matters beyond its experience.

Ted, still smarting from his altercation with the baler, limped to his truck but driven by ever strengthening resolve he charged towards the bank. His conveyance was a 1928 A model Ford pick up, purchased new from the cash windfall that came to him after his father died. Ted was quite the man about town – if you can count Dencubbin as a town – and Ted was 26 bone-shaking miles away from its throbbing heart, which in turn was 171 axle-shattering miles from the great city of Perth.

A banner with the slogan 'Support Secession' had recently appeared on a purpose-built A frame on the back of Ted's Model A pickup. Ted was passionate about secession. He'd thrown himself heart and soul into the movement; there was no doubt in his mind that making Western Australia a sovereign nation would usher in a golden age, and solve all the problems that seemed poised to throttle his very existence.

At a rocketing 40 miles an hour, the Model A raised the dust of the sleepy town. Ted, with the throttle held firmly to the floor rehearsed his speech for the bank manager. As Ted passed the newly established State Grain Authority his dust settled on the freshly painted but misprinted sign that declared it was 'The State Gain Authority'. Mr Anthony Carlisle, the new manager, looked out the window at the impending human tornado. Carlisle had seen Ted in action before, he knew he had not the temperament for farming, he lacked the brain for a profession, perhaps politics - he was after all; a one eyed, simplistic, xenophobic, jingoistic populist – positively unhinged, but despite all these fine qualities Carlisle knew that Ted lacked the killer instinct to actually succeed.

"Ted's in town."
"Sir?" said the nameless boy.
"Never mind son, just get on the phone and get me the figures from the silos."

The nameless boy dutifully rang each of the district silos in turn and took down their total intake for the week. He then entered the tallies in the ledger and calculated the grand total.

Carlisle, meanwhile mused on his meaningless existence and the strangeness of life. As a minor civil servant he had no influence on government policy; as a local manager of the newly established Grain Authority he was universally derided; and as a low achieving graduate of a premier private school he had no friends. And with no prospect of a romantic attachment with either sex he really did wonder what life was all about. Sometimes he drifted into a miasma of cynicism and was quite palpably the most quintessential public servant of the 21st century; such a pity it was 1932.

"Thirty tons, sir."
"What?" - he drifted back.
"The silo tonnages sir, they're done."
"Well add them up,"
"They are added up, sir."
"Thirty tons - for the whole district?"

Anthony Carlisle was about to explode with exasperation when Ted, fresh from educating the bank manager, came through the door, red faced with serious intent. Ted always had serious intent, his genetic code had a double helix brimming with serious intent. Carlisle envied his purpose and resolve, but totally despised his inane reasoning and fuzzy logic.

"Morning Ted."
"Morning Tony."
Carlisle bridled at the shortening of his Christian name.
"How's the harvest?" Ted smirked.
"Not great."

"Well there's a reason for that," Ted was never more supercilious than at this moment.

"And what might that be Ted?"

"We're on strike."

"You're a farmer, Ted. You work for yourself, you can't go on strike."

"Well we are and we're not sending our grain in – may as well dump it than give it to you mongrels, so make a better offer or... or... or... the bread'll run dry."

"The bread... will... run... dry?"

Carlisle slowly restated the mixed and meaningless metaphor taking perverse pleasure in forcing Ted to explain.

"It'll be dry, it'll be out, it'll be not..." Carlisle staunchly resisted any impulse to save Ted from the confused vocabulary that swallowed his attempts to make meaning from his halting explanations.

Ted was red faced with exasperation, constricting his musculature in an attempt to bring forth the right word, and then in triumph, "We're not bringing it in! And you can tell your bosses in Canberra that the sixpence a bushel bounty is about as useful as tits on a ... cow!" He meant 'bull' and the 'Grain Authority' was a State responsibility and nothing to do with Canberra and sixpence a bushel from the Commonwealth meant a staggering windfall of three million pounds to the WA wheat industry ... but this was Ted at his moronic best.

Ted stormed out, much as he had stormed in, leaving Carlisle relishing his pyrrhic victory.

The gormless, nameless boy looked on in complete confusion; "perhaps we should pay more sir."

"I assume you've heard of this minor irritation we're calling the Great Depression, commodities are through the floor, we can buy wheat cheaper in Iceland than here, Ted wouldn't have a clue what's happening beyond the confines of his own chook pen and even there he's outclassed in intellect."

"Sir?" This last polemic having escaped his understanding.

"Ring the Silos again, maybe it's raining wheat"

The witless, gormless, nameless boy ambled to the telephone.

Ted hurtled on. Seemingly endless paddocks of wheat stubble floated all around him like a golden carpet while he reviewed his morning, "gave that machinery dealer something to think about, opened the eyes of that jumped up little bank-Johnnie, manager, my arse and Carlisle he'll be wanting to hear more on the subject."

Without conscious thought Ted slammed on the brakes, stopped, found reverse gear, accelerated recklessly backwards and slammed on the brakes again. He looked out the window and his jaw dropped, he'd seen emus before, they were quite common but what seemed like 10,000 emus calmly grazing was a bewildering sight. Ted took it all in.

Power in Perth

It seemed that all of the 562 Perth policemen had been called out to control the riot at the State Bank of Western Australia. Policeman that were used to friendlier times, when the criminals were just the usual suspects and mostly in gaol and when the 150 or so Aboriginal people in the city were peaceable types despite their appalling treatment at the hands of the white invaders. It was a time when the average constable was regarded as a pillar of decency who played his part in holding the community together.

The increasing number of riots was confusing, it seemed they had only just dealt with the riot at the Treasury Building. These were the good people who should be swimming at the beach or at home playing parlour games and drinking beer but they were here, yelling abuse and trying to force their way into government buildings, pushing and goading the police who were now their enemies.

The adrenalin rush on both sides surged, push repaid with shove, abuse repaid with threat, fear and tension rising as the mounted troops, still holding back, stood ready to disperse the crowd should things turn ugly. They lived in interesting times. 2300 miles away in Sydney the New South Wales premier Jack Lang had defaulted on Government bonds held by British Banks. Lang had argued that the interest rate on their loans should be reduced to zero just as the Brits had convinced the Americans to reduce their rate to zero. Despite this rational, laudable and very credible argument, Lang failed. The Commonwealth Bank of Australia was refusing the States ongoing credit and the Commonwealth Government having agreed to pay off the British bankers, had started a recovery action against the NSW Government in the courts. Small wonder there was a run on the Bank of NSW and now Premier Mitchell was facing a similar crisis in Western Australia.

Premier Mitchell was not one for heroics, he watched the common men demonstrating their disgust for his government from the safety of a first storey window. Mitchell didn't like the common man, he found him, well, common. The Premier had waited until the mounted police arrived before venturing outside to address the crowd. He cursed his most senior minister, John Scaddan for going north to stir the possum at a secession rally at Jundulup, leaving him only the less impressive Hal Colbatch for support. The two politicians looked nervous, they had to put on the performance of their lives to calm the crowd, some angry over the mass unemployment and others worried that the banking system would collapse, all of them looking for someone to blame and maybe someone to hurt. Politicians are curiously allergic to pain.

Approaching the glass pane in the door Mitchell took a precautionary look through the unfrosted glass centre of the 'a' in 'Bank' and was reassured by 5 lines of burly constables between himself and the seething crowd. He took a deep breath opened the door and led Colbatch and two aides onto the steps of the bank.

The crowd erupted with, "where's our money ?" "where's our jobs?" Mitchell groaned audibly." He raised his hands for silence, there was no response, he tried the public address system with; "My good friends." Jeers and derisive laughter followed. He thought himself lucky at that point that he couldn't be ridiculed with working class doggerel since nothing much rhymes with 'Mitchell', but never underestimate the working class. Several hand painted signs appeared declaring 'This is Mitches Hell' (missing apostrophe noted) and 'Mitch comes just before HELL'. He persisted with his call for quiet and in a lull in the commotion he managed to break in with, "Good people of Western Australia, once again we have been forgotten by Canberra and the Lyons' Government *(they're listening, excellent scapegoat opportunity)* the Lyons' Government cares only for the Eastern States *(avoid specifics, speak in generalities)* our economy is being raped and plundered by unfair import tariffs. Tariffs that swell the cankerous coffers in Canberra *(hyperbole and alliteration, yes, keep it up, keep it up)* It is at this time in our history *(unfortunate cough, allowing interjection)*

"Where's our savings?" "Yeah answer that one!"

"Your savings are absolutely secure, guaranteed by the rock solid bank of Western Australia *(back to the scapegoating)* we stand firm, we will not have any fancy Eastern Bankers meddling with the savings of the good people of Western Australia *(god knows what that means, quick breath)* your Government has everything under control."

"You couldn't control your thirst in a brewery!"

(moronic remark, smile, ignore and move on)

"I personally guarantee your savings and the continued good management of this rock solid bank, I G U A R A N T E E *(spell it out for the dummies)* guarantee that Joe Lyons will join a monastery before one penny is lost from the savings of ordinary West Australians." *(at last a laugh, quick, more about Lyons)* "Joe Lyons, Ladies and Gentlemen, Joe Lyons needs that tariff money from your pockets, with 11 little mouths to feed he needs our support, I am assured Ladies and Gentlemen that no Canberra concubines were involved, Mrs Lyons did it all by herself, *(pause)* well almost *(laughter, excellent risqué joke now go for the jugular)*. As you all know, Joe Lyons has emerged as Prime Minister after a typical Labour bar room brawl *(good Catholic, must be a big drinker)* which left the remnants of the Scullin labour machine and those ratbags from the Lang camp, unconscious and bleeding on the tiles ready to be hosed out like the shiftless swill they are." *(they love it, I should write more of my own speeches)*. "If there is one singular difference between my conservative Government and the Labour Party, it is this: we know how to manage money, we know how to balance the books and we know how to keep your savings safe. Ladies and Gentlemen, this afternoon you can go home to your families, to your wives, husbands and children secure in the knowledge that Western Australia is under good management." *(applause, even a 'good on yer mate' and they're satisfied, mollified, pacified ... mission accomplished)*. Mitchell's aide was applauding wildly when he felt a jab from the Premiers elbow. "Set up a meeting with the Commonwealth Bank."

"Sir?"

"We're broke you bloody fool. Two more weeks and we're under and get Scaddan back here, we might just need his expertise to sort this mess, Christ why couldn't I be born in 1950!"

The future is always a brighter place; for Ted it was the baler, for Premier Mitchell it was good times with full employment, for Joe Lyons, even though he didn't know it, a leap to 1967 and a heart transplant would have been a cracking good idea.

Just to round out the Premier's day he returned to the comfort of his office only to find a telegram from a group of farmers declaring that they were on strike and boycotting the newly formed State Grain Authority. *Brilliant*. He slumped in his chair and mused on his feckless electors; poorly educated farmers, his so called power base, what did they know of the cost of mass unemployment, of struggling with the economics of Keynes or continuing with the conservative strictures of rigidly balanced budgets. What it meant to be in power was disturbing, for like the man he had just publicly lambasted for ineptitude he also wished for defeat so that he might share a little happiness with his wife before public life stole his soul as well as his health. Unknown to Mitchell, Lyons had written as much to his wife Edith. But the two men were locked in a foolish struggle for power, from which there was no obvious escape.

The Pub

Dencubbin had only one pub, unusual in alcohol obsessed Australia, east or west. The standard was at least two, one slightly more refined, the other where there was hardly enough room to swing a punch on a Friday night as eager patrons crowded the bar. The pub was strictly a male domain except for the female publican who dominated the proceedings; 'incongruence' is as much embedded in Australian culture as 'tautology' is in its political speeches.

Ted and his associates met at the Dencubbin Hotel. Australians commonly refer to their friends as 'mates', but mateship implies support, a close companion, and comradeship; which is all quite difficult because a close companion could be a homo and a comrade could be a commo. Anyway Ted had associates, namely Maurie and Bill that he used in pursuit of his current obsession and they met at the same table at the Dencubbin Hotel a couple of times a week.

Maurie could only be described as a kindly imbecile, easily duped and lacking in any kind of analytical ability. True he was a successful farmer with a good eye for stock but the fact that he had managed to hang on to 'Getalong', his family property, was more due to the incompetence of local con-men than to any innate common sense possessed by Maurie Mason.
Bill on the other hand was solid, sensible and talented and with higher education could have been a good engineer. Bill had known Ted since his arrival in the wheat country and found himself falling in behind what sounded to be the sensible causes that Ted put forward with irresistible enthusiasm. Bill had a

happy family, a devoted wife and a loving daughter, Janet, who was worryingly intelligent. Janet worked for the local paper and though she wrote mostly about the agricultural show, the local Red Cross, the Hospital Committee and freakish events like two headed calves, she had ambitions way beyond Dencubbin.

Ted called out, "The usual Molly" as he came through the door removing his Akubra and slapping it against his moleskins, an action more about his social status than the removal of any dust. He made for the usual table and Molly arrived with the usual 3 beers. "Pulled 'em just for you Teddy Bear," said Molly as she set down the tray and uncovered some complimentary cheese and biscuits.

When Molly had served the refreshment and hurried back to the bar, Bill said, "I think she's sweet on you Ted."

"Molly's just a barmaid, just a sweet talking barmaid," snapped Ted.

"Alright, alright." sighed Bill.

Ted reached for his beer and took a long sip as if to extinguish any further commentary on the subject.

Then, as if Molly had never existed, Ted launched headlong into the briefing. "Well we've got the Grain Authority on the run, that Carlisle never knew what hit him, told him there'll be no straw coming to the hive."

"What?" said Maurie.

"The grain Maurie. We're not sending it in!" Bill explained.

"How long are we not sending it in for Ted?"

"We've been over this Maurie; for as long as it takes!"

"Oh," squeaked Maurie.

Bill was always slow to speak and asked obvious questions: "Do you think the boycott will be enough Ted?"

"I told them we're as committed as two peas in the hand!" He hadn't.

"I said that we'd see them freeze in hell before we hand over any grain!" He grossly exaggerated.

"Now we've got to get the message to the politicians", he said.

Maurie gave his most puzzled look and having a premonition that he was again asking a stupid question, said "How do we do that Ted?" His premonition, although justified, was wrong, this was in fact the most sensible, if blindingly obvious question available. Maurie had popped one in at last, it was advantage server.

Ted was now thinking hard, looking for a quick return, he fumbled with "if we could just meet them face to face, Mitchell and Scaddan and talk to them man to man." The ball dribbled into the net.

Maurie smiled in triumph.

Bill's voice volleyed in "You know, I reckon we should get Janet in on this, she has connections with the papers in Perth and she's working late tonight."

Game set and match and the end of the tennis metaphors.

Janet

The associates adjourned to the building next door that housed the local paper and laid out their problem for Janet's consideration.

Janet was independent and opportunistic, she had grown up with all the toughness that comes from being part of a farming family in hard times. She embodied the 'catch and kill your own' mentality that makes good journalists and great entrepreneurs. Her eyes flashed as she suggested "The State Funeral, ... how about the State Funeral?"

"It died? I knew it was in bad shape but ..." Maurie was mercifully cut off mid sentence by three looks of complete derision.

Janet sailed on, "The State Funeral for Edith Cowan, it's next Tuesday."

Ted said what the others were thinking, "And who's Edith Cowan when she's at home?"

Janet gave a brief sigh, she was was used to the parochialism that dominated her world. "She's only the greatest woman of the century, first woman member of parliament, social reformer, welfare campaigner. She's just died and all the leading politicians will be at her funeral. You could grab them there. But if you're going, I'm coming with you."

The associates nodded their assent and very, very early Tuesday morning they assembled for the trip to Perth. Maurie's Chevrolet, that wonder of automotive comfort that was 'softer than the lounge chairs at home' was washed and polished, its bow tie marque gleaming, ready to make a good impression on Janet. Maurie made to open the front door for her while yabbering that this was the Chevrolet six cylinder that had been produced at the price of a four cylinder. Janet glazed over and darted into the back seat.

The gruelling trip over rutted roads was a full eight and a half hours, most of which passed in silence. Maurie's attempts at small talk with Janet met with monosyllabic replies, the Chev obligingly filled the silence with the drumming of rubber on road that seemed to prohibit conversation.

Maurie was unused to city traffic, so many streets, so many cars, so many wrong turns, with Ted yelling so many instructions that Maurie was reduced to a wobbling jelly.

Ted was still going on when they pulled up at the cemetery. "Over the bridge and turn left, it's not hard, Jesus look at the time!"

Maurie mumbled his protests as they walked toward the crowd. Janet had managed to get photographs of Mitchell and Scaddan, for everyone and they looked at them as they walked.

Both men had been photographed wearing black suits and black ties. As they surveyed the crowd they saw nothing but men in black suits and black ties.

Ted, feeling the thrill of being in charge, gave his final orders. "Everyone take a good look at the photos, we'll split up, whoever finds him try and give a signal, wave a hat or something, and we'll come over.

Now remember, it's 'Mr Mitchell we're the concerned farmers that keep writing to you, we think the grain authority is a bad idea and we want your commitment to dismantle it as soon as possible.'"

The troops spread out and encircled the flock like well trained sheepdogs while the priest droned through the service followed by a lengthy eulogy from an MP cashing in on Edith's lifetime of service.

The sheepdogs scanned male faces and compared them to their

photographs, Maurie thought he'd nailed it and approached a likely suspect and launched into "Mr Mitchell ..." Unfortunately he was not Mr Mitchell and the man's wife wheeled round on Maurie, koshed him with her umbrella and demanded he show some respect. Maurie suitably chastened, yelped and ran on. Janet meanwhile was distracted by the eulogy and started to see herself receiving similar accolades. In a dreamlike state she was a latter day Jean d'Arc riding through the adoring crowd. When the eulogy finished with "A Great West Australian Woman" Janet jerked back to reality and continued the search.

Ted was now accosting people, seeking Mitchell's whereabouts. To most of the mourners Ted was an irritating noise, until one slightly less grief struck gentleman pointed him to the official party. To Ted's great distress he was at least a hundred yards away from Mitchell and he could see Maurie approaching him. He surged into the crowd, a man possessed.

Maurie, confident he had his man this time, ran up panting "Mr Mitchell."

"Yes."

"Crikey it's really you."

"To be sure."

"Crikey, I'm Maurie, Maurie Mason" He grabbed Mitchell's hand and pumped his arm vigorously.

"Pleased to meet you Maurie."

"Crikey ... I mean crikey ... lovely day for a funeral."

"We're very fortunate."

"I'm Maurie, Maurie Mason."

"Without doubt."

"What do you think of Bradman?"

"Fine Batsman."

Ted arrived just in time to hear Maurie's final blathering and broke in with "Mr Mitchell I'm Ted Wainwright"

"Friend of Maurie's are you?"

"No ... Yes ... I mean... "

"Goodness me is that the time, I must be off, very important meeting" and with a tip of his hat he disappeared into a waiting car leaving an aide to deal with the hapless Maurie and the exasperated Ted.

The aide took their details and assured them the Premier would write to them and give their concerns his full attention. He didn't.

Ted was developing a nice shade of purple when he turned to Maurie. Angry, furious, enraged but really closer to apoplectic and verging on homicidal, Maurie was only narrowly saved from extinction by the arrival of Bill and Janet.

"You lost him, you had him right there and you lost him, ... 'What do you think of Bradman?'

I don't believe it, we come all this way and you ask him about Bradman."

The trip home was funereally quiet.

Hour after grinding hour, the Chevrolet jolted towards home, Janet fidgeted in her seat, Maurie offered her a cushion, she declined with a sardonic smile that had all the grace and charm of a bayonet. Maurie had never felt so stupid in his life, even more stupid than when he was trying to see how much petrol was in a 44 gallon drum, he had the match on the striker when his aging mother grabbed his hand, narrowly preventing his incendiary demise. She told the vicar, he told his wife, she published it to the world. He stayed at home for months to avoid the ridicule. If he had known anything about theology he would have realised that he was the special favourite of Ridic, the God of ridicule, the cruellest of deities and absolutely unshakable. In Maurie, the merciless Ridic had found the perfect vehicle for his malicious portrayals, worse than Puck who at least demonstrated a bit of humour at the expense of

Titania and Bottom, Ridic was just plain mean. The lesser known son of Hades would later laugh himself silly as he perpetrated a mining boom on Western Australia. Watching men spend their lives eating dust to gain the earth's supposed treasures, it really did tickle his fancy.

Meanwhile, Maurie was just too good to be true, Ridic hardly had to try.

It was dusk as the Chevrolet, trailed by its orange dust plume, was passing Baker's place. Ted had done his best to remain sullen, not a word in eight hours but now the sight that had intrigued him the week before, replayed before his eyes.

"Stop the car Maurie!"

"I really am sorry Ted."

"Just stop the car you ..., look out the window!"

As the dust settled and the scene came into focus the other three exhausted travellers looked in amazement.

"Christ", said Bill "I've never seen so many."

"There's thousands," said Janet.

"Millions," said Maurie. This particular piece of idiotic innumeracy passed unnoticed as they all took account of the feathered gathering.

"Emus," said Ted, I knew they'd come for a reason, they're going to help us win the referendum.

Janet had caught the plan as if by telepathic transfer. "Bloody emus!" she said with a sense of excitement, relishing the campaign ahead. Her father, always plodding two steps behind had an each way bet with a half angry, half expectant, "Bloody Emus". Maurie, still in the previous paddock offered a bemused and questioning "Bloody Emus?"

Janet sailed straight passed explanation and right into strategy.

"We'll make this the biggest story ever. First we make sure they hang around, everyone's got plenty of wheat put aside, so we feed them. Then we break the story that the wheat belt is being devastated by emus in plague proportions. We demand action from the State Government, we demand..."

"You've got it girl, we make a huge noise that only the Army can deal with this plague and that Canberra must come and help, they won't of course, it's completely stupid, but we ..."

"We tell the papers it's typical, the only time we ask for help and the Australian Government won't do shit for us..."

"Janet!..."

"Sorry Dad, anyway they won't come, it'll make Federation look like the farce it is and we've got the referendum sewn up. Somebody give me a phone!"

Maurie decided, despite the feeling in his stomach that indicated a completely contrary move, to remind Janet that they were in the car and that cars don't have phones.

More sardonic looks and rolling eyes, Maurie hastily crunched the Chev into first and drove on.

Dreams and Visions

Janet said goodnight to her father and dropped into bed, she looked around her simple room, her first published piece of newsprint framed and hanging proudly on the white lining boards, a picture of Edith Cowan and just to the right and on top of her drawers her childhood dolls sitting up having a tea party. She routinely packed the dolls away under the bed but her mother routinely ferreted them out again and put them on display, as if to say, you're still my little girl.

A 'little girl' she was not and had not been since early childhood. She had always preferred the company of men, the coarseness, the larrikin spirit but most of all the apparent freedom to do whatever you wanted. She shook her head at the dolls and smiled, tomorrow was Saturday and she had a plan.

In the open country that is the wheat belt the sun rises triumphant and early. Eight hundred miles to the South West the rise is more gradual as the early sun filters through the eucalyptus forest giants. Janet squinted at her east facing window, rose quickly, dressed and was out to the saddling yard before her mother could enforce the ritual three course breakfast.

Like most farms in the 30s Janet's family had a couple of Aboriginal stockmen. She loved them for their passion and skill with horses, was distressed that they worked for next to nothing and was fascinated by their secretive customs. She quizzed them and she heard their dreamtime stories but there was no language to explain the depth of meaning, the unbreakable connection to their people and their country. These things were autonomic like a beating heart and seemed not to require analysis, deconstruction, demythologising or remythologising or any of the other so called aids to understanding that were on an inexorable rise in white society. This morning she had persuaded them to take her to the dreaming rock. They had been reluctant. Steve claimed, "Secret Men's Business, Miss." Fred said, "mmm. "But these were friends of 20 years and they eventually agreed that she should climb by herself and never speak of it to anyone.

They mounted the chestnuts and walked them out the gate, Janet leaning down in the saddle to close and latch it without stopping, as she had done since she'd turned twelve.
She loved riding, especially with Steve and Fred, they were good company and told her the stories that circulated through the local shearing sheds. Steve was the teller of stories, Fred was the listener. Steve laid his reins on his horse's neck and sat back in the saddle with his arms folded. The story began, "you know that dickhead man?" Janet knew the one, an objectionable piece of work conveniently named Dickman. Steve told of a day that 'Mr Dickhead' had gone fencing. He towed a trailer with all the fencing gear behind his Fordson F model tractor ...
[The F Model was a steel wheeled labour saving wonder complete with optional mudguards. Who cared if Henry Ford was an industrial fascist, he sure made cheap tractors, he had exported thousand of F models to Britain during the Great War and his mass production technology just kept on spewing them out.]

... Mr D spent the day splitting and drilling posts, digging post holes, tamping in the posts and finally running and straining the wires. The sun was going down as he stepped back to admire his work. As he took his first step towards his beloved tractor he realised to his horror that it was on the wrong side of the fence with no way to get through, except to cut the perfectly strained wires. Steve had told this story many times and Fred had heard it just as many but he still laughed so hard that he nearly fell off his horse. Mr D was not popular, he mistreated his workers, refused to pay them unless they worked 7 days a week and generally behaved like a complete know all 'dickhead' during shearing. Revenge, although minor was sweet. Janet laughed and told them they were mean to make fun of such a nice man. They laughed.

The rock came into view, an unusual monolith that provided panoramic views of the district. Like many places that give you an instant sense of awe, it had a ritual importance to the local Aborigines. Not so different to the Europeans who conduct their rituals in places that give you a sense of awe. Venerated spaces that saw medieval bishop compete with medieval bishop to build the tallest monument to obsolescence. Workers regularly died as the non buttressed walls bellied out and collapsed; forced apart as the heavy roof timbers applied increasing and unsustainable pressure. Cathedrals were irony on steroids. Built to proclaim the GOOD NEWS to the peasants, but so many would die under the collapsing structures. Their exorbitant cost meant no money for the relief of the poor while bishops justified their excesses by pointing to the elaborate carvings that made bible stories accessible to the illiterate masses. The Dreaming Rock on the other hand was just there and made you go silent and listen, no payment or further intervention required.

The horses stopped instinctively at the base of the rock, the riders dismounted and led their ponies into the shade. Janet nodded her thanks to Steve and Fred as she handed Steve the reins, then turned to start the climb. Steve spoke softly, "You be careful up there Miss." Janet waved a hand in acknowledgement without turning around. She climbed steadily for about 15 minutes sweating heavily in the mid morning sun. The summit provided natural places to sit and look out over the surrounding country, she sat and looked and breathed in the view, a long intoxicating breath. She closed her eyes and it seemed as if thousands of years of planetary history both past and future spread out before her with such speed that her brain could not store it all. Countless generations before her had done exactly the same thing and their experience, good or bad, meant inevitable change. As she looked and breathed ever more deeply the kaleidoscope slowed, a band started to play 'Beyond The Blue Horizon' and she saw herself in a classy bar on the water's edge, 'lies a beautiful day', as she turned back to the table the drop dead handsome man seated beside her, 'goodbye to things that bore me', handed her a cocktail. They talked and laughed and seemed to be the most confident and complete couple on the concourse. 'Joy is waiting for me', the scene drifted into an art gallery where they walked arm in arm deciding what to buy. 'I see a new horizon', 'My life has only begun,' Beyond the blue horizon lies a rising sun'. Wow all this and set to music by Irving Berlin ... (of course Irving didn't write 'Beyond the Blue Horizon' but Janet knew he'd written what seemed like, just about everything else, except for that strange Gershwin music, so she felt safe in her assumption.)

The experience on the rock was not what she expected but she was far from disappointed, Janet was not the deeply spiritual type she, was more the wild and spirited type and the vision fulfilled her dream of big city excitement and success. A vision of the Rainbow Serpent's creation rampage would have been OK but this was so much better, this was her, really, deeply, truly HER. She knew that it meant a break with family and friends and much loved mates but she was ready. She knew that in Dencubbin she could only ever hope to write stories about the birth of two headed calves and endless tedium about soil moisture and power farming, it just wasn't enough. She was ready for the big editorials, the spin and sometimes even the truth, but definitely the issues that made history. Steve and Fred waiting patiently below could look back on 60,000 years of history that didn't need making, it just was and always would be.

Janet came down smiling, her companions asked no questions, they knew more than they showed and feared for her more than they said. The horses took them home as horses do and on the way they passed Baker's place and once again the incredible flock of emus. Steve and Fred spontaneously broke into emu imitations and they all laughed at the silly caricatures, just as children will laugh at a house brick or a finger once they are overtaken by a laughing fit.

Janet could readily appreciate the humour but she had more serious plans, she had already mapped out the first three stories, each building on the other to make the great emu plague an issue of national importance. She would carefully build public outcry at government inaction and create the environment where the State could only blame the Commonwealth and the Commonwealth would reasonably ignore public opinion to their ultimate peril. She had planned a local secession rally where Treasurer Scaddan would be invited as the keynote speaker. Scaddan's presence alone would allow her to turn an insignificant district meeting into what would seem like a major State event and with pictures of the Emu Menace to add to the drama, she had something that the newsreels would grab with both hands.

Janet had never tried Bayer's Heroin, quite legal in Australia for a short while around 1900, and didn't even know about cocaine or dexamphetamine but the adrenalin that was surging through her body was a feeling she liked very much.

The horses picked up the pace as they sensed the nearness of home and anticipated the very bearable lightness of being that would follow unsaddling and then, the rolling. No human knows what delights surge through the equine body and brain when the back touches the ground and the aching legs float in the air. Bayer's Heroin was two shillings and sixpence a pint, but rolling was free in every sense.

Steve and Fred never let the horses canter home, they were natural horsemen, always in control, their horses ever ready to respond to their subtle commands, the rein on the neck, the pitching of their body weight, and on occasion the jab of the spurs when their mounts momentarily forgot the usual protocols. They had explained to Janet when, as a child she complained that they would hurt the horses that, in a horse, the wire from the pain to the brain is very thin and often rusty. This had completely satisfied her childhood sensibilities and as an adult she knew that the need for equine control was ultimately for her own safety and overruled any foolish squeamishness. She smiled to herself as she mused on these memories but she had to get back for a planning meeting with Ted, Bill and Maurie.

"Thanks for a great morning fellas but I've got to get home." She clicked her tongue and raised her heels and she was into a canter leaving the two stockmen to their gentle pace. They smiled to each other, "Same since she was a kid", said Steve. "Mmm" said Fred.

Janet pulled up at the house paddock fence, swung down and tied her horse to a post for Steve to look after. The strategy for the emu campaign was brewing stronger than ever as she ran up to the house.

Ted, Bill and the Maurie were seated around the kitchen table with Janet's mother fussing over them pouring tea and getting fresh scones from the fuel stove. Maurie rose when Janet entered; his mother had failed to give him brains but she had drilled him till he dropped, in good manners. Janet pulled up a chair, assiduously avoiding eye contact with Maurie. "We've only just started luv", said her father, "You haven't missed anything."

"Thanks Dad."

Janet was still radiant from the excitement at the dreaming rock and her face flushed from cantering into the morning breeze. Her father smiled at her, conveying his pride and approval. Bill thought her the most beautiful creature on earth and was drifting along on a soft cloud of proud parenthood while her mother, observing these 'symptoms' and knowing that she had missed breakfast, thought in a horror filled moment, that she might be pregnant. Janet would normally have deferred to the men present to open the conversation but the recent confirmation of her future propelled her into action.

"I've got something growing in my (her mother dropped the sugar bowl) mind. Tell me what you think. We write to Scaddan and invite him out here for a combined election and secession rally. We let him know about the emus and that we can guarantee newsreel coverage, complete with an emu stampede. We throw him some Dorothy Dix questions and let him take the running on challenging the Feds to come and help."

Ted was a little peeved that it wasn't his idea but conceded that it was brilliant.

"Though," he countered, "we need a big crowd, how can we guarantee a good turn-up?"

"If everyone is willing to kick in … we put on a free feed, advertise lucky door prizes and I think I can get..." she held up a finger indicating that they should wait a minute, hurried to her room and returned with a handbill that she flattened on the table.

"Not Stiffy and Mo, that's brilliant." Ted could hardly say the words he was so flabbergasted.

"Well just Mo, they sort of don't get on any more and Fullers Theatre had to close but he..."

"Is that, Mo as in Mo from McCackie's Mansion on the radio?"
said Maurie.

"Yes, and he ..."

"He is so funny" said Maurie.

"Well he..."

"I'm sorry dear but I think he's crude!" her mother cut in.

"I know Mum. You say that every week."

"So unnecessary!" said her mother.

Janet finally continued, "NOW he's going to be in Perth and my
contact says he's pretty cranky with the Federal Government
after Jack Beasley refused to support out of work actors".

"Jack Beasley?"

Long story. He's a Lang supporter. I think he's a bit of a
commo, which makes no sense. Anyway Roy Rene, that's Mo,
isn't fond of the Feds and we might be able to get him out here
for a 30 minute show."

"We don't want communists here Janet," said her mother.

"Mo's not a communist mum that's ...oh never mind."

"Are you sure about all that?" said Bill sounding a note of
fatherly caution.

"No, but one way or another I'll get him here."

"Now we need to book the biggest pub in the district."

I'll do that."

"Thanks Ted."

"Mum could you get the CWA to cater?"

"I don't know dear, the CWA is non-political."

"Just think of it as entertainment for the community."

"If you say so dear."

"I do say so mum."

"Dad you're good mates with the local member, do you think he
could deliver our invitation to Scaddan in person and make sure
he accepts."

"Good as done."

"You never told me you were good mates with Harry Denison," said Ted.

"You never asked," replied Bill.

"And Maurie could you feed those emus and make sure we know where to find them when we want them."

"I can do that ... and Janet would you like to come over and cook dinner for me next week?"

"My cooking would poison you Maurie."...A long silent pause was finally broken by an irrelevant and intentionally diverting story from Janet. "Did everyone read about the opening of the Sydney Harbour Bridge, they're ready to cut the ribbon, Premier Lang and all the officials are there, thousands of people are waiting to walk across the bridge and that lunatic from the fascist New Guard, Captain de Groot, gallops in on a horse and cuts the ribbon with his sword. They actually tie it back together so Lang can cut it officially. Everyone was cranky as hell but God it must have been funny. And can you believe it the cameraman missed de Groot cutting it? Probably the most exciting thing he'll ever have the opportunity to film and he's facing the wrong way. Now, I'm going to write the articles announcing the events and get all the pre-publicity in place. Are we done?"

There were nods all round. Janet made a speedy exit and so began The Great Emu War.

The Rally

Janet was as good as her word, ambition was driving her like a drug, she hardly slept, she ran her parent's phone bill sky high and pounded her portable typewriter mercilessly. The articles came thick and fast as she churned out the kind of populist propaganda that she knew would unite the people of Western Australia against a perceived common enemy. She used the politics of fear as if it was inherent in her genes. Seventy-five years later another Western Australian woman would write about such politics as the incarnation of evil. Carmen Lawrence was probably the absolute antithesis of Janet but Janet was about to ride an unparalleled wave of success; quite the opposite of Carmen's much lamented and undeserved fall from grace.

Janet arranged for copies of The West Australian, The Geraldton Guardian, The Kalgoorlie Miner, The Fremantle Herald, The Sunday Times, The Mirror, The Sydney Morning Herald and The Canberra Times to be delivered for the next 8 weeks and although it went against the grain she eventually included The Westralian Worker, just to see if that 'Red Rag' would carry her stories.

With headlines like:

Emus Destroy Crops and Livelihoods
Canberra Sleeps While WA Invaded
WA Abandoned to Fight the Emu Menace Alone
Schools Consider Closure

Emus threaten Child Safety
Emu Numbers Worse Than Originally Feared
Lady Bowlers Chased from Greens by Excited Emu Drakes
Schools Threatened, Children Kept Inside
Joe Lyons Vacillates While the West is Eaten Alive

it was small wonder that she was well pleased with the circulation.

Janet sent telegrams to every news service in the world describing a plague of biblical proportions and offering an unauthorised syndication of the as yet unshot, unscheduled and in fact unintended, (except by Janet) Movietone Newsreel footage of the plague. She then wrote to Movietone including clippings of all her articles and return telegrams from foreign news services expressing interest in a syndication deal. She then 'plagued' her only contact in the Perth media gallery until he agreed to independently substantiate the story with Movietone, all in all a good morning's work.

Next she had to land the famous comedian Mo McCackie, known off stage as Roy Rene but legally as Harry Van der Sluice. She knew that Rene had a serious side and that he had married about 3 years ago but that was the sum total of her knowledge. She rang her Perth journalist colleague Herbert Potter, to ask yet another favour. She knew the goodwill was wearing thin and that as a woman she was playing a dangerous game. Intimating a libertarian attitude with a flirtatious turn of phrase was definitely a short term strategy that might buy one more favour from a randy journalist but after that her status would be downgraded to, 'uncooperative'.

Fortunately, Herbert's sex drive was still racing far ahead of anything that resembled common sense and after Janet's promise to get together for a drink, he rang Rene's hotel. He lied to the switch girl, saying he was the West Australian features editor, and was immediately put through. He then convinced Rene that he was the features editor and that he would like to write a serious story about Rene's life. The rest was easy, hook Rene on the need for secession, guarantee newsreel coverage alongside the WA Treasurer and then take him to the wheat country. Nice feature piece, a genuine exclusive, a very sexy girl and with any luck his boss might even make him the actual features editor.

Came the day, John Scaddan, Roy Rene, Movietone News, an agitated populace and the Emus, all the ducks were lined up. The free beer and sausages worked a treat, five hundred and twenty eight people imbued with Janet's populist journalism crammed into the pub, Roy Rene put them at ease and Scaddan twisted an ordinary event into a constitutional crisis.

"Ladies and gentlemen thank-you for your invitation to the real heart of Western Australia, as a senior minister of this great State and soon, God willing, this great independent nation, I am proud to be here with the finest farmers in the world. Ladies and gentlemen, I want to put before you this evening a vision for the future, for too long the West has been held back by the parochial interests of the Eastern States, held back by import Tariffs. Tariffs, who do they protect? Eastern manufacturers Who do they disadvantage? Western Australian farmers, that's right the people in this room who labour under the scorching sun to feed the Nation and export to the world. There is no doubt in my mind that the West will be a great nation, the bread basket of Asia and a quarry for the planet."

Janet nudged Maurie, cueing his scripted contribution.

"Too right"

Ted launched in with his question: "Mr Scaddan, in this region we are experiencing an invasion by the biggest mob of emus this state has ever seen. It's a plague. We're up the creek with our pants down. Crops are being eaten and trampled, they're moving like locusts, destroying everything in their path. What would an independent Western Australia do in such an emergency?"

Scaddan seized the moment: "As an independent power we would have our own army and we would use them immediately to counter such a crisis."

Ted's follow on, triggered an avalanche: "But Mr Scaddan this is happening right now and where is the Australian Army? No doubt doing marching drill. I reckon they should be called out now!"

"Call out the Army!" yelled various stooges.

"Use our soldiers!" roared the planted agitators.

"Get the job done!" cried at least 10 provocateurs.

"Call out the Army!" chanted a growing mob of completely spontaneous citizens.

"And the Navy!" This last triumph, from Maurie.

Scaddan took the only course open to him: "The Federal Government … The Federal Government … The Federal Government. Those indolent self serving politicians will do what they always do for Western Australia …

Absolutely Nothing. That's right. Nothing.

The usual run around, the red tape and excuses.

Too costly,

Too hard,

Too far away!

But we'll ask, be assured of that.

We'll ask!"

Movietone got great footage of the rally, Rene's imitations of the progeny of lady bowlers sired by emus caused near hysteria as he attempted to walk straight, but due to the inherited bowling bias kept turning to the right. The crew were then treated to a carefully arranged Emu tour, complete with broken fences, devastated paddocks and weeping farmers. The freight train was rolling and gathering momentum with incredible speed.

In Perth

John Scaddan was feeling incredibly pleased with himself. He was in that glorious political situation where he just could not lose. He laid it out for Premier Mitchell. This was the issue they had been searching for, a chance to embarrass the Federal Government, bolster their electoral position and put the secession movement in the spotlight. In essence they would send a request for troops to Canberra, if Canberra rejected their request it would underline the failure of Federation and in the unlikely event that they did send troops it would be because they had been bludgeoned into it and the Mitchell/Scaddan Government would drive home the fact that they had to drag the Federal Government kicking and screaming into the The Great Emu War.

Mitchell took the bit between his teeth and tabled a non-existent report in parliament on the extent of the emu plague. He laid down the gauntlet to the Federal Government to send in the troops to deal with the emu menace. No one would ever read the 'report', not when the movietone news feature had been playing in cinemas around Australia and overdubbed for syndication in five languages.

Janet had already prepared a story for simultaneous publication. It read like a press release from Mitchell's office and Mitchell's press secretary would later take the credit for this firebrand rhetoric and the intense public reaction that it stirred.

In Dencubbin

The celebrations were in full swing in the pub. Janet had just delivered the West Australian which featured her actual journalist's story complete with her byline.

The Great Emu War
Action at Last

by Janet Cole

Ted, Bill and Maurie had sat stunned for some minutes while the breadth of their success slowly dawned.

Ted finally opened his mouth, "we did it, we bloody did it!"

"Shout the bar Maurie." said Bill with a wry smile.

"The Drinks are on me!" shouted Maurie.

Maurie's enthusiasm was short lived as thirsty patrons thronged the bar, he corrected the directive with, "Just middies, all right fellas ... and no seconds." But as always, free alcohol spawned a playful spirit and Maurie was wilfully ignored, raised shoulder high and paraded round the bar, still shouting something about restraint. Of course he couldn't be heard over the continuing chorus of 'Hooray for Maurie, Hooray at last, Hooray for Maurie, he's the horse's arse.'

In Canberra

The newsreel had been seen, the telegram demanding an armed response to the emu menace had been received and was about to be given to the Prime Minister, Joseph Lyons. The PM was enjoying a rare pleasure; his wife and 13 children were at the Lodge about to dine with a former Prime Minister Billy Hughes.

The Lyons family lived mainly in Melbourne for, while Canberra was the National Capital, there wasn't much there. The Temporary Parliament House hadn't opened for business until 1928 and the funds available to realise the dream of Walter and Marion Griffin to build a modern city that drew on its natural surroundings for inspiration were thin indeed. The Griffins were outstanding American architects. Having met while working at the renowned Frank Lloyd Wright Studio in Chicago, they had won the contest for an Australian National Capital design in 1912. Things moved slowly for the Griffins. Construction had commenced on the ambitious Australian War Memorial, but it was not to the Griffin's ziggurat design nor was its function what they had described and to add insult to injury it didn't take pride of place on Capital Hill.

The Griffins officially withdrew from the Canberra project in 1921 after an acrimonious dispute with the government which saw Prime Minister Hughes remove Walter Griffin from his supervisory role.

In the city centre, the East Block was finished in 1926 and West block in 1927 ready to house the national public service. Meanwhile shoppers would have to wait until 1946 for the Melbourne and Sydney buildings to open their doors to a long awaited retail Mecca.

And so in this architecturally sparse environment with its small population of politicians and public servants, the Lyons family were together for a brief visit.

Dinner was eventually served after the Lyons children had finally been quieted and seated in order of age with the older Billy and Sarah near their mother so they could listen to the adult conversation. Former PM Billy Hughes sat on the PMs right and Enid Lyons on his left.

Hughes's turbulent political career bore many similarities to that of Lyons, both having left the Labor Party to lead successful breakaway groups. Lyons had recently resigned as Treasurer and deserted the Scullin Labor Government which was disintegrating into that most entertaining Australian sport; public factional brawling, over ... well ... not much at all really. Then in a merger with the Nationals and 6 Labor defectors the United Australia Party was formed. Lyons had become leader, won the next election in a landslide and was now Prime Minister with a comfortable majority and with the great depression almost spent, he was a completely happy man.

Joe Lyons, was a devout Catholic and led the family in grace. With adult heads bowed and eyes closed, the younger Billy taunted his sister Sarah by mouthing "Sarah loves Michael," and puckering his lips in a kiss. Sarah poked her tongue out at Billy just as the 'Amen' was uttered, prompting a disapproving look from her mother. Billy, in retaliation flicked water at Sarah from the finger bowl prompting, "Stop that Billy" from his mother which in turn prompted a confused look from the partially deaf Billy Hughes. "No, not you Mr Hughes - children, God's gift, questionable generosity don't you think, proffered

Enid, who breathed a sigh of relief as they were interrupted by the extraordinarily handsome Michael Fleming, the PM's private secretary. More smirking from Billy followed by faux disinterest from Sarah that quickly transformed into a wide smile for Michael.

"Sorry to interrupt Prime Minister but I think you ought to see this telegram."

Joe read the telegram. Michael waited for a response and returned Sarah's smile. Billy imitated her smile and received a kick under the table and a sickly smile from Sarah for his trouble.

Joe finished reading and said, "Thank you Michael, have the Minister for Defence come for a nine o'clock meeting tomorrow." "Very good Prime Minister." Michael was then smiled out of the room by Sarah while Billy made heart thumping gestures under his shirt.

"Trouble in Europe, Joe?" said Enid

"No, just our own Western front, the secessionists are trying to goad us into action on an emu plague that they are well able to handle themselves."

In a superhuman effort of annoyance Billy reached for the salt cellar and 'accidentally' knocked it over onto Sarah's plate.

"Sorry," said Billy

"Plague of what? … Billy, just ask and she will pass it to you," said Enid

"What?" yelled Hughes.

"Not you Mr Hughes," said Enid

"Emus dear," said Joe

"He did it on purposefully!" said Sarah

"'purpose' dear," corrected Enid.

"They have a purpose alright," snarled Joe.

"Emus, ridiculous," said Enid.

"Had emu once, didn't go much on it," mumbled Hughes
"It's a plague Billy," said Joe.
"Sure is Dad," said Billy the younger.
"Not you Billy," said Joe.
"Steady on," said Hughes.

The gabbling finally subsided under the weight of its own confusion and Joe explained the emu plague and the secessionists ulterior motive, thinly disguised as a cry for help.
"Anyway, they can't secede, it's clearly excluded by the constitution," thundered Hughes.
"That's my position entirely, the political union is inviolable," replied Joe at the same volume.
Enid in her usual measured tone observed "We'll all be deaf at this rate. And I thought it was you two who were the experts on breaking up political unions."
And then almost in unison: "that was a matter of principle and for the good of the country."
"Mum, Billy is teasing me."
"That's enough Billy go to your room. Not you Mr Hughes. You two must learn to get on! Not you Joe. But don't you see that the secessionists could well insist that this is a matter of principle and for the good of the state? Perhaps it's time to stop behaving like children and mend some fences," Enid concluded.
"Alright, I'll arrange a WA visit as soon as we have the troops in place, but I'll need you to come with me and you too Billy."
Enid smiled, she would enjoy this trip, there would be plenty of influential wives for her to impress and plenty of parochial politicians to charm from their burrows into the light of the modern world. The more she got involved in politics the more she liked it. To her great surprise the cultural maxims of women and power being incompatible were waning very quickly, as she hurtled down the runway enjoying the pressure under her wings

41

lifting her into the air.

Joe called out, "Fleming, are you listening just outside the door? "

"Yes sir," came the reply.

"Well get in here, this has to be well planned with plenty of prepublicity. I want press releases about helping in time of need, our national family, the Commonwealth at work, that sort of thing and a couple of sympathetic journalists to come with us. Enid my darling, I'll show you how to mend a fence." He smiled as they rose from the table.

The Military

The Commonwealth is very big on displaying the Australian coat of arms which features the Emu and the Kangaroo and, true to form there it was on Defence headquarters. The addition of a farmer with a gun would have been very apt, especially if the nation's fauna lay dead at his feet. Beyond the main entrance and with a surprising lack of security there was the steady hum of military efficiency driven by the hierarchy and protocol that are part of all great defence systems.

Among the officers arriving were Captain Brown and Lieutenant Robert. They shared an office, they were intelligent, they were handsome, they definitely had 'dash' and they really knew how to wear a uniform. Brown desperately wanted to make a significant contribution to the Australian Defence Forces, he was a serious soldier, he had applied for this position in the desk army because he wanted to see how it worked and how it could be made to work better to support the real army. He was learning slowly, like all public servants, that reason and logic always play second fiddle to politics and ego - but he was still young enough to think that fundamental change could be achieved by persistence and hard work.

Robert on the other hand was more the realist and had concluded that a desk job gave him more time to pursue his other interests like planning a successful life strategy.

Approaching their shared shoebox they passed two privates carrying a door marked Major N. O. Bullen, Logistics and two more carrying a door marked Col H. Market, Materiel. The temptation to ask about the doors was irritatingly great but previous experience suggested that in the interests of sanity, tacit acceptance trumps investigation.

Brown and Robert commenced their respective morning routines; Brown read his memoranda while Robert devoured the financial pages of the newspaper. The tea trolley arrived on cue and both took tea and biscuits while they bantered with the tea lady about her wild children and her 'carefree' life. Maureen, the tea lady, had more cares, pound for pound, than the ADF. Her children were almost feral, her husband was a casual labourer. The family lived in public housing in Reid and while it was better than Sydney, it was socially isolating, for in Canberra the working class was a minority. Clearly, entrée to Canberra society, where interest in public service level was obsessive and the desire for social advancement intense, was firmly locked and barred to Maureen the tea lady.

Brown and Robert returned to their desks, as Robert picked up the financial pages once more, Brown asked, "anything interesting?"
"Just looking for the golden opportunity," replied Robert.
"Your name came up yesterday"
"In relation to?"
"The Port Moresby Liaison position"
Robert shuddered, "mosquitoes, dengue fever, crocodiles, headhunters. Small wonder the Brits were so keen for us to take over the protectorate."
"Golden opportunity, next step up the ladder and you're smart enough to make a difference."
"It's not me you know, too independent, I don't even know why I'm here. I hate taking orders."
"You're here because you come from a military family, it's in your blood. You just need to discover what your father discovered when climbing ..." Brown was interrupted mid

sentence by a messenger with an envelope marked Urgent, Security level high. Leaving Robert dangling along with the participle, he read the message and laughed out loud. "Come on, the General wants both of us in the briefing room right away. Read this on the way." Brown handed the paper to Robert as they gathered coats and caps and hurried to the briefing room.

General Morefield had come to prominence for heroism in the Great War, he had risen through the ranks and was well respected by his junior officers. Although he didn't suffer fools gladly he did have a good eye for talent and knew how to use it. "What is this Brown, some kind of April fools day joke?" barked Morefield
"It seems not sir, it's straight from the PM"

It was an unusual step for the PM's office to specify how the army should achieve an objective. Planning and implementation was what Defence was good at, but now they read with incredulity that they had been ordered to reduce the 'Emu Menace' by executing a cavalry attack using machine guns mounted on lorries.

The General was livid, "go skidding around through the Western Australian wheat fields shooting at emus while they scatter all over the place, we'll be lucky if we don't shoot ourselves in the crossfire. It's absurd, a complete misuse of men and resources, an insult to the ANZAC tradition, we'll be a laughing stock, I can hear them in Whitehall now. Oh the Colonials, aren't they amusing, making use of their independence, flexing their military might, that'll give the Japo's a fright, show them who's boss in the Asia Pacific." The General finally drew breath, giving Brown the opportunity to inject a dash of his personal brilliance before the next salvo was launched. "Couldn't agree more, Sir. This is petty politics not the defence of the nation but if we can do the job quickly and safeguard our reputation at the same time ...".

"You obviously have a plan Brown, spit is out and stop hedging," demanded Morefield. "Sir, publicity is unavoidable but publicity is exactly what the PM wants out of this, so if we can dodge sideways by finding a leader for this expedition who isn't quite a part of the ADF, someone who enjoys the limelight, someone who will believe in the importance of this mission, someone with an ego so large that he will attract all the adverse publicity personally and protect us from any damage."

"You're an evil man Brown, remind me to keep a close eye on you. ... Do you really think he'll fall for it?"

"Let me see Sir, ... sun comes up every morning, tide goes in and out, rocks roll downhill, ... it's a fair bet."

"Set the trap Captain, but I want someone we can trust to be our eyes and ears on the ground, what about Robert here? About time you started to earn your keep lieutenant." Robert and Brown acknowledged the General's decisive action and beat a hasty retreat to put the plan into action.

Battling another flotilla of doors in the corridor Brown and Robert finally made it to the office of Major d'Camry. On secondment from the British Army, d'Camry was a self important nuisance who was meant to be parked out of harm's way while his superiors decided what to do with him. Unfortunately, for his superiors, d'Camry was extremely well connected within the British establishment and had to be treated with care for all the wrong reasons. d'Camry was pompous, overbearing and singularly untalented in the military sense, he had been assiduously kept away from actual leadership positions by politically adept superiors who had occupied him with a series of high sounding but meaningless tasks.

Brown knew that d'Camry couldn't be told what to do, he would have to 'discover' this opportunity all by himself. Brown knocked on the door and Robert started to laugh. Brown kicked him sharply in the shin as the door opened. Brown saluted and requested a few minutes of the Major's time and was invited in. Robert limped along behind. "Nasty limp you've got there old man, shrapnel is it?" asked d'Camry. "Too young for the Great War I'm afraid sir, cricket injury, yesterday," replied Robert. His somewhat sarcastic tone earned him a scowl from Brown and on they went. "I've just come to take up your offer to act as a mentor for younger officers while you're here Major" said Brown "I thought it most generous of you sir". "Always glad to give a helping hand to a struggling junior," d'Camry replied, giving fresh meaning to pompous condescension.

Brown in a deliberately halting manner began his approach, "I have a rather difficult task sir. General Morefield has asked me to identify a range of officers for a very sensitive assignment, it's straight from the PM's office and I'm not quite sure how to start." "You've come to the right man me-boy, now give me a summary of the objectives and the skills required." d'Camry was off and running, the energy of self importance accelerating his speech and fuelling his use of personal superlatives.

The pain in Robert's shin was waning and he could not contain his delight at this circus spectacular. Brown saw his ever widening grin and quickly distracted him by requesting the mission folder and simultaneously turning to Robert and crushing his toes under his heel. Brown estimated he had bought another five minutes of pain induced seriousness and sped up his delivery accordingly. "Well Sir, this is a very politically sensitive assignment, more than one government to keep happy and a military component that requires surgical precision. It seems that thousands of Emus are causing havoc in Western Australia, damaging crops even threatening small settlements. They have to be stopped and quickly, it's an absolute top priority. The right man has to have excellent organisational and logistical skills. My first thought was Blamey, but he's caught up with this New Guinea thing. We could use Parsons but there's some doubt about his ability to keep his mouth shut. We need someone who won't let a completely free hand go to his head, a good planner, experienced campaigner." Brown's contrivances were again bringing Robert close to peel of laughter and it was either knock him unconscious or speedily extract them both from this farce. "I'll leave you to mull it over Major," he said as he steered, the by now helpless, Robert to the door, pushed him out, managed to salute and close the door before the eruption of the inevitable howls of laughter that they tried hard to stifle by covering their mouths with their hands while they double timed it down the corridor.

d'Camry was not a subtle man. He waited for Moreland's secretary to go home and then barged into the office blathering, "look here old man, I know you're in a bit of a fix, too many emus, not enough top men, what?"
"Quite so," said the General.
"Well, now that I've tidied up my paper on the benefit of static gun emplacements in Singapore, I might be able to help you out," said d'Camry.
"Let's hope the enemy doesn't come by land," the General demurred.
"It's a naval base old man, absolutely impregnable," d'Camry replied.
"I'm sure you're right, but surely you've got other important projects Major," said Moreland.
"Well yes, but I feel I should make myself available if it will get you out of a jam," said d'Camry

"As long as it won't jeopardise your work in the longer term, we would be grateful indeed, a very generous offer. I'll write up the orders tonight." said Moreland clicking a ring binder shut.

"What was that?" said d'Camry.

"Something snapping shut, I think," said Moreland.

d'Camry in Charge

The Major had his orders.
Rescue the embattled communities of Western Australia from the Emu menace.
Delegated to his command were:
Captain Brown HQ Liaison Officer to be based in Canberra
Lieutenant Robert as head of Planning and Community Liaison WA

d'Camry was so exhilarated, he was verging on joyous apoplexy. His first ever real command, he would show those doubters, those detractors, those malignant War Office know alls that had suppressed his talent all these years. He despised them all, keeping him tied to a supply desk from 1914-1918, were they jealous that he knew more about artillery than Howitzer himself, commanded a comprehensive knowledge of battlefield strategy that would have made von Clausewitz cringe and knew in his heart that he was destined to be a lion in battle, greater than General Gordon, he would show 'em this time. Unfortunately for d'Camry, there was nobody called Howitzer it was some strange English, German, Polish, Swedish and Dutch strangulation of a Czech word meaning 'crowd', von Clausewitz wrote 'On War', as a philosophical treatise on the nature of war and military ethics not battlefield tactics and General Gordon perished at Khartoum at the hands of some very cross Arabs.

d'Camry had scheduled a briefing for his staff for 0900 hours, he had been up for hours developing his strategy and had just finished writing his agenda on the blackboard as Brown and Robert entered.

Pre-embarkation agenda
TASKFORCE EMU
1. STRATEGY
2. LOGISTICS
3. PERSONNEL
4. TRAINING
5. PROPAGANDA AND INDOCTRINATION
6. COMMUNITY LIAISON
7. MATERIEL
8. HQ LIAISON

Brown and Robert congratulated d'Camry on his appointment and took their seats in front of the board.

d'Camry, swagger stick in hand, stepped up to a small podium and addressed his staff of two. "Right men, this campaign is going to be run by the book. The British Army has a new procedures manual, incorporating the lessons from the Great War, the advances in artillery, cavalry and mobile infantry. This will be a rare glimpse into modern warfare, you'll be the envy of all your peers. This is your chance to look and learn; I'll show you how an operation should be run.

Captain Brown was finding it hard to contain his common sense response to this drivel. Morefield had warned him several times that reason and logic were often not the faculties that an officer applied when interpreting orders. There were times that blind faith was far more useful to a military career and indeed if carefully applied much more comfortable. It allowed one to sleep at night rather than being tangled in the endless mental review of the many permutations and combinations, contained in 'orders'. Brown was still trying to balance these competing sensibilities and in the end blurted out, "Sir do you think that

British procedures from a European war cover these unique circumstances?"

d'Camry was affronted, "I suppose you think you know better than the Imperial General Staff."

Brown suddenly wished he had just let it go, "No Sir."

d'Camry continued, "we are very fortunate to have such a comprehensive guide Brown. Let's see, ... Emus, ... that would be a lightly armed mobile force.

"Actually Sir they don't have arms at all, in fact they've hardly even got wings" replied Robert settling in to play the game.

"So, we don't need to worry about air attack and won't need to cooperate with the air-force," said d'Camry, laughing heartily at his witticism but never stopping to wonder why the others were silent.

"If you say so, sir," sighed Brown

"Moving on. Strategy," said d'Camry "If the Great War showed us anything, it showed the effectiveness of the machine gun especially against irregular forces. I think we can assume that emus are irregular."

"Very irregular sir." Brown's sighs were becoming elongated, almost dirges.

"In that case it's all there in chapter 22. Right, I'm in overall command, responsible for strategy, training and operations. Robert you'll handle community liaison, materiel and personnel and Brown you look after propaganda and indoctrination from this end. I think you'll find those chapters in the manual very illuminating, follow them carefully. We fly out in 2 days, Robert, I'll leave the arrangements to you."

The meeting ended, Brown and Robert saluted and made for the safety of the corridor. Robert had been under strict instructions not to speak and not to laugh, in his haste to get away from this surreal situation he crashed into an oncoming door parade.

"Heavy door traffic today private," said Brown.

"It's Major d'Camry sir," offered the private.

"It's Major d'Camry, what?" asked Brown.

"He's in charge of office reallocation sir, he said it would be more secure and efficient to change the doors rather than exchange keys."

"Very good private carry on," said Brown.

"He's barking mad you know," said Brown, "exchanging doors and running a campaign against emus by the book. Don't let him do anything too silly Robert or it's New Guinea for you."

The office of Brown and Robert, now door-less, was a welcome haven of sanity, they recalled the enthusiasm of 1914 when everyone believed that the war would be over in six weeks. They tried to buoy each other up by suggesting that surely this time, they could do it in a week, just a bunch of emus after all, what could possibly go wrong. They settled into their chairs with their respective copies of the British Operations Manual. Robert found it highly amusing as he transposed 'emus' for 'enemy' in the indoctrination chapter.

"Sir, listen to this, 'Men, you are about to go into battle and God is on our side! But remember it is not enough to fight these **emus**. You have to hate them! These **emus** are not normal law abiding men like us. They are evil! They have been raping Belgian nuns and have no respect for the laws of God or man!', it's too much"

Brown laughed and said, "Do you think Belgian nuns are entirely appropriate given that the operation is in Western Australia?"

"Good point sir", replied Robert, "Perhaps we should substitute the 'Sisters of Charity' or 'our virginal daughters'."

"Do you know any virginal daughters Robert?"

In a slightly sheepish manner Robert replied "well, fewer than I used to…sir."

Brown was still laughing but resigned himself to the situation, knowing that whatever he devised couldn't possibly be taken seriously and would hopefully be lost to history as soon as this ludicrous campaign concluded.

Their jocularity was interrupted by a messenger with a 16mm film canister. It was marked 'URGENT' and was addressed to 'The Campaign Leader, Project Emu'. Originating from the PM's Office it had been redirected to Captain Brown. Brown duly signed for the package and taking Robert with him went off to the viewing room to watch the movie. The PM's staff had been monitoring all the emu news from WA and were surprised to find that the issue had escalated considerably and was a subject of interest to the foreign news media.

The film rolled.

Italia CineGiornale

The camera panned over a huge mob of emus gorging themselves on Western Australian wheat, zoomed in on broken fences and finished with an obviously angry crowd of protesters. This last was actually the demonstration at the Treasury Building but it had been beautifully melded into a believable story of avian carnage and public outrage that had captured world attention.

The scene was repeated in:

The French
Cines Actualites

The German

Wochenschau

The British
WORLD NEWS

There was even footage of a Javanese shadow play of a man being chased by two rather jerky emus to the strange tones of a Gamalan orchestra.

Not even World War I was accorded this sort of fanfare, on that occasion the press gallery had simply been summoned to the PM's office and informed that war had broken out with Germany.

Brown was worried, whoever or whatever the enemy was, he had seriously underestimated them.

Janet's Campaign

Back in Dencubbin Janet was packing to go to Perth, Maurie was seeking advice from Janet's mother on how to succeed in romance without having a snowball's chance in hell, while Ted and Bill were discussing the prospect of happier times when wheat would be worth something and Western Australia could pursue sensible policies designed to rightly benefit those who toiled to feed the country.

Janet went to her tallboy for more clothes to pack but stopped short as her childhood dolls looked at her accusingly from its top. The dolls were having a tea party with the best china and clearly called her to join them. Janet stopped and smiled, "not this time girls, this is the chance of a lifetime"
The dolls and their pride of place was an ongoing issue between Janet and her mother, Janet would pack them away, her mother would get them out again and arrange them in novel poses. It was sweet and cute and Janet was increasingly irritated by this 'doll telegraph' that her childhood was still in full swing. This time it would be different, instead of packing them away she would let them stay there and pack herself off to Perth. She mused on sending them a postcard saying "Dear Dolls, thanks for helping me grow up, I'm a big girl now and ready for the world, don't wait tea for me. Love Janet"
In the end she knew that she would have to find a way to gently give her mother that message without destroying all the maternal affection that she cherished so much. As an only child, in the isolated farm environment, she had always been the centre of attention, and had enjoyed the company of adults from an early age. Her mother blamed herself for not being able to

have more children and had strived and was still striving to provide a normal childhood. Despite having plenty to be proud of she increasingly felt that time was defeating her and she couldn't or wouldn't accept it.

Out in the kitchen she could hear her mother telling Maurie that Janet loved riding, that Jane Austen was her favourite author and that Ranunculus were her favourite flowers and then spelling it out for him as he wrote it down. Janet groaned, forced her leather suitcase shut, smiled at the messianic gold embossed 'J.C.' initials and went out to face a difficult goodbye.

Janet's appearance with a suitcase was a pretty obvious trigger for her mother to ask, "where are you going dear?"
"I'm going to Perth for a few days to interview the Prime Minister; the West Australian has offered me a stringer deal, they want me to keep writing about the emu plague, it seems my articles have caused quite an uproar,"
"Oh that's too bad darling," said her mother.
"No mum, that's a good thing when you're a journalist." "But you're not a journalist dear, you just write little stories for the local paper."
"That is journalism mum and this is a great opportunity." "But your father needs you here." said her mother sensing that Janet was asserting a level of independence for which she was absolutely not prepared.
"It's only a few days mum" said Janet, skating horribly close to caving in, "besides this is what we've all been working for, building the case for secession and getting Western Australia on its way to prosperity."
"She's doing a great job love," said her father, "we're all proud of you Janet. The PM, it's quite a step up in the world. The cars ready, I'll drive you in."

Janet took that as her cue to leave when Maurie looking forlorn murmured, "I was going to ask you to dinner on Thursday."
Janet was not without compassion but she knew it was kinder to cut this off at the knees. "You just feed those emus Maurie" and with that she winked at her father, kissed her mother and made for the door.

Perth Barracks

Despite his appearance of complete indifference to the mission, Lieutenant Robert had made all the arrangements necessary for the beginning of operation Emu. He had acquainted himself with Sergeant Wilkins who as the Perth based leader was informing his men of the machine gun platoon about the impending active service. The three lance corporals were together as usual and apparently cleaning and polishing their gear, but actually playing their favourite game that required intense concentration. Their seemingly random babbling about numbers was an enigma to the Sergeant, he knew they played often and that the chalkboard showed the results, they had explained it to him on other occasions but he just didn't get it. As he walked across the parade ground he had to give way to a troop of light horsemen returning from their cavalry games, they were an elite group, always going on about how you could take off a man's head by detaching a stirrup and swinging it round as a high velocity weapon or the endless tales of repulsing the Turks at Romani and pushing them back across the desert into Palestine in 1916. They had an aura about them that emanated from their unwritten code of no surrender, a code that had no appeal at all for the highly pragmatic lance corporals; Cox, Ford and Down.

Peak hour finally passed and the Sergeant approached the men as Cox said, "one",

"two" said Ford,

"four, that's a point to you Ford" said Down.

"I wish we got to wear ostrich feathers like the Light Horse, three" said Ford.

"And charge into enemy fire wielding a sabre? One" said Cox.

"No, just to impress the girls at the dance hall, four" said Ford with a wry smile.

"They don't need impressing, they're all over you as soon as you walk in." Said Down

"Yeah, all over you, I need more of what you got," said Ford.

"No you don't, said Down, … and another point to you Ford, you better lose soon or you'll get too far ahead."

"You men still at that stupid game, piggy in the middle is it?" said the Sergeant.

"Med-i-oc-rity, sarge" said Cox, emphasising each syllable. The Sergeant looked quizzical and slightly embarrassed.

"You know, where the aim of each round is to call the middle number. It's a sophisticated game of subtle strategy." said Cox.

"How's that?" Said the Sergeant feeling that once again he would fail to comprehend and be left wondering if they were just taking the piss out of him.

"Well mediocre, like not good or bad just in the middle."

"And what do you do about ties?" asked the Sergeant.

"They're decided on alphabetical order. But the real subtlety is that the ultimate aim of the game is to end up with the middle number of points. So if you win each round, you lose!"

"Sounds like the army," mumbled the Sergeant and then more powerfully, "I think you lot have been sniffing the boot polish again."

"It passes the time." Said Down.

"Well time is about to speed up, we're going on active service," declared the Sergeant.

"Not bloody Gallipoli again," said Ford.

"Not quite," said the Sergeant "we'll be fighting emus."

"The emu Hun?" said Down.

"Only not so bright," said Cox as he opened his notebook ready for any further details.

"Just ordinary emus corporal, the kind that destroy wheat crops and upset the farmers and the farmers upset the government and the government upsets the brass and the brass are upsetting us. Fucking useless bastards! Why not just poison the mongrels? Never mind, they didn't ask me! Indoctrination and drill at 0800 hours, let everyone know."

He turned to go as Cox closed his notebook and said, "Three, now, this will be fun."

In an office overlooking the parade ground Lieutenant Robert was on the phone trying to explain his current dilemma to Captain Brown back in Canberra. It was true, d'Camry had ordered an indoctrination session based on Robert and Brown's comical rewrite of the absurd propaganda manual, followed by bayonet drill in full battle dress. "He's as mad as a coot sir, I couldn't stop him, ... yes I've put a blanket ban on all publicity and convinced him of the need for absolute secrecy, he thinks it's to ensure that nothing leaks to the enemy, the enemy, Christ does he think they can talk. I'll do my best to keep the journalists well away from all this. ... I seem to be hearing a lot of laughter from your end sir, I can tell you it's not so funny over here. I'll kill this bloody fruitcake before I risk getting sent to New Guinea."

0800 hours came on Robert like a dry electrical storm, the Sergeant's declarative commands, were the rolling thunder threatening his impending doom by d'Camry, uncontrollable as lightning and just as dangerous.

Robert shook himself as the Sergeant boomed his instructions, "platoon, fix bayonets, first line charge!"

They didn't.

"Are you men deaf as well as stupid? When I say charge the dummies I mean charge the dummies."

"Sorry sarge," said Cox "it just seems a bit daft to charge chaff bags that have those dopey emu heads."

Sergeant Wilkins was career army, the real McCoy, a veteran of the Boer War and the Great War, he had a genuine sympathy for the opinion of the men. Wilkins had disobeyed orders himself in 1918 when, heartened by the uniquely Australian wildcat tactic of 'peaceful penetration'; surprise attacks, unheralded by artillery or tanks that took many German positions. Sgt Wilkins and some of his AIF comrades had refused the British order to break up the badly depleted divisions to reinforce the remaining ones. This moderately rebellious cohort, appointed their own officers and fought on in their original units to the end of the war.

Notwithstanding this classic larrikinism, Wilkins was a great fan of Lieutenant General John Monash, who was appointed as Corps Commander of all the Australian troops in Europe in May 1918. He stood in awe of his basically intelligent approach to modern warfare. Monash could not see the point of sending countless waves of infantry to their certain death. His approach was to use *the maximum possible protection of the maximum possible array of mechanical resources, in the form of guns, machine-guns, tanks, mortars and aeroplanes; to advance with as little impediment as possible.* This was key to his success at Hamel in July 1918.

Wilkins had the larrikin spirit but recognised that the big battles were won with meticulous planning and high level integration of resources demonstrated by Monash.

Right now he had to show his men that he supported them without destroying morale or inciting insubordination.

"Look men, were here to do a job and by hell we're going to do it, if it means a bit of harmless play acting to get things started then, that - is - what - we - will - do. Just thank your lucky stars they're not shooting back, now first row, with enthusiasm, - charge!"

They did, some even gave the wild blood chilling cries of murderous mayhem, thought to be so effective in battle. By the end of half an hour the emu dummies had been cut to ribbons and there was a sense of camaraderie of which Wilkins was duly proud. D'Camry had witnessed the final charge and was impressed but instead of congratulating the men he launched straight into his indoctrination speech.

"Men, I am glad to see that Sergeant Wilkins is instilling you with the right martial spirit."

"Right martial spirit?" whispered Ford.

"Too many gin slings," said Down. Cox smiled and took notes.

"You're about to go into action and God is on our side. It's not enough to fight these emus, you've got to hate them. These emus have been raping the members of the Piesseville CWA and the Balingup Ladies Bowling Club. Are you going to let them get away with this?"

The silence was palpable.

"Are you going to let them get away with this?" he repeated at greater volume.

Cox put away his notebook and murmured "Well if they enjoyed it." There was a ripple of convulsed laughter in the ranks as d'Camry, clearly ruffled, screamed, "I will not tolerate insubordination, put that man on report." Unfortunately he pointed to the wrong man.

Robert interjected with "Don't you mean..?"

"I know what I mean!" said d'Camry scornfully cutting him off.

Parliament in Perth

Australian parliaments are not always rowdy melees but question time is traditionally regarded as more of a sporting opportunity for those with a quick wit and a thick hide, rather than an opportunity to ask questions that need answering. Ironically it is the least informative part of any parliamentary session with much interjection, disorderly comment and gavel banging.

"The house will come to order! The honourable the leader of the opposition."

Philip Collier took the call ready for some parliamentary sparring.

"Can the Premier explain to the house why his totally incompetent government has done nothing about the plague of emus that is currently threatening the livelihoods of farmers across the wheat belt?"

The usual voices in support and calls of shame echoed round the chamber.

"Order, order, the house will come to order! The honourable the Premier."

"I thank the honourable member for his question. I would remind him that just two and a half years ago the voters decided that **his** was a totally incompetent government. But to return to his question. We have not been inactive on this issue. My government has made representations to the Federal Government in Canberra and requested that the army should deal with the problem. Emus are clearly a Federal responsibility."

The usual jeers rose sharply and fell again with the speaker's gavel.

"Clearly a Federal responsibility since they form one of the supporters of the National coat of arms. If the honourable member wishes more immediate action perhaps he should approach his treacherous cronies in the Federal Government. Or perhaps he should start listening to the electors of Western Australia and support 'secession' in the forthcoming referendum."

More jeers.

"Yes Mister Speaker, find out what the ordinary people of this state already know, that the Federal Government has absolutely not one jot of interest in our people, our resources or our future."

General uproar and calls of traitor reverberate.

"Order, order, the house will come to order! The honourable the leader of the opposition."

"Will the Premier concede that his previous answer was the biggest load of obfuscation that he has ever inflicted on this house and that in fact he has no policy or plan of action to address this plague and that he will in fact leave the wheat farmers to fend for themselves while he strips away their income with his ill conceived Grain Authority. Mister Speaker, this man and his Government are a disgrace and the electors will tell him so at the forthcoming election."

"Order, order, the house will come to order! The honourable the Premier."

"The answers to the Honourable Gentleman's questions, in order, are No. No. And no.

We will win the election, the referendum will succeed and the Honourable Gentleman may need to migrate to seek a new career. Go East young man, go East!

Mocking calls of 'King Mitchell', 'King of Kings' and 'Lord of Lords'.

"Order, order, the house will come to order, the honourable

65

member for Fremantle will resume his seat. Order!"
Speaker of the house is a thankless task.

Flying Circus

The flight from Canberra to Perth via Melbourne and Adelaide in a 14 seat De Havilland Hercules DH 66 was an ordeal more tiring and less fun than crossing the Nullarbor with an Afghan camel train. The Prime Minister with his wife Enid, ex PM Billy Hughes and a small entourage, apprehensively approached the aircraft.

"Joe, I'm not sure I like the look of this, are you sure we shouldn't have gone by train; Bradman's just arrived in Perth by train we could have ridden the same wave of popularity," said Enid.

"How do you know that my love?" replied Lyons

"It's in this morning's Canberra Times."

"Well bless my soul, but look this thing has three engines and it's modern and fast and shiny, I'm sure it'll be alright."

The party boarded the plane and took their rudimentary seats. Billy Hughes unaffected by the noise of the aircraft engines due to his deafness pointed out other articles in the Canberra Times that morning. "Look at this Joe, Mussolini wants the yanks to wipe Italy's war debt, bloody little twerp I wouldn't trust him as far as I could kick him."

Lyons was settling in his seat looking over his briefing notes for Western Australia when Hughes chimed in again. "And Herr Hitler's on the wane, look, this says: 'that since the last general election in Germany, Herr Hitler has been losing his adherents faster than he made them a few months ago.

The numbers attending his meetings have dwindled in a remarkable fashion.

The East Prussian campaign was a fiasco. The need for funds is so great that uniformed Nazis rattle collection boxes under the noses of passers-by in the streets, although the practice is of doubtful legality. The Government hostility is also increasing the cost of Hitler's propaganda. I knew it couldn't last, a man like that thinks he can lead the most cultured nation in Europe, absurd."

Hughes sat back smugly in his seat.

The flight was long and torturous and the party arrived looking more like refugees than a visiting delegation from the national capital. The plane landed at Mayfield aerodrome, shuddered down the runway and taxied up to a galvanised corrugated iron shed bearing the glorious emblem 'West Australian Airways'. There was no welcoming party, no refreshments and no sign of Major d'Camry who was supposed to rendezvous with them at 1500 hours. Lyons was visibly put out as Hughes reminded him that they were both completely 'on the nose' to both sides of politics in WA; the conservatives wanted to secede from the Commonwealth and the labour party always hates a rat; or in this case rats.

Enid pushed them toward a more positive frame of mind with her schedule of teas and luncheons with significant parliamentary wives, insisting that tea party diplomacy could be very effective. This was a prophetic announcement regarding their American cousins although 'The Tea Party' and 'diplomacy' would be mutually exclusive terms 80 years hence.

Lyons and Hughes planned to visit the operational headquarters, be thoroughly briefed by the commander and hold an Emu Press Conference followed by a rally for the Federation and the unity of the Commonwealth. Lyons would make a passionate speech, that presented the United Australia Party as; 'a party to represent all Australians', 'One Nation for the good of all' and other hopefully meaningful epithets. Lyons hoped that Hughes could rouse the Australian spirit, he was still remembered for his role during the war and his voluble performance at the Versailles Peace Conference and he had the authority to call forth the spirit of mateship and unity of purpose that was ANZAC.

It was anything but the spirit of ANZAC that they saw coming toward them in a Model A Ford. It was d'Camry with Lieutenant Robert and Sergeant Wilkins in tow. Robert was fuming, the PM's visit meant his efforts to keep the press completely uninformed would prove futile, Wilkins was livid that his platoon had been humiliated and to top it off it was clear that the seating logistics in the Model A would be a fiasco. Without waiting for Robert's guidance, d'Camry addressed Hughes as 'Prime Minister Lyons' and had to be corrected, proper introductions were eventually completed and Wilkins volunteered to stay with the remainder of the party and wait for another vehicle while the PM with Enid and Hughes piled into the Model A Ford with Robert and d'Camry. Robert prayed fervently to all the gods for d'Camry to be killed by lightning, knocked unconscious by a falling Koala or simply struck dumb, but the gods were on holiday and as always the koala's role in diplomatic affairs was restricted to pissing on foreign dignitaries. In the awkward silence d'Camry launched into a diatribe on static gun emplacements followed by the performance of his men at the morning's bayonet drill. Lyons and Hughes were the ones struck dumb while Robert gripped the steering wheel as though it were d'Camry's throat.

In the safety of the hotel room, Lyons, Enid and Hughes were finally able to vent their frustration.
"They assured me he was a top man. ... Shoot some emus, champion the Commonwealth, what could possibly go wrong?" said Lyons.

"This could hurt us badly," said Hughes.

"Will you two stop it," said Enid, "the media just need to be fed, play up the Commonwealth rally, keep that idiot major away from the reporters and definitely away from me, tell the press that the Commonwealth has the beginnings of a naval presence in the Indian Ocean, a battlecruiser, three cruisers, four destroyers and 4 submarines, tell them that it is often hard to see the benefits of the Commonwealth because as in this case they're out at sea, letting the world know that we are a fiercely independent nation, not just a rag tag collection of colonies cum state."

"It's not a lot compared to Japan,' said Lyons.

"DON'T MENTION JAPAN," said Enid.

"I agree" said Hughes, "well not in this arena."

And so it was that 'Operation Emu' led by the redoubtable d'Camry quietly left Perth for the wheat country well ahead of schedule. Lyons gave the press conference of his life, telling the press gallery that he understood the concerns of the West, reinforcing the response that the federal government was making to the emu plague, pledging further support for population growth, repeating with gusto, 'a battlecruiser, three cruisers, four destroyers and 4 submarines' and finished with a fervent urging for people of good will to embrace the ideals of Commonwealth.

Janet was there asking the hard questions about tariffs and the effect they were having on struggling farm communities. Lyons countered, arguing that any advanced economy needed a manufacturing sector and that Australia had to support that sector through its development phase. Janet was not to be fobbed off, she asked what milestones the Commonwealth had set for manufacturing to reach in order to receive ongoing assistance. Lyons had to retreat once more to the safe haven of defence and the necessity for on shore manufacturing in time of conflict. This particular debate was destined for many future iterations without any improvement in the quality of the argument.

Enid meanwhile was making genuine inroads with the parliamentary wives, she charmed them with her devotion to family and amazed them with her knowledge of world affairs and Australia's place on the world stage. When she spoke of the Commonwealth as a family that had to learn the art of compromise when it came to family spats, there was genuine acknowledgement of her point of view.

"Oh yes, I know 13 children sounds a lot but a bit of organisation and handing some responsibility to the older ones seems to work and Joe is such a family man. He speaks to them every night by telephone and lets them know he is interested in their sport, their schooling and their friends," said Enid.

"When's the next one due?" ventured Mrs Davy, attempting a deliberate provocation.

"We have let nature take its course up till now and I do so love all my children, but you know I think that if priests had to give birth then nature might be subjected to a bit more control."

"You surely don't support that awful American, Mary Sanger and her immoral interference in private family matters."

"Mrs Davy, I don't think this is the time or place for a discussion on morality but I will say this; that if I had 13 children without a wonderful man like Joe who is able to provide and help care for our family I would be wondering why God had placed me in such precarious circumstances where the best I could hope for was hunger, charity and an early death."

Just as things were looking precarious Mrs Mitchell saved the day with, "well said, Mrs Lyons, it's high time that women took charge of their own lives especially in family matters. I don't know about the rest of you but I am sick and tired of being preached at by men who have no idea what they're talking about." Mrs Davy coughed her disgust and retreated to the ladies room while the rest of the gathering found renewed courage and the afternoon took a definite turn for the better.

After Enid's triumph and a passable performance by Joe and Billy at the press conference, the delegation escaped what could have been a media catastrophe.

d'Camry of course was another matter.

The Campaign Begins

Both sides were making preparations. At Bill's shearing shed cum bulk grain storage facility, the 'emu wranglers' were filling sacks with wheat. The two Aboriginal stockmen were puzzled. Steve asked, "hey boss, we take the wheat and feed the emus, what for? Last year we shoot the bloody emu."

"It's complicated mate, white fella's politics," said Bill, "we'll feed out after smoko." He turned toward the house.

Steve and Fred looked at each other in silence, Steve made a well known move followed by Fred as they spontaneously reworked their ceremonial emu dance to include the eating of the wheat. After several rounds they fell back against the shed wall laughing at their own interpretation of the strange ways of the white fellas. Had they been privy to the whole story, the emu dance could have developed into a world class comic ballet.

In the house Janet, having returned the night before and slept in, was now waiting on her father to give him directions.

Meanwhile the men of Operation Emu had loaded their supplies, ammunition and weapons. They had been on the road for two days in search of emu country and this, evidently, was it. The intelligence report, gleaned from the newspaper, strongly suggested the Dencubbin area as a likely centre of operation. d'Camry scanned his map, all soldiers can read maps but some are better at it than others, d'Camry was not one of those.

"Robert, I think we'll make camp by this river", said d'Camry.

"I think that's a contour line sir," replied Robert.

"I know that man, it's this thing here I'm talking about," d'Camry replied fractiously, stabbing the map repeatedly with his finger.

"That is a gorge sir," said Robert who by now had lost all interest in keeping up the façade of making d'Camry feel important. Robert's disdain for d'Camry had reached a point that roused his forgotten feelings about being a good officer, he recalled his father's bravery, his ability to command the respect of the men, his tactical brilliance, his devotion to an army that he saw as protecting the populace in peace and in war. On behalf of all professional soldiers Robert felt insulted by this buffoon.

"Perhaps we should ask one of the locals to host us on their property," suggested Robert.

"Very well and if they won't comply hit them with a billeting order," said d'Camry with a vomitous swagger.

"Don't you think that might be a bit inflammatory sir?" said Robert.

"Damn it man, this is war," said d'Camry.

"Not against them," Robert hissed as he saluted, turned and walked away.

Robert took one of the soft top Model A Fords, that had been hastily requisitioned in Perth, the Australian Army had been very slow to mechanise and by 1932 had no tanks and certainly no passenger vehicles. Robert took Cox as driver went in search of a suitable property, preferably one with a water supply adequate for his men. He passed several prospects but considered them a bit down at heel to be lumbered with the demands of the machine gun platoon. After an hour or so they pulled up at a white weatherboard farmhouse with wide fly screened verandas. It was rare to see a well cared for European style garden in this part of the world but the incumbent had gone to great lengths to establish a flower garden with many species that needed a great deal of extra care in this harsh environment. The magnificent display of dahlias protected from the sun by 20 or so umbrellas attached to garden stakes brought a smile to his face. Someone trying to bring their idea of beauty to what must have seemed an inhospitable land. The local native flora had adapted over millennia to the infertile soils and without any gardener to help them would display their spectacular beauty when the rains came. Wildflowers would attract many tourists in the years ahead but right now Bill and Elizabeth Cole, the property owners, were just reminding themselves of the green and pleasant land they had left thirty years ago.

The initial isolation had nearly killed them and was still having a profound effect on Elizabeth who longed for the closeness of an extended family, and now with her only child, Janet, testing her adult wings, she felt the shadow of long days alone creeping in, taunting her, threatening her sanity. Her garden was a poor substitute for a daughter close at hand and a tribe of grandchildren to dote on. Bill on the other hand, had the all absorbing work of the farm that kept him from thinking too much, though the current wheat prices had worn him down as their bank balance dwindled in an ever diminishing spiral. It haunted him at odd hours of the night when he was without the distracting protection of the farm hands or his somewhat strange neighbours.

Robert strolled up to the house, stepped onto the veranda, felt its welcoming shade and used the brass knocker which had a donkey at its centre and 'Clovelly' written in the curve underneath, a piece of memorabilia from the green and pleasant land.

Janet opened the door, saw the uniform and jumped back in fright as if the army had discovered all their clandestine plans and her arrest was imminent.

"Sorry, I know I'm very frightening," said Robert.

"More than you know," said Janet with a recovering laugh.

Robert hesitated for a moment considering another funny line (I'm a secret weapon or, or … (he couldn't think of another) and then completely disarmed by Janet's laughter not to mention her stunning good looks he simply said, "I'm with the army."

"Go on," said Janet.

"Yes, of course, I am. The uniform, hard to miss really. We're here to deal with the emu plague and we need somewhere to bivouac and if you'll have me, I mean us, that would be very convenient, for me, us, that is," said Robert breaking into an idiotic smile. Being tongue tied and looking stupid was a new experience for Robert.

Janet's adrenaline was fairly pumping as she invited Robert in, activating her muscles and sending her brain into overdrive. Scrambled messages flashed from neurone to neurone, axon to dendrite; *ENEMY HANDSOME UNIFORM, string him along, don't let him get away, take him to bed, erotic screams, heavy breathing, don't faint, act sensible, don't trip and* on and on and on. Somewhere in that cloud of pheromones she managed to say, "would you like a cup of tea and some shortbread kisses, I mean biscuits, well they're called kisses because they're soft and sweet and buttery." *God I'm blathering*, she thought.

Robert survived 'soft' and 'sweet' but 'buttery' sent him into a blushing funk that radiated enough heat to start a bushfire.

Janet felt it and pulled him through to the kitchen, "I think you'd better meet my mother before (*I throw you on the floor and jump you*) we go any further, … with the bivouacking, … of the troops that is (*CHRIST!!!*) mum this is … a man, a soldier, a person, he wants to stay, outside, well not now, later and he needs a cup of tea. … What's your name?" she said finally turning and speaking to Robert in the most sheepish tone that sounded more like one of her dolls than the whirlwind of action that had been fomenting political turmoil for the last eight weeks.

"Lieutenant Robert," said Robert making a pathetic salute. "And your first name, Lieutenant Robert?" said Janet almost smoothly. "Robert," said Robert.

"So, Robert ... Robert?" said Janet.

"My father thought he had a great sense of humour, ... he didn't," said Robert, managing to say all the words without stumbling. Elizabeth stood silent, seeing her daughter as an adult sexual being for the first time and remembering when she met Bill when they were both on holiday at Clovelly.

"Mum ... mum!" said Janet "Teeea."

Elizabeth drifted back and automatically moved the kettle onto the hot plate of the slow combustion stove.

"So, Robert, will you be staying long?" she said.

"Well it could take a while, this is quite a new experience for me and I do want the mission to succeed," said Robert looking at Janet.

I'll be in her backyard, thought Robert.

He'll be in my backyard, thought Janet

I'm still in love with Bill, thought Elizabeth ... *Maurie and Janet, where did that come from?*.

No-one thought to mention consulting Bill on the subject of accommodating soldiers in their house paddock, it was all quite secondary to the romance that was unfolding in the least likely of circumstances. Of course they must stay, the continued existence of the universe depended on it.

After exhausting every possible excuse for extending his time with Janet, Lieutenant Robert Robert reluctantly returned to the Model A to find Cox asleep. He shook him gently and Cox sprang to life.

"Is it a goer?" asked Cox

"You might say it couldn't be more perfect," said Robert with a stupid grin.

Cox made a couple of notes in his pocket diary and drove back to the temporary HQ with Robert quietly singing,
♪Blue skies smilin' at me, Nothin' but blue skies do I see...♪
as he gazed love struck out the window.
They passed Bill on the road coming towards them.
Bill thought, "hmm I'll have to be more discreet about feeding these birds now that the army's here."

Robert reported to d'Camry and Operation Emu headed for the Cole farm.

Janet raised the alarm that the army was moving in and reorganised the insurgency's emu feeding schedule. She explained that it couldn't be better, they would know in advance where they would be and could easily take the emus out of harm's way thus embarrassing the Federal Government with the complete ineptitude of their efforts. It was only after dealing with the immediate demands of the Great Emu War that Janet took notice of the strange feelings in her stomach, feelings brought on by the young man in uniform who was unsettling her, taking away her certainty and raising significant incongruity; always a worry for a completely rational person. What do you do when your whole view of the world is challenged by feelings that you previously declared trite and decried to your friends as meaningless pap? What do you do when it won't go away and the feeling is so delicious that you beg it to stay despite its complete lack of coherence with your declared values and life plan? What do you do?
In line with other great philosophers Janet did nothing, she held on to the conflicting feelings as if one were in each hand and she went forth into life not knowing how any of this could be resolved. All she did know, was that she wanted everything and that she would fight against reason to have it.

Was this the verge of schizophrenia? The descent into irrationality? The fraying of the psyche? Only one thing was sure, she was going to find out.

As night fell, the army was settling in, erecting a tent city, well town, well village. The heat of the day lingered on as the earth gave back what it had collected from the scorching sun. Robert was dreaming up excuses to visit Janet, Sgt Wilkins was making sure the weapons were secure, Ford, Cox and Down played mediocrity and talked of whether there was a future outside the army while d'Camry wrote despatches to Canberra embellishing their establishment of a base of operation into a major logistical achievement.

Robert chose to sleep on the shearing board, away from the others, he lay on his cot looking up at the Moffat Virtue overhead shearing gear illuminated by the dim light provided by the 32 volt generator. A shearer's handpiece still loaded with comb and cutter hung by its tension knob on a 6 inch nail. Robert remembered his father telling him that David Unaipon of South Australia had designed and patented a significantly improved hand piece in 1909, that his improvements had been misappropriated by British manufacturers and that his genius was not recognised, well, not by 1932 anyway. The poignancy of this immoral tale had stuck with Robert and now mixed with thoughts of Janet which were simultaneously erotic, loving and benevolent, it seemed to amplify his indignation on behalf of a fellow human being who had been so poorly treated.

As Robert's growing social conscience fought with his professed self interest, sleep eluded him, he tossed and turned, partly from the unwelcome dissonance, partly from heightened sexual arousal and partly from wondering who the hell he really was.

The morning parade brought further dilemmas when d'Camry, without any consultation addressed the men and ordered them to dig in, to actually entrench, to prepare a front line. Robert was gobsmacked. The men were confounded. Cox made a note in his diary as the parade was dismissed. Robert approached d'Camry, he questioned the wisdom of entrenching, especially in the Cole's house paddock and secretly wondered whether an accidental death from friendly fire would be a solution to this madness. d'Camry was not to be denied, "you can't have an effective campaign without a line, Lieutenant. Do you think you know better than the Imperial General Staff?"

"I do not have the experience of the Imperial General Staff, Sir, but I do know know that emus are notoriously stupid and have no knowledge of modern warfare." said Robert on the verge of losing his temper.

"Hate to pull rank old man but in this case experience wins out, you'll see the benefits once the campaign starts."

Robert recalled the sage advice of Captain Brown that applying reason and logic was pointless in cases where status and power had blocked the common sense receptors. He saluted and walked off to see if he could get Brown on the phone, perhaps the General might intervene before this idiot brought disgrace to all concerned.

Having promised Mrs Cole that the Australian Defence Forces would pay the telephone bill he placed a call to Canberra HQ. The local operator, who had never travelled beyond the district, thought it must be a prank and asked him to put his mother on the phone. Robert did his best to persuade her that he really was an adult and a serving Australian Officer but she insisted and he finally had to capitulate and hand the phone to Mrs Cole. He suffered through a lengthy conversation while the two women caught up with all the local gossip, peppered with titbits from overheard telephone calls.

But finally "Oh yes, Lieutenant Robert, he's the real thing alright and a charming young man, feels like he's one of the family. She'll put you through now."

"Thanks," said Robert "good thing we're not trying to organise the invasion of Greece, though a bit of delay there might have been a good thing. Captain Brown please, ... Brown, thank God, you sound like you're in a tunnel, this mission is turning into a farce, ... it's d'Camry I can't control him Sir, he's ordered the men to entrench, ... yes entrench! against emus for God's sake. Stop laughing Sir, ... please. I was thinking that maybe the General could rein him in a bit before this thing goes completely pear shaped. ... In London? What's he doing in London, Christ what a mess. ... Back when? ... Alright I'll do my best but this needs intervention as soon as possible."

It was then that Janet took a break from her typewriter and emerged from her room.

"Intervention, that sounds very serious, lieutenant."

"Very serious business the army," he replied with a smile. "Janet, I was wondering, could you possibly spare some time to show me round the district, it's just intelligence gathering and maybe you could inject some actual intelligence into the operation."

Janet had to take a deep breath to disguise her excitement as she replied "yes, hurrah, just us, lovely that would be ... lovely and ... good. Tomorrow? Soon? Now?" She was smiling broadly and internally cringing at her continuing girlish ineptitude.

"About half an hour if all goes to plan, I'll come and pick you up about 11.00."

Robert called a 'thank you' to Mrs Cole who had returned to the kitchen and went to find d'Camry to see if he could lever him towards common sense. He found him inspecting the beginning of the trenches and looking extremely self satisfied.

"Construction's going well Sir" said Robert. "As well as can be expected," replied d'Camry, lacking the confidence that allows the acceptance of a genuine compliment. "Good, good, ... Sir, I was thinking, ... your intelligence ... um, ... plan, does it include a preliminary reconnoitre of the area?"

"Of course," snapped d'Camry.

"Well sir, we can't use all the men on the digging so perhaps we could send out five scouting parties to familiarise ourselves with the area and identify possible lines of attack," said Robert.

"Four will be quite sufficient lieutenant,"replied d'Camry, for no particular reason except to have the last word.

"Shall I get that underway Sir?" said Robert.

"Very good," said d'Camry.

Robert briefed Ford, Cox and Down to lead three of the scouting parties and went to find Janet to make the fourth.

Robert and Janet set out in dazzling sunshine to gather intelligence or rosebuds or get wisdom or find felicitude or ... in any case their motives were very mixed.

Since they were the Western party Janet immediately wanted to show Robert the Dreaming Rock, she wondered what he would see, would it include her, would it be significant or just a tourist attraction. They passed the wheat country and went on into the scrub without even sighting an emu, the rock loomed on the horizon and Janet explained it's significance to the local Aboriginal people. Robert was clueless about Aboriginal culture, he had seen Corroborees performed at official functions in Canberra and knew David Unaipon by reputation as an inventor and preacher. He knew that legislation had been passed that excluded Aborigines from suffrage and indeed from holding office. He didn't know that William Ramsay Smith the somewhat famous anthropologist had taken David's unpublished work about Aboriginal legends and published it as *Myths and Legends of the Australian Aboriginals* under his own name in 1930 or that suffrage would not be restored to Aboriginal people until 1967, but then he could be forgiven for that.

From his brief exposure Robert had not gleaned any of the richness of the culture, he thought the percussive music and the monotonal chanting to be bland and reflective of a primitive stone age people. When he said as much to Janet she came close to biting his head off. "You've got to know the individuals," she retorted, "they are just as human and clever and funny as any of your men."

"Not much competition there," Robert admitted.

"And Corroborees are living histories!" said Janet.

They drove on in silence for another ten minutes, Janet hoping that she hadn't blown away any possibility of romance in the first hours of their 'relationship' but feeling at last less like a schoolgirl and enjoying the return of her usual confidence. Robert was hoping that he hadn't alienated this beautiful creature who had just demonstrated the sort of backbone that he prized and wished he had more of himself.

In this fragile state they pulled up close to the rock. The rock that had never known fragility or doubt or rank or status, not even fear of failure or the lure of egoistic success, it just was and had been for a very long time.

"Would you like to climb it?" said Janet in a calm even voice that put Robert at ease.

"I would," said Robert in a voice that acknowledged Janet's superior understanding.

Janet lead the way and as they started the ascent Robert looked at her shapely buttocks and smiled. Yes, he thought, this is very sexual but there's something else going on here, something a bit more scary, something deeper. At a tricky ledge Janet found a secure handhold and extended her hand to Robert and pulled him up in front of her so that he would be first to the top. As she followed him up the last hundred yards she looked at his shapely buttocks and smiled, he was a very sexy man and she wanted him and if the interchange in the Model A was what she thought is was, she was looking at someone who displayed more respect than ego, ... remarkable.

Robert walked out onto the wind worn top of the rock, a stunted shrub clung to the side of a depression that would hold water when it rained, he marvelled at the toughness of this land; how did plants survive here, how did anyone survive here? Janet walked toward him, stumbled at the last step and had to steady herself on his shoulder. They laughed as they straightened themselves and looked out over the surrounding country, they held hands as they pivoted a full 360 degrees, breathing in the history and the pheromones. They kept turning and instinctively closed their eyes.

"I can see us," said Robert, "in a fancy office, people are signing papers and shaking our hands."

"I can see us too," said Janet, "now it's a gallery, lots of modern art, we're drinking Champagne. I can see the bottle, it says Krug and I see a bronze replica of an emu, do you?"

"Yes, but why?" said Robert.

"Not everything makes sense," said Janet.

"That's the first thing you learn in the army," said Robert.

They laughed as they turned minuet-like on the ancient rock. When they stopped and embraced, it was with all the ease of lifelong lovers.

The visions faded gently as the lovers focused on each other.

"That was ... I mean ... it ... when ... God ... I thought you were having me on."

"Not me lieutenant, would a journalist mislead a soldier on a critical mission?"

"Probably, but would a soldier find meaning with a beautiful girl on a rock?"

"Absolutely unbelievable."

"Do you believe this?" said Robert as he kissed her gently.

"I'm a believer," said Janet as she pulled him back to her lips and held him there until they both trembled and laughed and cried and ... here they were on a rock, talk about right time wrong place. "Soon," said Robert. "Soon," said Janet.

The climb down allowed them to use their bodies and explore their unity, each one in turn being an anchor for the other, each feeling the other's weight and strength, the clasping of hands creating trust and confidence and the inevitable touching of sexual parts brought sweaty pleasure as one squeezed past the other.

Cox

Cox's patrol was not having nearly as much fun. Without an emu in sight, they surveyed an open landscape that gave new meaning to the word 'flat' and an equally flat tyre that gave old meaning to the word 'bugger'.

Cox did not take easily to command, he took no pleasure in telling other people what to do, it made him feel uncomfortable. When he took out his notebook and started writing, his two subordinates didn't wait for instruction they gave each other a knowing look and simply got on with what the situation demanded.

"Why do you suppose it's called a jack?" said subordinate one, whose name was Harry.

"Dunno," said subordinate two whose name was Jack.

"I would've thought you'd know the answer to that," said Harry.

"Hilarious," said Cox. "The word 'jack' apart from being a name derived from John, is used to describe men or masculine things or things that vaguely resemble penises in a deprecating manner. For instance; a 'jack rafter' is a shorter rafter, a 'jack plane' is a rough planing tool and a 'car jack' is shorter and gets longer the more you … the more you ... wind it. So Jack, get winding, I'd stay back a bit if I was you Harry."

Cox returned to his incessant writing, Harry and Jack were too dumbfounded to laugh. They didn't understand Cox, his learned ramblings seemed to miss the point with them, why couldn't he just say, 'cause it's up in a flash like you Jack'? That would've made them laugh.

If it wasn't for the company of Ford and Down, Cox would probably have left the army. Inexplicably, uncannily and possibly absurdly he had found a couple of soul mates in Ford and Down, they supported the same jaded world view and found enough meaning in friendship to sustain them in what some might think was an anti-intellectual, rabidly jingoistic and totally inhospitable environment. The trio, held together by friendship, created an opportunity for all three to stay long enough to actually appreciate the army, the undeniably great feeling of being a part of something important, the knowledge that an organisation of committed human beings that could act as one, rapidly and effectively. And on top of all that it gave Cox the opportunity to write about everything he saw; the smart and the stupid, the brave and the cowardly, the skilled and the useless – it all passed before his eyes as if ordered for his entertainment and delight.

Cox's parents had come to Australia after the great war, they did not become cattle barons or senior public servants or property developers; they lived from hand to mouth and moved from job to job, his father, tormented by the lingering horrors of the war in France and his mother trying to love the stranger that had returned to her in 1918. An itinerant lifestyle meant a scant education in the company of rough shearers and farm labourers. But in this turbulent, brawling, drunken sea of humanity there was the odd one that was a thinker, the odd one that took an interest and with the tutelage of his mother he started to learn and embrace the world of ideas, albeit in a narrow way with huge gaps in the knowledge of his casual mentors. It was during an unusually long stint on a Northern Territory cattle run that he met Mildred Carter. She was cheeky and boisterous, a year older than the gangly John Cox and beat him in their first arm wrestle. Mildred was the cook's daughter and after a bit of cajoling came to share in the daily lessons provided by John's mother. Mildred and John developed a strong bond. They competed; to use new words, to yell out answers to mental arithmetic and read aloud with meaning even when the meaning was obscure. They tried their best to outdo each other. They loved it, a rare time of connection for two souls denied access to a 'proper' education. Their bond was strong and it was miraculous that it didn't become sexual in that pubescent year – it may have been fear or perhaps respect for the opportunity to learn or maybe they were just having too much fun to worry about all that excitement of sexual arousal.

When the families finally moved on, John Cox and Mildred Carter vowed to stay friends and to write to each other every week. The addresses of itinerant workers are of course forever changing but each family had the benefit of a stable relative with a regular address who could forward mail as soon as they were informed by their itinerant relatives of their new location. And so the voluminous correspondence of John and Mildred began.

John Cox didn't know anyone that had been to a university, his few friends had not even completed primary school. And so, he was a talented man from an impoverished background with no idea of where to go in the world; the antithesis of a Patrick White endowed with privilege, talent and willfulness. Both men were 20 in 1932 and White from his own account could walk from Victoria to Queensland without getting off a White family property. Two men who could do nothing but write. They never met and Cox didn't read White until 1939 when 'Happy Valley' was panned by the Australian press and Cox knew he had to read it. It is doubtful that White ever read Cox.

"Hey Coxy, the Model A 's ready," said Jack.
"Hey Jack off ... we go." Jack didn't get it and Cox kicked himself for being obtuse, mean, superior and not funny.

True, Jack was not very bright but he was a good mate, affable and dependable.
Sometimes intelligence is a curse.

A Country Garden

Janet's mum was the soul of hospitality, but starved of regular company she descended on these visitors like a hungry jackal. The isolation of the farm had created a desperation for human contact that exploded in a disconcerting effusion of welcoming ceremonies. Elizabeth wandered among the troops with a tray, offering tea with scones, jam and cream.

"Good morning Corporal …?"

"Ford, ma'am Henry Ford, not the car maker."

"And where are you from Corporal?"

"Born in Bristol ma'am."

"That's nice, do have another scone, they don't keep you know, does your mother bake scones?"

"Fraid not ma'am, she has to work you see. My Dad died in the war."

"How tragic so many good young men lost to their loved ones."

"Mum says he was a drinker and used to hit her regular, so I don't think she was too upset."

"Still he managed to serve his country."

"Not really, he were court-martialed for cowardice in the face of the enemy and because he were in the British Army they shot him, ma'am."

The hostessing was not going entirely to plan.

"Goodness, I'm so sorry … oh Major, a cup of tea?"

"Splendid, thank you, d'Camry's the name, this is just what the chaps need, home away from home, a bit of feminine congeniality."

"I was just a bit worried about Corporal ..." but before she could finish d'Camry cut across her

"Don't you worry, not one little bit, they've all been worded up to behave like gentlemen so no need for any concern, not that you'd need to worry."

"Well no, ... it's just that ..." d'Camry cut her off again and looked her up and down..

"Must have been a bit ... you know ... , and after I had made it perfectly clear that fraternisation was simply not on, I mean, damn it, this is a military mission not a night at the local bordello. The very idea that ..."

Fortunately for d'Camry, Robert returned at that moment and came to the rescue of the woman that he was pretty sure would be his future mother-in-law.

"Mrs Cole, what a marvellous thing to do, did you bake these just for us? You're a gem."

Relief flowed like a river.

"Corporal, I want a word with you!" Bellowed d'Camry, as he marched off to support the chastity of women everywhere. This generally unwelcome chivalry he referred to as the Tenth Crusade, and in line with the success of the previous nine would quite soon be added to d'Camry's list of consummate cock-ups.

Mrs Cole smiled broadly at Robert "Thank you lieutenant, did Janet show you her ... (d'Camry had managed to heightened everyone's sexual awareness) ... rock?" She said nervously. "She's quite absorbed by it, something to do with native ceremonies, I think."

"Yes, it was quite wonderful, I've never experienced anything like it."

"Mrs Cole, may I tell you something?"

"Certainly you may and please call me Elizabeth."

"I didn't want this mission, in fact I tried very hard to get out of it but after today I think this might just be the best thing I've ever done."

"I'm glad to hear it Robert, would you like to have dinner with us this evening, just you, not that awful Major."

"Thank you Elizabeth, I would be delighted, d'Camry does have his good points but they are, shall we say, as yet undiscovered."

As they chatted on about Elizabeth's garden and life on the land, Robert simultaneously mused on his uncharacteristic charity toward d'Camry, minor as it was, he wondered where it had come from, was this another 'rock' experience or was everything rosier and brighter in the afterglow of 'Janet and Robert'.

Elizabeth foisted the last of the tea and scones on Corporal Down who had a lovely family, a happy home life and really no skeletons in the closet at all, but Elizabeth was too afraid to ask, so she simply smiled and as he opened his mouth to say 'delicious' she filled it with the last scone in a race to return to her kitchen.

As she started the preparations for the evening, she entertained very girlish feelings about weddings and babies and family dinners; hopefully they would live close by, not in Dencubbin, maybe on the coast in that glorious country South of Perth. Elizabeth loved the ocean, she longed for the breeze and the salt air, would Bill like it, he had loved Clovelly, their walks along the coast, the romance of its long history. Surely, it wasn't too much to dream about.

The Emus Strike Back

Maurie had been delegated by the all powerful central committee (Ted) to take care of the first diversionary wheat run (DWR 1). He had co-opted Fred to help load and then gradually empty the bags off the back of the truck as he drove into the least likely location for emus, well away from the open paddocks of the better farming country. Maurie and Fred had loaded his farm truck with bags of wheat at Bill's 'depot' that morning and driven off to the north, as per the master plan, which aimed to keep the emus as far away from the army as possible. Unfortunately, the bags had not been stitched across the top and Maurie had not taken care to stack the bags so as to stop them falling over. Almost as soon as he was out the gate the first bag fell onto its side and started to dribble its contents onto the floor of the truck. Unfortunately the tongue and groove boards on the floor of the truck's tray were old and weathered and now had gaps between them that let the wheat fall through to the ground as Maurie drove on over the bumpy tracks. Unfortunately several more bags fell over and most unfortunately, created a perfect trail from the destination of the feeding grounds back to Bill and Elizabeth's farm.

Feeding the birds sent them into a frenzy and Fred was lucky not to lose an eye. He yelled to Maurie to speed up and keep ahead of the bloody birds but Maurie was surrounded, he was bogged in emus. Emus have long necks and they could easily reach over the tray of the truck forcing Fred onto the roof of the cab and Maurie to speedily wind up the window. Maurie blew the horn and Fred yelled obscenities but it was no use, they just had to wait it out.

When the clouds of feathers finally cleared a little, Fred made a leap off the roof and seemingly rebounded into the truck and slammed the door. "Drive through there boss," yelled Fred seeing a gap in the dense throng. Maurie responded, crunching the truck into first and planting his foot on the accelerator. They cleared the iron ring of birds and made for home. With the dust and the failing light they drove, unaware over the trail they had laid on the way in.

Later that evening Maurie dropped Fred off at the shearers quarters and thought he would call in and see Janet. He made a list to ensure an interesting, if somewhat contrived conversation.

Tell her about the emus.
Ask her to dinner.
Get on the piss with Bill.
Ask Mrs Cole how the flowers for the show are coming along.
I love you Janet.
I love your writing and that, Janet.

With this fulsome preparation under his belt Maurie banged the Clovelly door knocker. Elizabeth opened the door. "Maurie, come in, we're all in the dining room." Maurie followed dutifully down the hall. As he came to the doorway he saw Janet across the room and blurted out, "The emus are under ..."
"Maurie, how nice to see you, come in, this is **Lieutenant Robert**, from the **Army**, Task Force Emu, the ones who are here to help us with the **emus**," said Janet underlining every word and trying desperately to convey to Maurie that he should, shut up!
"Maurie, nice to meet you," said Robert as they shook hands. "As you were saying ... about the emus, they're under ...?" said Robert.

"Yes, emus, under, no not under, in or out, yes out, they're out..."

"Of sight," interjected Janet. "Have a drink Maurie," she said, quickly pouring a large Scotch and pressing it into his hand. "Drink up, that's the way, warm you right through, brr, cold out," blathered Janet.

Maurie never drank Scotch and a big gulp made him gag.

"Oh dear are you alright? Too much excitement, he's just a country boy, probably wants to go home." Janet was raving as she refilled Maurie's glass.

"He only just got here," said Robert. "And the emus are under … ?"

"Oh they could be, ... Under Milkwood for all he'd know," Janet was losing composure.

"Under Milkwood …?" said Robert.

"On the rock, small man, drunk, poet, ...I don't know."

And when it looked like everything was cascading into oblivion, Maurie waded in with, "they're outside!"

"Thank God," said Robert with a laugh, "another Scotch Maurie?"

Robert took Maurie's quizzical look for a yes and plied him with a third double.

Maurie was now doubly confused and close to legless but determined to stick to his list said, "How about dinner Janet?"

"But I've only just eaten, Maurie."

"Then how about getting on the pi.." Maurie stopped just in time, realising that he had discounted that possibility, "on the porch, how about it on the porch. It's lovely out."

"No it's not," said Janet, "it's cold, brrr remember."

The Scotch was cooking Maurie's brain.

"Your writing, no, the flowers next, the flowers are writing to our mother."

Robert could see exactly what was happening, at least with

Maurie, so with a gentle arm around his shoulder he guided him to a seat by the fire and sat down next to him and moved him into the comfort zone of wheat farming. "Did you plant a lot of wheat this year Maurie?"

The wheat crop was definitely not in Janet's comfort zone, but Maurie was beyond her immediate reach. She looked to her Father with panic in her eyes and signalled that he should get Maurie out.

"Maurie, your mother rang earlier, ... when ... that is ... before, before Lieutenant Robert ... arrived." Bill was a hopeless liar. "And she wanted you ... to ... help."

"With what?" slurred Maurie. "With the er ar ... chooks," said Bill.

"We don't have chooks," said Maurie.

"They just arrived ... from ... town and she needs you to get them ... in the pen," said Bill.

"We don't have a pen," said Maurie. "Well, bit of work to do then, need a hammer?" said Bill.

"Better hurry, don't keep her waiting; chooks on fire rollin, down the road." blurted Janet.

"On fire?" said Robert.

"The rock .. again, wheels actually, bloody weird that," said Janet.

"Janet!" reproached her mother.

Janet shook her head in an effort to get her thoughts back in order.

"Sorry mum, let's get Maurie under way shall we, sounds urgent." And with that, Maurie was dispatched to his truck and sent to confront the flaming chook crisis.

As Maurie rattled over the grid, Robert reluctantly made his goodbyes knowing that he had to be up at 4.00am for d'Camry's predawn briefing for the officers and NCO's, Janet longed for him to stay. He longed to take Janet with him. Bill and

Elizabeth finally went inside. Janet walked with Robert the 200 yards to the shearing shed, an enormous moon hung low in the sky, they stopped at the stairs, the silhouetted lovers kissed, seen only by the horses who nickered in approval.

o-o-o-o-o-o-o-o-o

"Surprise and intelligence, intelligence and surprise, that's what we need" roared d'Camry as if he had just discovered the inner workings of the atom.

"So we should find out where they are and surprise them?" said Robert as if he was paraphrasing genius for the benefit of the layman.

"Exactly," said d'Camry, "in my opinion these birds are more cunning than we originally thought. They have been taking evasive action, leaving false clues, leading us up the garden path and down the rabbit hole."

"They've been reading Lewis Carroll" whispered Cox

"Something to share Corporal? said d'Camry.

"Well yes," said Cox "It's an interesting observation sir, do you have any further insights?" Robert had to turn away at that point to control his laughter. Cox pursued his baiting.

"Do you see the emu as a more sophisticated enemy and if so should we be taking our security more seriously?"

It was at that point that the cook rushed in waving a spatula yelling, "we're under attack!"

Without stopping to ask, 'by whom', 'how many' or even 'where from' d'Camry gave the order to "man the guns!"

The emus had in fact made a preemptive strike; following the grain trail they had come upon a feast that was clearly meant for them. Cook had been laying sausages on a steel plate while an emu standing behind him would remove them when he turned to get more. More sausages, more emus, more bread, one terrified and hysterical cook and complete chaos in Elizabeth's garden. The emus it seems were expert tent peggers and frightened into an uncoordinated stampede, by the cook, collapsed most of the tents onto the waking soldiers. Bleary eyed gunners stumbled into the trenches and watched in amazement as their breakfast disappeared down the throats of the voracious birds. The ensuing melee of screaming soldiers and squawking emus prevented them from firing any shots at all so they leaned back to enjoy the spectacle. When the emus eventually retreated, the depth and direction of the trenches meant that no effective retaliation was possible and the gunners sat dumbfounded while d'Camry screamed repeated orders to fire.

Cox had plenty to write about.

The d'Camry Line

At parade the following morning d'Camry kept the troops waiting while he finished his notes. The sun was already hot and by the time d'Camry finally addressed them they were feeling ... less than receptive.

"The first battle of this campaign is over and the result can only be regarded as indeterminate. It seems that ... *rave, rave, sun hot, sun hotter, when's breakfast ...*

... It is without doubt that my assessment of the enemy's capability has proved correct, an enemy with guile and cunning which ... *stop, no more, how much longer, we fucking give up*

... Men, after a complete analysis of our defences I have decided that we will now implement stage two. I think you will all agree that an enemy that moves with such speed and precision can only be effectively confronted by more flexible and extensive fortifications. We will extend the trenches ... *not more fucking digging you fucking useless dick ...* so that we have the ability to deliver a volley in any direction. When complete I will personally be checking the enfilade angles. If this one small detail had been checked before the previous strike we would have inflicted severe casualties on the enemy despite their duplicitous raid. Detail, detail, detail, it is detail that will win in the end. ... *counting the minutes, must be near the end, give me breakfast or give me death.*

Everyone was counting the seconds that brought them closer to the conclusion of this self serving tripe, every man knew that silence and tacit assent was the quickest escape route and when Cox sought permission to speak there was an audible groan.

"Sir, I am sure I speak for all the men when I say that I am honoured to serve in this command, the chance to acquit oneself in a theatre like this is the dream of every professional soldier. To say that we fought the emu, to tell our children and our grandchildren that we made that world a better place, a safer place .. *we're fucking going to kill you Coxy* ... a place where sheep can roam free and the ladies of Baling Up can have one right on the jack .. *now that's funny thought Jack* ... without risking their chastity. Sir I ... *one more word and it's the garrotte for you mate* ... just wanted to say, thank you.

"Well said corporal, ... *fuck, he's responding, this better be quick* ... my subordinates have always enjoyed a certain reputation, ... *for suicide in the face of ineptitude* ... they are well known throughout the empire for ... *fucking stupidity, you cockhead* ... excellence in logistics and solid detailed planning and execution. *execution? don't tempt us* ... Sergeant dismiss the troops." *thank Christ for that.*

Cox, knowing what was coming, bolted up the water tower trying to escape retribution but you can never escape your peers; Cox now suffering a fit of laughter was hauled down and indecorously thrown in the horse trough. Only Jack and Harry held back, indulging in some self congratulations for getting all the jokes.

Breakfast finally followed.

Work recommenced on the trenches, the men were uninspired, the sun was hot and the grumbling was constant.

"A lot of men just disappeared beneath the mud in the French trenches ... never seen again," said Cox.

"Anyone in mind?" said Jack, as he swung a pick, striking a rock and jarring his hand.

"Perhaps one of the Majors while checking the enfilade angles," said Cox

"We only have one Major and ..." said Jack pausing with the realisation that he was once again stating the bleeding obvious, "and what are enfilade angles?"

"It's just an arcane way of saying, have the guns set up so you can actually shoot the bloody emus," said Cox.

"And what's arcane then?" said Harry as he heaved another shovel full of dirt from the trench.

"It means 'mysterious'," said Cox, "like the workings of d'Camry's brain, though 'working' and 'brain' might be overly generous."

Jack and Harry smiled politely. They needed to learn about sarcasm next.

With Jack's next blow Cox noticed a glint that he thought was probably just a spark caused by the friction of iron on stone but unlike those common little sparks it persisted momentarily until falling dirt covered the gouge.

Jack swung again but Cox had a reflex action and grabbed the handle of the pick at the top of the swing which sent Jack sprawling forward.

"Very funny,' said Jack wiping has face and spitting dirt from his mouth.

"Sorry," said Cox as he lunged forward to the face where jack had been digging, "I saw something," he brushed the dirt away with his hand 'it was glinting in the sunlight.

"I saw it too," said Robert who had been doing the rounds of the new earthworks.

As Cox removed more and more dirt a nugget emerged from the earth like a Michelangelo sculpture from its marble prison. The mark of the pick was now clearly visible and the bright gold of ... GOLD ... reflected sunlight on the stunned soldiers.

"I've never seen ... do you think .... are we ..." It was Cox's halting speech but it was everyone's immediate thoughts.

Robert knew exactly what to do; "at this point I think we keep this to ourselves, keep digging, see if there's a seam and … follow it, I'll work out the legalities, we could all be very very rich." This last he said in hushed tones.

There was an instant increase in productivity from Cox's team. Corporals Ford and Down looked over in amazement, not so much at the productivity but at the breaking of the unwritten rule of working at a median pace. This was a universal law in work teams, not so much the pace of the slowest but a standard derived without discussion that everyone could meet without the onset of exhaustion or accusations of tardiness. It had worked for thousands of years, what was Cox thinking; a work ethic that mirrored their game of mediocrity was suddenly under threat and this from its firmest adherent and brightest son.

The Cox trench meandered somewhat, yielding occasional nuggets and then a seam so rich the excitement of the diggers was impossible to conceal. Robert casually sauntered up to check the progress, there was no need to ask the result, it was writ large in dirt, sweat and smiles.

"You are, on track Corporal?" asked Robert.

"I'm a bit worried that we're headed for the tank stand sir," replied Cox

"I think you're right on the money there Corporal, just keep going … I've brought you some water, have a bit of a cool off," said Robert, as he splashed a bit from the bucket on each man causing providential muddy puddles. "Best to keep covered up in this sun, don't you agree? Try these wet bandannas," said Robert as he made subtle trowelling motions. Jack and Harry looked back at the Lieutenant as if he were a piece of cheese speaking Arabic but Cox led the way and smeared mud over the persistent sparkles.

By day's end the Cox trench was outstripping its rivals by more than double and had seriously undermined one leg of the high tank stand. Cox was thinking about reinforcing the structure, when d'Camry came to inspect the days progress.

"Excellent work Corporal, and well done on the curves, bound to confuse the enemy," said d'Camry.

"Confusion's what we had in mind Sir," replied Cox

At that moment the tank listed ever so slightly, letting loose a spray of water from the overflow pipe. Several drops hit d'Camry who instinctively looked into the clearest of skies for the offending cloud. Despite all the evidence pointing to continuing dry weather d'Camry immediately ordered duckboards to be made ready for installation in the trenches and declared, as he marched off with his swagger stick under his arm, "we won't be caught with our pants down." At that moment in what seemed like pure insect spite, d'Camry was bitten on the leg by a green ant, he slashed at the suspected spot on his trousers with his swagger stick and hurried into the nearby latrine to disrobe and investigate further. With all haste he removed his trousers in search of the offending ant when he heard a creaking sound follow by the crash of the tank stand collapsing and then with no further warning a wall of water carried away the hessian privacy barriers of the latrine leaving d'Camry with his pants definitely down and struggling to get them back on. Thousands of gallons of water then surged down the trenches and ploughed through Elizabeth's prize dahlias.

In a panicked attempt to recover some decorum d'Camry managed to get both his legs into one leg of his trousers and then unwilling to drop his pants again as Elizabeth and Janet came rushing out to see what had happened he hopped briskly to the safety of his tent with his swagger stick still under his arm.

Elizabeth was too devastated by the loss of her dahlias to even notice the hopping Major but Janet convulsed in laughter, stifled it then laughed again before finally breaking into a fury over the destruction of their garden and the loss of the water supply. Janet took a perverse but totally forgivable pleasure in immediately confronting d'Camry. She marched into his tent where d'Camry was still struggling to get his pants off but upon Janet's entrance was forced to stop and pull them back up again still with two legs in the one trouser leg. He stood there sheepishly as Janet berated him. "Major d'Camry," she hissed "you are without doubt the most incompetent, rudest, over-promoted, egoistic fool I have ever had the misfortune to encounter. Our garden is in ruins, you have destroyed our water supply, your trenches are a farce, the emus have more collective brain power than you are able to display and pants come as a pair for a reason!" Without waiting for a reply Janet turned on her heel and left.

Steve and Fred looked on in disbelief. "One fella trouser, two fella leg," said Steve as they walked away. "And hops like a kangaroo," said Fred. They laughed.

A Little Child

On a rainy, cold, grey, miserable Canberra day the Lyon's children played happily in the Prime Minister's Lodge, the older ones indulging the younger ones in simple games. Eight year old Edward had hauled out the jigsaw collection, Sarah had guided him away from a 500 piece puzzle that looked like the great southern ocean on a dark night and they settled instead on a map of Australia complete with kangaroos, parrots, koala bears, dingos and, of course, emus scattered across the continent. An Aboriginal man stood commandingly in the middle dressed in a scarlet lap-lap and throwing a boomerang decorated with dots in imitation of a popular Aboriginal art style. Over this unlikely scene King George V looked down from where New Guinea should have been with a smile that conveyed that all was well across his vast realm.

And so it was, except for those damned Indians always carrying on about independence, those damned Iraqis cranky about being under a British mandate, those damned Kurds who just couldn't be satisfied even though they had been 'liberated' from Turkish rule and those damned Irish... *hmmm maybe that's a different story* ... and that damned Edward, Prince of Wales and his playboy lifestyle ... anyway George was smiling because his second son, Albert, had married a lovely gal and so far had presented him with two adorable granddaughters Elizabeth and Margaret. They helped to take his mind off that scallywag Edward.

Edward (Lyons that is, not the Prince of Wales) had secreted several pieces of Western Australia under his cushion so that he would have the honour of placing the last piece. As the puzzle neared completion, all the animals had found their place and the states all had their boundaries except for Western Australia which was missing its entire coastline.

"Come on Edward I know you've got the last pieces, just put them in," said Sarah.

"What if I don't want to," retorted Edward.

"We all want to finish the puzzle Eddie," coaxed Sarah

"Dad says the West Australians are a pain in the arse and I'm not going to have them in my Australia," said Edward with a superiority that accurately reflected the hubris of some of the real players in the game.

"Don't let Mum hear you talk like that or you'll have your mouth washed out," warned Sarah.

"I don't care, Dad said it and he wouldn't say it if it wasn't true," said Edward standing his ground.

"I don't think he meant you to hear that little mate," said Billy.

"Well I did and I'm throwing Western Australia away," yelled Edward as he grabbed the remaining pieces and ran towards the window.

Edward hadn't counted on the speed and agility of his older brother; as he ran Billy ankle tapped him and he went sprawling headlong into a lounge chair, Billy then picked him up and worked him like a puppet, putting the last puzzle pieces in place. Edward wailed and pouted and generally behaved like an eight year old child. He was still sobbing indignantly when his mother came in and asked what on earth was going on.

"Oh, Eddie's just upset about what's going on in Western Australia,' said Sarah quickly.

"Really?" replied her mother, "such awareness for one so young. Have you quite recovered from your upset Edward?" Edward nodded, preferring the rough justice of his siblings to the fearsome retribution of his mother.

As she left the room, the atmosphere dripped with maternal

sarcasm and sibling relief.

"Anyway," said Sarah, "Australia wouldn't be complete without the West, it wouldn't make any sense, Dad said that too, you little shit."

"Mouthwash!" yelled Edward as they all fell about laughing.

The Election Campaign

The Western Australian State election campaign for 1932 was now in full swing with both parties haranguing the electorate at every opportunity. Opposition leader Phillip Collier had been hard at it selling the same message in every small town and community hall across his vast state. It was Dencubbin's turn and Collier cranked himself up knowing full well that this possible handful of votes was not his just for the asking and hardly worth the trip.

It was a far cry from the big politics of Roosevelt vs Hoover or Hindenburg vs Hitler but the rhetoric was remarkably similar. It was said of Hitler that at a regional rally he promised that; "Under my government every German Girl will find a husband." The authenticity is doubtful but it mirrors the political desperation of those who would be king … or queen.

Promises promises promises …

"Labor is the party of the working people of Western Australia, we have a proud history of fairness and reform. We have championed worker's rights and created enterprises that have not only provided employment but challenged corrupt monopolies. This is a difficult time for an export economy like ours, we need the strength of a united Australia to compete in world markets.

I know many of you sincerely believe that an independent Western Australia will see the dawn of a golden age of prosperity, this is an illusion. We are part of a large country with a small population on the edge of Asia. Without continental unity our security would be seen as a farce and in any attempt to exert our influence in Asia we will be seen as a very junior power that can be easily ignored. My friends, the workers' cause, the farmers' cause and indeed the cause of every Western Australian will not be served by breaking our ties with our brothers in the other states. United we stand, divided we fall. Unity is strength and the Nationalists only offer division."

"What about the emus?" yelled Bill.

Collier knew this was coming, Dencubbin was after all the epicentre of the Emu plague.

"An excellent example of the ineptitude of our current government. A Labor government would have acted decisively to eliminate the emu menace before it got out of hand. Thank you for your attendance this evening, let's make this coming polling day one to remember."

The scattered applause was more than he had expected and gave him some confidence that even in this conservative heartland people were tiring of the Nationalists.

Bill was not to be denied this opportunity and even though Collier had wrapped it up he yelled, "and we want more details about fixing the Grain Authority and the tariffs…"

"Too right," echoed Ted and Maurie.

Collier smiled through gritted teeth and muttered to himself as he came off the platform, "do something about the emus, maybe I should promise them that interest rates will never rise."

Secrets

Bill, Ted and Maurie came home together for supper at Bill's and a quick meeting. Ted was livid at Collier's defence of 'continental security'.

"They don't care about the West. They'd sell us to the Chinese if the price was right."

Bill was tiring of Ted's hyperbole, "steady on Ted, the Federation's been going for over 30 years and no-one's ever suggested anything like that."

"They'd ditch us like a hot spud," said Ted.

"Drop us! It's 'drop us like a hot potato'." said Bill

"Exactly!" said Ted.

"I'm not agreeing with you Ted, I'm correcting your idiom."

"What?" said Ted, angrily, mistaking 'idiom' for 'idiot'.

"All I'm saying mate is, just calm down a bit, alright, we need to maintain a bit of perspective."

"Perspective? Where was their perspective when they put sky high tariffs on farm machinery?"

"I agree on that, you know I do, but we can't go round saying things that aren't true or we look like ignorant idiots."

"There it is again!"

"What?"

"Idiot, you called me an idiot!"

"I didn't"

"You did, Maurie heard it didn't you Maurie?"

"I think … I don't … because the … is Janet home?" Maurie was very far away.

"No, she's working late at the paper, reporting the Collier rally," said Bill.

"Do you think she'd like me better if I could make speeches?"

"Who?"

"Janet."

"I don't think so mate, Janet's impressed by,... well it's complicated she, ... Look she's my daughter and I'm surprised she's stuck it out here as long as she has, she's not really the 'farmer's wife' sort of girl, mate, if you know what I mean."

"You mean she's not a farmer's wife yet, Bill?"

"I mean Maurie Mason, you are the world's most guileless person and she's, ... well she's not." Just as Maurie opened his mouth the phone rang and saved Bill from the escalating awkwardness that could only end with *mate you have as much chance with Janet as a ram in a goat paddock.*

Ted was the last sage available and predictably Maurie asked, "Ted, what's guileless?"

"It means less guile, it means your liver produces less guile."

"So Janet produces more guile?"

"Yes mate that's about the size of it and it all balances out in the end, some more some less, you know." Ted was on fire, Maurie was fully informed about the human guile balance and Bill was off the hook and off the phone.

"That was Elizabeth, she and Janet are staying in town tonight. So what's our next move with the emus?"

"We need to make the Army look like complete idiots, next time they head to the Northwest we round up as many emus as possible, use our grain truck to start them in the right direction, get them going at high speed and lead them straight into the Army convoy and away again before they know what's hit them." Ted swung back on his chair ready to receive the appreciation of his peers.

Bill was slow to respond, he liked Lieutenant Robert and could see the growing affection that was developing with Janet. "Keep your enemies closer," he mumbled, shaking his head.

"Yeah good idea," said Ted.

It's a bugger when they're close and you get to know them and you like them and then they marry your daughter and then the truth comes out and it all falls apart. "Sorry Elizabeth love, it was all my fault we don't see Janet and Robert and our grandchildren any more." Bill mused as Ted raved on and on about times and logistics.

Bill could see the value in the plan but without it being captured on film it would have precious little impact. He kept his mouth firmly shut.

o-o-o-o-o-o-o-o-o

Outside in the cool of the evening Ford, Cox and Down had joined the stockmen Fred and Steve at their camp fire. The stockmen were shy of these newcomers and feared intolerance and violence, after all they had good reason to fear complete stupidity and irrational behaviour based on what they had seen so far of the d'Camry mission, let alone the madness that seemed to have overtaken their boss.

"Mind if we join you?" said Cox.

"Emu chasers always welcome round the campfire," said Steve.

"We haven't been doin' too well," said Down. My name's Michael by the way and this is John Cox and Henry Ford."

"Steve and Fred; Henry like the car man?" said Steve.

"My father was drunk when he registered my birth, I guess it was the first thing that came into his head," said Henry.

Everyone shook hands and settled down by the fire.

Curious, Cox opened the batting. "Are you fellas really called Steve and Fred, I would've thought you'd have names like Umba Jumba or something?"

"Oh you're thinking of my uncle Umba Jumba Roomana," replied Steve.

"Really?"

"No fuckin' way, that's the stupidest thing I've ever heard."

112

Steve had a way of making people laugh and putting them at ease.

They laughed, and laughed and laughed.

Cox laughed till he cried and his sides began to hurt.

"But really, you must have names in your own language," said Cox, before he dissolved into another fit of laughter. 'What was I thinking, Umba Jumba."

Uncharacteristically Fred broke his silence to say,"It's Jaril, his name is Jaril. Jaril is Owl, smart bird, night hunter."

"And what about you Fred, what are you called?" said Down, suddenly interested in something that had depth and meaning.

"I am called Jarli,". said Fred.

"Means ... friend," said Jaril pushing his friend off balance.

"Makes sense," said Ford.

They all settled round the fire and heard stories of tribal lore, army life, massacres, stolen children, moronic commanding officers, horses and mustering, shearing and lamb marking, planting and harvesting, the stuff of their daily lives except for the emus and the gold.

"You fellas want some tea, billy's boilin'," said Jaril.

"Thanks," said Ford.

Jaril added the tea and sugar and gave it a stir and poured out a single enamel mug full. They passed the mug around and sucked in the sticky sweet liquid.

"How much sugar is in this stuff," said Down.

"'Nough to bring the life back after a hard day ... my old father used to go for miles to find the bee's sugar bag, now it comes from missus Elizabeth's kitchen ... never runs out," said Jarli.

Jarli was unusually relaxed, he was feeling something new, white fellas that just wanted to talk and laugh and listen, it was different to his experience in town where he was barred from the hotels, had to sit at the back of the picture show, always regarded with suspicion by the police and never spoke to anyone more than to buy something in a shop.

"You fellas married?" said Jaril venturing on to more sensitive territory.

"Not me," said Henry, "my parents fought all the time. Father was a drunk and it kind of put me off the whole concept."

"I'd love to have a family," said Down, "but army life and marriage don't go together too well, especially if you're just shitkickers like us."

"Hopping Major, is he ...?" asked Jaril

"Married? I don't think there is anyone that stupid on the planet," said Cox, "stupid, conceited, arrogant, self important bloated buffoon!"

"He's not your friend then?" said Jarli

"Well ... no ... sorry, I get a bit carried away sometimes," replied Cox "He is such a prat, god knows what he's doing in the army apart from making us look completely stupid. I read a piece in the West Australian about shooting emus with machine guns, it's been tried and failed, they just disperse and disappear into the scrub and once they are in good condition like they are now you can't even drive them towards the guns. The same thing happens, they just break up and hide."

"They in good condition alright, they ...." said Jarli, getting a cautionary look from Jaril that stopped him mid sentence.

Jarli really couldn't see what all the fuss was about, these were goodfellas, why not tell them what was going on.

Cox had his suspicions that things were not as they should be but rather than push the point he changed the focus of the conversation back to love and marriage. "You know, I've thought about marriage but it's not for me, I like my freedom, I can do what I want without a wife and kids to think about and who would look after these two if I went off and got hitched."

"You a bunch of bum fuckers then?" said Jaril with a big grin. This time Jarli shot back a censoring look.

"These two are, I just watch," said Cox ... he held a poker face for all of five seconds and then burst out laughing which of course set everyone laughing again, partly as tension release but also because they had touched a delicate part of each other and implicitly decided that nothing was taboo.

Cox mentally turned over the gold issue, of course he should tell them, what happens later when they find out that their new friends deceived them? Is trust more important than wealth? Which is of greater value, gold or friendship? Why the reticence, fear of loss or fear of what others would think? Who did the gold belong to anyway, was it finders keepers or did these people, who had been here so long, deserve to be included or did anyone 'deserve' anything? He cursed his brain as it rattled on and on. What was he: the father of the faith, the manager of morality, the doyen of decency or patriarch of paternalism ... and where did all that come from? He was an atheist after all, didn't that protect him from these quasi-religious feelings? Clearly not.

Jaril was not immune either, he saw Jarli's desire for openness, but what of their implicit agreement with their boss, Bill was a good man, he had treated them well, he had made them a present of the horses they loved, he understood when they went home to their people, often without warning. Would they take on new friends and risk alienating the old ones? He was the wise owl but he didn't feel so smart right at that moment. He looked at Cox, a long and penetrating look, that said, *I have a dilemma please understand me.*

Cox gave a discreet nod then looked down indicating that *he got it and had no answer.*

It was Down, unencumbered by the hard questions of life who broke the long silence, thanking the hosts and telling them how much he had enjoyed the evening.

o-o-o-o-o-o-o-o-o

Robert had sought leave to attend the Collier Rally. He had seen Janet scribbling shorthand and noted her father's strident, seemingly out of character comment on the emu plague. He caught up with her as she walked toward the newspaper office.

"Need a fast typist," said Robert.

"I am a fast typist," said Janet

"Then I'm redundant."

"Fraid so."

"I make good coffee."

"At last a man with useful skills."

"Will you give Collier a good rap?"

"Always fair and fearless, Lieutenant."

"Your dad might have certain expectations."

"He knows what to expect."

"I bet he does."

"Are you trying to influence the press?"

"Absolutely."

"Then come this way." Janet unlocked the door and led Robert to the corner that she called her office. "Palatial isn't it, kitchen's through there, toilet's out the back."

Janet sat down on the bentwood chair and recycled an old galley proof into the Underwood with the blank side ready to receive her story.

Robert looked for coffee and something to make it in. The great Italian fad for espresso coffee invented in 1884 and commercialised in 1905 with the first machine from La Pavoni, had not quite reached Dencubbin. Robert found an aluminium percolator and a gas ring with which he managed a fairly bitter tasting brew that was pretty much the standard in 1932.

He delivered the stimulant to Janet who hammered away on the

Underwood, and went off to explore the mysteries of newspaper production. The Dencubbin paper had been over-equipped by an enthusiastic owner who believed that Dencubbin would one day be a regional centre. The Dencubbin Star boasted its own Linotype machine, the typesetting marvel invented by Ottmar Mergenthaler that removed the tedium of hand-setting individual letters and revolutionised the printing industry. Invented in 1884, the same year as the espresso machine, which one would be more enduring? All bets were on the Linotype ... wrong. Moving down the production line a Furnival printing press loomed up with its paper feed platform and seat for the feed operator at least 4 feet above his head. It was the only press capable of printing a broadsheet outside Perth. It was an older model still run from an overhead drive shaft connected by leather belts, Robert pulled on the belt and realised it was on the idler pulley side so he pulled it harder and harder till he got the drive shaft spinning then flicked the lever so that the machinery engaged and the momentum proved sufficient to make the great cogs, flywheels, push rods and rollers turn for a brief moment. It was like some giant beast stirring slightly and then falling back to sleep. He would like to be such a giant but he would not sleep easily, always alert, always planning, always winning, always with Janet. Two people who loved to win, it couldn't be better. Was it time to tell her about the gold? He passed the guillotine with its 5 foot blade of brightly polished hardened steel that could slice through five hundred sheets at a time. The machine did not scare him as it sometimes did other newcomers who contemplated its awesome destructive power and then made the obvious imaginative leap to a hand being accidentally severed. Robert saw its power and had only thoughts of respect and how to harness such power in his life endeavours. He came back to the secret of the gold. He wanted the shiny yellow stuff, the stuff that Joe Stalin said he would use to line public toilets.

Robert knew exactly how he would use it - would Janet be with him? - was now the time to take the risk?

As he walked back toward her, she ripped the recycled galley proof from the Underwood and started to read it over. 'Philip Collier Campaigns in Dencubbin.'

"Leave it for a minute," said Robert

"Can't stop, the news never sleeps and ... and ... other aphorisms."

"I have something to tell you."

"What? You want to be a printer, everyone does ... it wears off ...takes about thirty seconds."

"I don't want to print the news ... I want to make the news."

"Oh my God you're going to kill the Major. I've been reading about this untraceable poison, easy to make, absolutely foolproof, then we can still ...."

At that point Robert grabbed her and kissed her, a long, wet, passionate, silencing kiss. It left her speechless long enough for Robert to say, "get married? YES but before that I have a secret."

Janet finally broke the silence. "Two families one in Canberra and one in Melbourne, I knew it..."

"For Christ's sake will you please s h u t u p."

"OK," Janet bridled.

"Thank you..."

"But that was funny wasn't it?"

"Shoosh, hush, be silent, stop speaking, desist in your communication!"

Silence reigned.

"We're in the gold business."

"You have a second job?"

"No. Well yes. It doesn't matter, we found gold on your parent's farm."

"And you didn't tell me?"

"I'm telling you now."

"When?"

"Three days ago, the reef is extensive it runs right under the water tower, which explains why ..."

"A very sore point, ..."

"I know ... I wanted to tell you straight away but, whether it was greed or that I wanted to look after the men that found it or that I didn't know what your reaction would be or that I just needed time to think, I don't know. But what I do know is I'm telling you now and I want to spend the rest of my life with you and ... of course I care about the gold, who wouldn't ... but I care about you a great deal more."

"Let me get this straight, gold,.."

"Lots of gold, vast amounts, the mother lode."

"On Mum and Dad's place? And we're all filthy stinking rich."

"Yep ... all we need to do is register a claim. I rang my solicitor today and told him to set up a company, and arrange a line of credit to pay for the lease and other incidentals until we can start production, we need to figure out who the directors will be, what share structure we will have and then we can register the claim in the name of the company. In the meantime we need to keep this as quiet as possible."

They stared at each other in seeming disbelief, everything had changed in the last thirty seconds, it was like watching a storm break, blocking the sun, deafening you with thunder, scaring you with lightning and drenching the earth with rain.

"So, ..." began Robert.

"Not so fast,"

"What?"

"I have a secret too and mine is ... awful ... I mean really ... awful."

"Your a foreign agent sent to steal d'Camry's military secrets."

"Close." Janet fell silent as the full impact of what she knew she must confess descended upon her, would Robert laugh it off and forgive her or would he see it as a deep character flaw that would destroy their fledgling relationship.

"Come on, it can't be that bad." ... ... "Can it?"

"Yes. I feel just terrible. I thought I was playing a clever game but now it's not so clever, it'll wreck everything."

"Come on Marina, spill it."

"Who's Marina?"

"I don't know, Marina Lee, it's another flashback from the rock, some sort of Russo/Norwegian ballerina/spy for the Nazis, whoever they are, just seemed like the right thing to say. How much did we see up there?"

"Probably too much ... and maybe ... not enough, Steve and Fred said to be careful. Do you really want to hear this?"

"Of course I want to hear it, whatever it is, the future seems certain, if a little blurry."

"It's the emus, I ... we ... created this hysteria about the emus, the newspaper articles, the newsreel footage, everything, then Dad and his mates have been feeding a huge mob and leading them around so you can't find them."

"But why?"

"It's all about the secession movement; we didn't think Canberra would respond so it would be just another snub to the West and more reason to secede. But then Canberra sent you, which was very nice of them, I must write to Mr Lyons and thank him for the best present ever. Once the Army was here we decided to make them look incompetent and make the Federal Government look stupid by association. And then there was you and me and the rock and ... I love you Robert, please don't be angry, I think I'd die if you went away." Janet's voice trailed off as she heard these uncharacteristic words from her own mouth. It struck her that she was compromising her rabid independence. "Love is compromise isn't it," she blurted.

"So it seems, that's the blurriness in the future, will we trade some freedom for some happiness ... oh that sounds so callous," this time Robert's voice trailed off as he realised the threat to his selfishness, the very thing that he thought would be the key to his success. "Will you marry me, right here right now?"

Janet nodded as Robert swept her up in his arms, they held each other a long time without speaking, their hearts pounded like jungle drums carrying messages of fear and love, commitment and reticence. They increased the strength of their embrace as if to squeeze out the doubt, they immersed themselves one in the other until their blood surged and their joining parts enlarged, their juices flowed, their clothes fell to the floor and against the dust and grime of the printery wall they joined themselves and instead of words they groaned and screamed their marriage vows.

The quintessential modern couple had performed the primeval rites, they had no need of church or state. Beyond the law, civil or canon, they took courage and faced a partially known future.

As the leftover juices dripped from their bodies they took no care to wipe away the residues but let it run down their legs as an affront to the propriety of a society cloistered in clothes, swamped in scent and mired in manners. They continued their naked rite and communed with coffee and biscuits until the discomfort of nudity in a printery and the need to return to their tribe forced them to dress.

Janet forgave Robert for keeping his secret and Robert was mightily impressed by Janet's deceptive brilliance. Both secrets lost their power and the previous owners grew a hundred feet in stature. The release from the evil of secrecy was like bursting out of a shell or standing under a waterfall or purging the body by running it to exhaustion. *Hang gliding would have been an excellent simile but in 1932 it carried unacceptable risks. NASA 'solved' the problem in 1957 with the invention of the Rogallo wing.*

The Mobile Emu Shooting Squadron

d'Camry addressed the men at the morning parade. "Men we have underestimated the emu menace. I have reassessed our strategy and effective immediately we will actively hunt the enemy instead of awaiting an opportunity for engagement. We will henceforth be known as the Mobile Emu Shooting Squadron."

Cox made notes and underlined the letters that formed the acronym, MESS, he nudged Down and subtly indicated the new entry. Down had to call upon all his military discipline to keep from laughing out loud. Cox had written LOL underneath; an acronym he had coined at the beginning of the d'Camry Mission and one that had proved its value on a daily basis. *Etymologists take note.*

"Are there any questions?"

"Sir," said Cox, "should we fill in the trenches?"

"No time soldier, run some rope around them so that no one falls in and that will have to do. We depart at 0900 hours on our first sortie to the North East. Take over Lieutenant."

Robert stepped forward, "men report to your work groups, Corporal Cox, secure the trenches and be thorough very, very thorough, we don't want anyone looking, I mean falling, in. Corporal Down, load the ordinance and the guns, Corporal Ford, fuel the vehicles and whatever Cook needs for a day in the field. Sergeant make sure that nothing is overlooked, double check all the inventory."

The men went about their assigned tasks with Cox's squad smearing mud over any likely glints from the trenches and then roping off the area and affixing hastily made signs saying '

DANGER KEEP OUT'.

All was in readiness for departure at 0900 and d'Camry smiled as if his logistical brilliance had forged this efficiency. Just as he opened his mouth to give the order to move out, Elizabeth came running from the house to tell d'Camry that Canberra was on the phone. Agitated at the delay but pleased at the obvious importance of his position he ordered the convoy to depart and told them he would catch them up. d'Camry sauntered toward the house making sure that Canberra was kept waiting a sufficient length of time so as to underline his status. Meanwhile his driver settled down in the car as the convoy rattled away to its date with destiny.

d'Camry finally picked up the receiver and started an elaborate briefing that highlighted his observations, intelligence gathering and consequent detailed and implicitly brilliant planning.

"... and so we have redoubled our intelligence gathering with surprising results. The emus are more intelligent than we first thought, they have been able to predict our movements and take evasive action. Now that we know what we are dealing with we have made some diversionary sorties to confuse them and we are confident of a significant engagement within a very short time frame. We also ..."

At this point the caller broke in to advise the Major that he was an acquisition clerk wanting to confirm the proposed expenditure on a new water tank and stand. d'Camry was furious at his time being wasted by this desk jockey. "Yes, an unfortunate accident, push it through ASAP will you."

The lorries meanwhile rolled toward 'fortress emu' closely observed by Ted, Bill and Mauric.

"This is it," said Ted, "they picked the least likely direction first up. I reckon they'll get to the Boulder Country by lunchtime, we can take the stock route and have the emus ready for a stampede.

"So now we're going to let them find the emus?" said Maurie.

"If we time it right we'll hit them while they're having lunch and the emus will be out of sight and into the boulder plains where the Army can't follow them. Then the emus will circle round back to the feeding grounds where they started. I should have been a logistician," said Ted. "Tactician." corrected Bill but went no further.

"No sign of d'Camry," said the Sergeant.

"Quite a good sign," said Robert, "are you feeling peckish?"

"On this mission, any time is a good time to stop for lunch Sir."

They chose a shady spot and called a temporary halt to the grinding bumping drive, the dust settled and the Cook set up for a basic lunch. A camp fire was soon underway with water boiling for tea and damper cooking in the coals. Plenty of butter and some bully beef made a generous lunch and the men were glad to have a 10 minute sleep in the shade of the stunted Eucalypti.

Who says Eucalypti? We all say Eucalypts, actually we all say gum trees, which is really wrong.

Cox was making notes on the flora and making a few sketches. He noted the boulders that had been increasing in number as they progressed on the journey and mused that they were in a very poor position in the case of an ambush, but then an ambush from whom, some camel herders perhaps? That was just silly.

Ford rolled over on a sharp rock which woke him up. He pulled himself to a sitting position and leant back against a tree, he looked at Cox's notes; "nice work, mate, you ought to put that emu in the sketch."

"What emu?"

"That emu and that emu and fucking hell, there's shit loads of them. Emus! we're under attack, set up the guns," yelled Ford as he roused the men.

Robert woke, from a blissful dream that discretion demands should not be recorded, in time to see a column of emus at least 20 abreast, coming round the bend in the road at a cracking pace. The men moved like a well oiled machine and set up the machine gun. Cook retrieved his pans and billies, he had encountered these vandals before.

The emu numbers were increasing every second as more and more came round the bend, there were a couple of thousand at least and closing fast on the camp.

"Are you ready with that gun?" yelled Robert.

"We can't find the third leg, Sir."

Well oiled but not well organised.

"Use a rock man."

"Ready to fire, Sir."

Robert checked everyone's position and just as he was about to give the order, d'Camry's car came hurtling round the bend, seemingly pushing the emus towards them and moving into the direct line of fire of the machine gun.

Inside the car d'Camry was apoplectic, "It's them, ... those ones, ... the enemy," he screamed as he reefed his sidearm from its holster, he fired immediately, without aim and certainly without checking the enfilade angles ... unfortunately there was a windscreen in the way ... well not for long.

"Hit the deck!" yelled Robert as d'Camry's shot whistled overhead. Soldiers leapt into the dirt as more shots pinged off rocks and emus overran their camp. d'Camry was finally out of ammunition as the car pulled up. Robert ordered the machine gun turned around to fire on the birds as they fled, the crew turned it round, moved the rock and started firing but the recoil sent the gun sideways off the hastily placed rock support and a hundred rounds sprayed the side of one of the lorries, wrecking the sideboards and shredding the tyres.

"After them," screamed d'Camry, "follow them to the gates of hell. I need to get back to HQ and send the dispatches to Canberra, first engagement and all that and I want to see plenty of emu feathers as evidence of the kill."

Cox had been having a quiet word to d'Camry's driver who gave a pantomime version of events; the wrestle with the holster and the shooting of the windscreen featuring large in the telling. The driver thought he might be able to claim for Post Traumatic Stress Disorder, unfortunately PTSD was not recognised until the 1970s so he had to struggle along with a pat on the back from Cox for surviving the event, possible battle fatigue and the rich compensation of the best war story ever. Before d'Camry left, Robert requested his driver, a skilled mechanic, stay with them to get the damaged lorry back in service. d'Camry agreed and roared off in the now 'very open' car by himself.

Ted's plan had worked better than expected for just as they led the emus onto the road into the rocky gully d'Camry's car came screaming up behind and as the birds began to overtake the feed truck Ted pulled off the road shrouded in clouds of dust, the emus passed them at an ever increasing speed with d'Camry closing on the birds as he dealt them non-fatal blows consisting of glass shards and misguided projectiles.

Robert ordered the serviceable lorry and machine gun after the emus but only 200 yards away they were halted by the size of the boulders on the imaginatively named Boulder Plateau. As the truck returned to the camp Robert was furious, an impossible mission, a CO who shoots at his own troops and a lorry that will take hours to repair. This farce must end and life with Janet must begin, he thought, as he planned his next move and made a note to self: *issue d'Camry with blanks and shove emu feathers up his arse.*

"Anyone not involved with fixing the lorry or squaring away the gun, see if there are any emu feathers lying around'" said Robert.

The feather collectors returned empty handed, not one feather, these birds were in the peak of condition.

"I give up," said Robert, "why are we doing this anyway? We'll all be sitting pretty when the gold mining starts."

Sergeant Wilkins was a practical man, he may not have appreciated the subtleties of Cox, Ford and Down's Mediocrity but he thought he knew where there might be a few emu feathers.

"Sir," said Wilkins, "we need to keep the Major out of our hair for the next little while and we need emu feathers to do it, right?"

"And...?"

"Well, the Light Horse have emu feathers on their hats and I was thinking, ..."

"Sergeant, you are a genius, take a car and the men you need and get to Perth and back as fast as you can, ... and Sergeant, ... don't get caught."

"Right now Sir?"

"Right now my dear Wilkins."

d'Camry - A Macbeth Moment

Blurry visions; all great soldiers have them. With d'Camry it wasn't so much witches and bloody daggers but a broken windscreen and dust in the eyes as he drove like a maniac in unfamiliar territory. As a largish tree loomed in front of him he swerved violently and found himself well off the road next to a towering rock formation. As he skidded to a halt his body lurched forward and then violently slapped back against the seat. He waved vigorously as if to clear the dust from his personal space, the dust took its own good time and when the wider landscape finally came into focus he realised that he was completely and hopelessly lost. The degree of unfamiliarity made him shudder; it was the kind of dissonance that occurs when reason cannot make sense of the immediate environment, fear ensues, adrenalin flows ... d'Camry leapt vertically out of his seat and climbed the rock at a cracking pace, his heart raced and when he reached the top his respiration rate caused a dizziness that made him feel as if the whole plain spun around him like a giant disc. At least that's what he thought in retrospect; a fully reasoned explanation for an unreasonable phenomenon.

"Must find my position, my place, my way." He panted heavily as he reached the top. The last several yards required extreme perseverance and concentration as if he was trying to enter an unknown realm without an invitation, without a password, without the correct authority. It was like a marathon runner hitting the wall, he had to decide to go on, to force his arms and legs to act and confront the forces that sought to prevent him. He finally emerged as if from the womb into another world, as if the air was somehow different and he could fill his lungs and feel the elation of uninterrupted breathing. His life thus far had been heavily constrained, as if he was still connected to his umbilical cord – someone must have forgotten to sever it – as if his breathing was ever hampered by a redundant biological restraint.

His first sight was an endless plain and his heart sank, no hills, no trees, no creeks, no markers at all; lost in the infinite, how was that possible. He began to turn taking in the vastness of unfamiliarity, he felt concurrent fear and excitement, depression and hope, hatred and love.

He stayed.

He turned but the landscaped turned faster, it blurred and he strained to focus and he saw a treasure map; he felt a boyish thrill. He sped backward in time, a long way back, before his father dragooned him into the family business AKA the 'British Defence Forces'. He was in bed, he was sick with the wretched bronchitis, listless and struggling to breath. His nurse had subtly put the tin soldiers and papier maché battlefields out of reach and placed an illustrated copy of JM Barrie's Peter Pan and Wendy, her own 1915 edition, on his bedside table.

d'Camry, whose name was also Peter, was an avid reader. He had been steered in a very narrow literary direction of boys own adventures, war stories, war histories and armaments magazines. The family library contained almost no fiction, a scant collection of *more serious* children's books and a vast collection of war histories. It was among the latter that he discovered the Greeks and Romans and developed a strong interest in the ancient world.

He devoured Peter Pan and Wendy and was moved to uncontrollable sobbing when Peter was faced with the terrible choice of either leaving Neverland forever and growing up or losing Wendy, her brothers and the lost boys, who, having returned to the Darlings in London would now grow into adulthood. Through his teens Peter d'Camry frequently visited the Peter Pan statue in Kensington Gardens and relived that emotional moment when Peter Pan made his choice to abstain from the adult world. When he arrived in Perth so many years later he was surprised to find another casting from the original mould while walking through Queen's Gardens; once again it brought back such raw emotion that he started to choke and tears rolled down his cheeks before his adult self turned away and hurriedly dried the tears as he pretended to blow his nose. No one was watching; he was quite alone.

The treasure map was not about pirate's gold, or indeed about gold at all, but it was like all maps, something to help the traveller; avoid obstacles, visit interesting places and then find his way home.

He had wanted to study classics, to explore ancient texts, perhaps even indulge in some archaeology, and enjoy the life of a Don.

But he had been raised and shaped and moulded and brain washed and convinced that he was destined for a great military career. When he spoke of battles and strategies his father smiled and sometimes touched him affectionately on the shoulder. When he spoke about the library at Alexandria his father ignored him or left the room.

He knew his father had planned his life in detail, he would go to The Royal Military Academy in Woolwich and train as an Officer Cadet. He would gain his commission and through the extensive d'Camry family connections have a steady rise through the ranks.

He saw it all; the unremitting appeals to 'common sense', the belittling of philosophy and indeed anything to do with the life of the mind. "It's your duty, it's your destiny, "it's in your

blood, be a man my son", make us all proud. Your Grandfather died alongside General Gordon at Khartoum, your Great Grandfather was at the charge of the light brigade at Balaclava, your Great Great Grandfather was with Wellington at Waterloo, your Great Great Great Grandfather was with Colonel Goddard in the First Maratha War and I, yes I, fought the Boer". d'Camry batted these assaults away as if swatting flies, with each one his anger rose. "Enough!" he yelled. "How could you?" he screamed. "I cannot, I will not, I am not," he sobbed.
"How could you be so wicked, how could you corrupt me, how could you ruin me?!" The fury, like a volcano, came from deep within; pushing aside the 'common sense', trampling the carefully layered guilt, flaying the pretence that had been his life thus far.

Discovery and loss, insight and emptiness; who was he, how would he act, how would he be, how would he survive; if he buried his military persona he would be lost.. Like one of the Lost Boys he would be in need of adoption by a kindly family; but he was a man, not the kind his father revered but a man nonetheless, a man who had to start again, was he up to it, did he have the courage? He was after all on a rock two hundred feet in the air. He could end it, it was appealing, no shame, he just slipped and fell, all would be dark, no more demands, no more disgrace, no more blunders, just the dark.
His vision on the rock turned black, blacker than a moonless night with heavy cloud, no stars, not a single ray of light. At first he felt comfort, no responsibilities, no demands, he breathed slowly and regularly, he discovered he could slow his heart rate just like the holy men of India, he wanted it to last, he wanted it to stay just like that, maybe forever. It was the cold that startled him, the cold that clawed at him in the blackness as he drifted towards death. It was the sudden realisation of the

impending nothingness, the eternal vacuum, that jolted him into action. Just as his inertia seemed complete, as the last erg of energy was draining into the rock he reached for the handbrake, engaged the clutch and propelled himself toward the distant memory of sunshine. He must concentrate his way out of the slough of despond, the confusion and self pity that had made him wish his life away. This supreme effort was at last genuinely heroic. There would be no medals or parades but a smile on his face and a spring in his step and much work to do. He turned to leave, but the rock was not finished with him yet. The swirling turned to emus hundreds, thousands, possibly millions, his nemesis come to taunt him. He instinctively reached for his sidearm, but why? He relaxed, he watched the flightless creatures and they watched him, giving him quizzical looks straining their tiny brains to make sense of what they saw. A British Major who loathed soldiering, lost in Australia while hunting emus to bring glory and honour to his family. It was then that he had another new experience, he began to laugh. The laughter was spontaneous at first but as he reflected on the incongruence, the absolute lunacy of what he was doing his reasoning reinforced the laughter, till he guffawed and howled and held his aching sides. He tried to stop, almost managed it once but then it broke out again as if he was a school boy laughing at his own crazy actions. He laughed without restraint or decorum or care, he laughed until he couldn't stand. He collapsed onto the granite and completely surrendered his body to the nonsense of his own life.

When he emerged from the grip of the rock the light was failing and he saw in the west a faint light that he knew by instinct was Bill and Elizabeth's farm; he took a rough bearing and scrambled down the rock. The vehicle was still drivable and he set off at a steady pace to start his new work; whatever that might be.

Promises Promises

"My good friends, so good to see you all again, as soon as I see that golden grain I know I am among friends. The farming community is the backbone of Nationalist support.

I am here tonight to talk to you about the future of Western Australia - your future - your children's future. We are the largest state with the smallest population but that population has a will to work, a dynamism and a resolve that others can only dream about.

We are constantly overlooked by Canberra and the Eastern States, their tariffs on manufactured goods destroy the profitability of our farming sector. We could be a farm and a quarry for the world. Our endless toil and ingenuity is the envy of all, but we are being penalised by the very Commonwealth that is supposed to support us. 'Commonwealth'? Ladies and gentlemen 'Common Wealth ' is a farce. Call it 'New South Wales Wealth' or 'Victoria Wealth', be honest, call a spade a spade. Western Australia must free itself of these shackles and strike out on its own. The time has come, we are ready to be a nation. On the world stage we will represent our farmers and graziers our miners and fishermen - we will succeed! Our children - your children will enjoy the harvest of independence because we will build a world class education system that will provide us with doctors and lawyers, engineers and architects. We will invest in transport infrastructure that will speed our produce and minerals to ports and onto ships.

Yes ladies and gentlemen it's ours for the taking and I urge you to vote 1 for the Nationals and YES to secession.

I will be happy to take your questions."

Ted stepped forward, he had always been a conservative and

this was his party but he needed to push the case against the Grain Authority. "Premier Mitchell, I am glad you mentioned Commonwealth because we have an impediment to wealth known as the Western Australian Gain Authority. Yes Sir that is correct the sign on our local office says GAIN Authority. It's a very telling slip of the sign writer's brush. This so called step forward means that grain prices have fallen through the toilet (Bill winced) and we have no other way to sell our grain. In this district we have joined the farmer's strike and our grain will continue to be stored on farm until the Authority comes to its senses. When will you get rid of this dimple on the backside of grain growers and disband the GAIN Authority?"

Dimple? On whose backside? Who is this idiot?

"I completely understand your concerns, the GRAIN Authority was created to provide certainty in the market and curtail the scurrilous practises of some of the private grain traders. It has run into two problems; one is the Great Depression which has seen record low grain prices worldwide and the second is the Commonwealth Government which penalises us with unfair tariffs and taxes at every turn. The only way forward is to secede from the Commonwealth and forge our own future."

"And the Emus what about the emus?" yelled Maurie.

"Another example of Federal incompetence. On Election day you be the judge!" Mitchell left the platform with a wave and smile - *What about the emus? Maybe I should promise them that interest rates will never rise. God I am tired and I have to spend the night in this one horse town.*

The Charge Of The Night Brigade

Sgt Wilkins was a career soldier, he loved active duty, it made sense to him, he knew how to do it. He had been offered the reward of an admin job after the Great War but after careful consideration, lasting fully five seconds, he turned it down flat. He had always derided the 'desk army'; his experience of administrators had not been positive. They seemed obsessed with paperwork and box ticking, they lacked trust in their counterparts who were risking their lives at the sharp end of the conflict. It seemed to Wilkins that trust developed under pressure was like diamonds squeezed from carbon. He and his comrades had an enduring hardness, an unbreakable bond that administrators and their ilk did not understand. Wilkins was confident and self assured, the satisfied son of loving parents. His father had loved him more than life itself but having pursued unattainable dreams he came to the end of his life with no tangible assets and so could only pass on the intangible maxims that he loved so much. These were not mentioned in his will or secreted away in a box under his bed but they were burned into Wilkins' brain by frequent repetition; 'know thyself' and 'to thine own self be true'. Wilkins had come to increasingly value the paternal bequest as he grew year on year; he knew who he was, what he could do and why he was here. He was proud of his actions in the Great War, even though he knew in his heart that it was a war about nothing. He wasted no time on wondering about the absurdity of the conflict itself but was a champion of mateship and camaraderie. The value of good men might not be bankable but it sustained Wilkins and gave him satisfaction beyond telling.

Wilkins, as always, had given his best to the Emu Mission but now, at last, here was something where his skills and training were really needed. He handpicked the men he could depend on and set out. The vehicles were slow, the road rough and long. They changed drivers every hour to keep fatigue at bay but it was impossible to sleep sitting bolt upright while the cars jolted and rattled their way to Perth.

The barracks had little security, a high wall topped with barbed wire and a couple of night sentries were all that confronted them at 3.00 AM. All the men knew the layout of the barracks from the few days they had spent there at the beginning of the mission. They parked the cars at the back of the barracks and quietly unloaded their gear, then with the precision that comes from well practised and well trained soldiers they chose the section of the wall that they knew had an adjacent building on the other side, they hoisted their lightest man onto the shoulders of their tallest man, others used a pole to push up some heavy canvas folded into half a dozen layers so that the man at the top could flip it up and over the barbed wire and so provide protection for the invaders. The same pole was then used to push up a rope to the top man who could then take it with him and using the stability of the pole make the final move to the top of the wall. Protected from the barbed wire he crossed easily over the wall and dropped catlike to the roof beneath. Moving quickly over the roof and down a drain pipe he attached the rope to a tree in the courtyard then signalled with three sharp yanks on the rope that it was safe for the others to follow. The remaining men fastened the other end of the rope to one of the cars and then, single file, the squad came over the wall and gathered near the Light Horse barracks.

The entry to the barracks was not locked and the squad slipped inside leaving one man at the door as a lookout. Down the first corridor they found a hat rack with two long rows of hats each bearing the signature emu feathers of the Light Horse. As if garrotting an enemy the squad moved deftly along the rows. "How many should we take?" whispered a young private. "Take the bloody lot, son," Wilkins whispered back.

And so it was. Each man using a knife, they removed the feathers from the hats and stuffed them into one of several duffel bags brought along for the purpose.

Wilkins scribbled a note saying "Thanks for the Horse feathers," and pinned it to the hat rack wall.

Carrying the booty the squad decamped as silently and quickly as they had come. The last wiry soldier released the rope from the tree pulled himself to the top of the wall, caught a length of cord tossed to him from below, attached both the ends, one to each of the two D rings on the barracks side of the canvas and threw the remaining cord back to his mates below. He then used the pole to ease himself onto the waiting shoulders and came down like a monkey. Six men pulled vigorously on the cords attached to the canvas and it came down with only minor tears.

With all the gear and booty back in the cars they took off for Dencubbin leaving the cryptic 'Horse feathers' note as the only evidence of an unknown presence in the barracks.

Parliament Of Howls

The Lyon's government had come to power on the back of a landslide of voter support but that didn't serve to blunt the opposition lampooning their actions and ridiculing their mistakes.

Lyons had tried to keep a lid on the Commonwealth's efforts to curb the emu menace which once in progress under Major d'Camry revealed itself as a comic opera ripe for parody. There was no doubt that his ex-colleagues in the labour party had not forgotten his disloyalty and duplicitous actions that brought down the Scullin government. Labor could now see clearly the support of right wing business and media interests that had backed Lyons in his move against the party and Lyons could see clearly the support of unions that caused so much factious strife and policy difficulties for Labor. It seemed that no-one saw clearly any common sense route for establishing government by the people, of the people and for the people. It was business as usual with gamblers both right and left prepared to risk everything in a winner take all adventure.

d'Camry had reported to Canberra on a number of occasions that emus were highly intelligent cunning birds that, "are capable of leaving false clues and laying traps for the unwary". Defence had rephrased this lunacy into 'a form more palatable to press sensitive ministers and senior public servants'. Viz. "In such a vast expanse it is difficult to pinpoint prime locations for meaningful engagement."

" … leading us up the garden path" became " … ducking and weaving through ravaged crop-lands" while "... down the rabbit hole" became " … disappearing quickly in unfamiliar terrain."

In 2005 the book Weasel Words would be published, based on

Australian political speak it would be a rich verbal harvest of twisted phrases, misleading emphasis and oblique obfuscation. A rich diatribe of wonderful words about nothing, encapsulating the very best in their class from masters past and present.

When d'Camry's unedited reports mysteriously landed on the desk of James Scullin, the labour opposition leader, it was clear that they contained no 'weasel words' at all, they were plain as day and embarrassing as hell. Scullin could not believe his luck, it had been a dry time for damaging leaks, but this, this was gold.

Question time in the Australian Parliament is what might be described as a non-contact blood sport, a confusions in terms perhaps but a daily ritual on sitting days that is relished by the sharp tongued and thick skinned. Points are scored according to the damage inflicted and the proponents firmly believe that the outcome has a serious effect on voter sentiment. A remarkable belief given that the words are only heard by the parliamentary chamber, a handful of journalists and some senior public servants.

Scullin rose to his feet to receive the call, "Thank-you Mr. Speaker, my question is to the honourable member for Wilmot. Can the Prime Minister confirm that the commander of Operation Emu is firmly in control and pursuing a credible plan of action?"

"The Honourable The Prime Minister."

"Thank you Mr Speaker. I thank the honourable member for his question, the expedition to control emu numbers in Western Australia's wheat belt is an initiative of my Government that recognises the importance of the developing wheat industry in Western Australia. It is highly appropriate that the Commonwealth uses its resources to support its citizens in time of crisis especially where so many pioneers have laboured under the harsh Australian sun to create a viable industry in a challenging environment. We may be a long way from them when the distance is measured in miles but when the measuring stick is graduated in mateship and nation building they are our next door neighbours.

It is a matter of some pride that my government has taken this plague seriously and acted with all speed to minimise the damage to crops and infrastructure. The expedition is under the leadership of Major d'Camry, an experienced officer on secondment from the British Army. Major d'Camry has been in regular contact and while the mission has some logistical problems in such a vast area, with emus in plague proportions, a detailed strategy has been developed and that plan is now being vigorously pursued."

"The honourable member for Yarra"

"Thank you Mr Speaker. The opposition supports the Government's commitment to the provision of assistance to the wheat farmers of Western Australia but my question was clearly about the competence of the leader of the expedition and by extension the effectiveness of the intervention.

I have here the original reports from Major d'Camry which I am sure the Prime Minister and indeed the Australian people will find enlightening."

The press gallery suddenly came to attention.

"But let me quote directly; ' the emu is a highly intelligent and cunning bird, capable of leaving false clues and laying traps for the unwary, they have on occasion led us up the garden path and down the rabbit hole.'"

The house erupted in laughter.

"Order, order ..."

"He goes on Mr. Speaker; 'when engaged these birds have a larger lead carrying capacity than tanks, they are like Zulus' ..."

Interjections flew thick and fast as the press gallery scribbled down these gems for tomorrow's edition.

"Will a medal be struck for The Great Emu War?"

"Order"

"How many emus will be recruited into the Australian Defence Forces?"

"Order, order, the house will come to order."

It didn't.

"The Honorable the Leader of the Opposition."

The leader of the opposition resumed, "The Government clearly has no idea of what is going on in the West, it is wasting taxpayers money with no clear plan or objective. The incompetence is beyond belief even for a Government that is led by an opportunistic rat ..."

A predictable eruption of, "shame, shame," followed by much laughter and abuse.

Order, order the honourable the leader of the opposition will resume his seat. The honourable the Prime Minister on a point of order."

"Mr Speaker, I ask that honourable the leader of the opposition withdraw his unparliamentary remark."

"The honourable leader of the opposition will withdraw his remark without reservation."

"Mr Speaker, I withdraw my remark, the Prime Minister is not a rat. Rats are actually quite smart."

"The honourable leader of the opposition will leave the chamber."

Mr Speaker was trying very hard to control his own laughter and maintain a sense of decorum in the house but nevertheless took great delight in expelling the leader of the opposition.

The newspapers repeated it all again the following day and reported that the Department of Defence while contacted several times for comment had declined the invitation.

The PM's fury at being caught so woefully ill-informed and unprepared set off a tidal wave of departmental anger that rolled down through the ranks and finally dumped its vengeful spite on d'Camry and Robert.

Thrashed With A Feather

The severe dressing down from Canberra accompanied by implicit threats of ruined careers and public disgrace fell so lightly on d'Camry and Robert as to barely be perceived. It was as if they were in another world and this sudden reprimand was a laughable nonsense. They had both listened quietly to the tirades coming over the telephone wires from Canberra, neither offered any excuse or explanation. They simply waited for it to end, apologised for any inconvenience caused and got on with more important business.

d'Camry was in a quandary, his life had changed in an instant, he was in uncharted waters, unmapped territory, unexplored space. What would he say to the troops, to Robert, to Elizabeth and Bill who must all think him a complete ass. And that was only in the immediate vicinity, there was still his British superiors, his father, his mother, and a regiment of military relatives to consider.

Robert was more blasé, he had been mentally leaving military life for quite some time. He had a road map, he knew where he was going and how to get there. Robert of course knew nothing of d'Camry's epiphany and so things must continue as usual for a while at least. The duty of daily soldiering, the pretence and seriousness of Operation Emu and the stolen feathers, that would convince d'Camry of the kill, must all continue while the mining lease was registered, companies formed and gold mining commenced.

d'Camry wandered back to his tent after receiving the early morning phone call. How much should he tell, how much would anyone want to know? - perhaps nothing. For the first time in his adult life he worried about being boorish. But he must make a start. Robert was certainly the right person to begin with, that was simple courtesy and reasonable protocol. Do that and see what comes next, no need to plan too much, his previous planning had after all 'taken him up the garden path and down the rabbit hole', he smiled to himself as previous words came back with a somewhat different meaning.

Robert was eager to keep d'Camry occupied and out of his hair and to that end he approach the Major's tent.

"Sir, I'd like to give you an update on the battle yesterday."

"Certainly Robert, come in, I need to talk to you as well."

"Thank you Sir."

"Please, sit down, we haven't had much of a chance to talk on this mission, all rush and tear."

Robert was somewhat taken aback by this completely normal behaviour, it immediately put him on his guard.

"No Sir, not much of a chance."

"Well tell me me how did the day finish up, I got a bit lost on the way back which made me horribly late and terribly tired for some reason and I went straight to bed."

d'Camry admitting to getting lost ... is the sky falling? Robert overcame a powerful urge to look outside and see - "I see, well Sir, the day finished quite successfully." Robert felt so ill at ease; lying through his teeth when d'Camry was so ... so ... human. "We chased the mob into a blind canyon and opened fire, there were no survivors, it was just on dark when the last bird fell so I detailed Sgt Wilkins to go back this morning and collect enough feathers to substantiate the claim. You know what HQ is like Sir."

"I do indeed Robert, I do indeed." Here was the perfect remedy, his way back, a successful mission, public gratitude, family acceptance ... it was all too ... tempting, no need to change, no gauntlets to run, just carry on as if nothing had happened. The thought filled silence was making Robert extremely uncomfortable. d'Camry wondered whether this hesitation meant that he would face this kind of dilemma over and over, an eternal struggle between his two lives, a never ending series of decisions. Could he sustain the effort involved in this monumental change? Robert shifted in his seat as d'Camry's brain swirled in his skull. *Decision required ... NOW. Yes forward, but is this the time?* d'Camry's rule book on social propriety had been shredded. *It must be the time, deception must end and not be allowed to take root even for a moment.*

"I've been thinking quite a lot lately Robert, well in the last 18 hrs anyway."

Remember to pause and give the other chap a go.

d'Camry paused.

"Sir?"

"This mission, Robert, it seems a little crazy, I mean why are we here, what's the point? It should be the farmers making the decisions, calling the shots, as it were."

Robert was discombobulated *(Aunt Doris's favourite word)* which in turn meant he was disarticulated, which in essence meant he was speechless for the second time in a week.

"I, er .. emus ... feathers, ... boxes ... much ... quite full ... no need to worry." Robert was pre-programmed to deliver the feathers, which would send d'Camry scurrying to claim the credit and leave him free to become filthy stinking rich. This was all very disconcerting, he had no idea what was happening.

d'Camry was in no hurry to do anything, he wanted to engage Robert in meaningful dialogue.

Robert was in a great hurry to do ... everything else ... and meaningful dialogue was the last thing on his agenda.

"That sounds like Wilkin's car with the feather's detail now, Sir. Shall I arrange a viewing?"

147

"Yes I suppose so," said d'Camry, unenthusiastically, as he felt his opportunity slipping away.

Robert bolted, pleased with the distraction that moved his plan along.

Robert was a tad anxious about the success of the mission and ventured, "everything in order Sergeant?"

"Everything is very much in 'order' Lieutenant."

"Well bring it on Sergeant, let's not keep the Major waiting."

Wilkins had placed the tea chests covered with the ever useful canvas in front of d'Camry's tent. As d'Camry stepped into the sunlight Wilkins dramatically pulled the canvas aside revealing the booty. d'Camry stepped forward and inspected the evidence. To the onlookers he seemed distracted even disinterested but it was more than that, his stomach was churning as he reflected on the slaughter of the innocent birds. He was well acquainted with the destructive power of artillery but that power now seemed to have been abused. He fingered the feathers fighting back the tears, the raw emotion that had been pent up for thirty years was swelling somewhere in his chest. He managed a "well done men" as he turned to escape the embarrassment.

As d'Camry disappeared into his tent Wilkins and Robert looked at each other with questioning expressions, "do you thinks he suspects anything Sir?" said Wilkins in a hushed tone.

"I don't thinks so," replied Robert, who was now visibly perturbed. "We'll have to wait and see, but well done Sergeant, you're a magician."

"Thank you Sir, most fun I've had in years. Hopefully I won't be mentioned in dispatches."

"If there is an Emu War medal, you will definitely have one but if not you'll just have to settle for excessive wealth and a life of unconscionable comfort."

Wilkins smiled, ordered the feathers sealed and stored and the 'Light Horse Raiders' to get some sleep.

The tea chests of feathers had not escaped the all seeing eyes of Jaril and Jarli and they wondered how they had been collected and why they were so important. Jaril's natural reserve prevented him from asking but Jarli wanted the openness of true friendship and was willing to take the risk.

Jarli approached Down as the white man with whom he felt the greatest affinity. Down was nearby and smirking at the proceedings of the morning.

"Hey Michael Down, what's going on with the feathers in the tea boxes?"

"Come over here," said Down as he drew Jarli out of earshot, and a safe distance from any would be observers. "It's crazy but we needed the feathers to make the Major believe that we shot a lot of emus."

"But you didn't shoot a lot of emus, not in that country, they just run away where you can't follow."

"How did you know where we were?"

"I - know - a - lot - of - things, cause … cause, … the spirits of the country tell me."

"That's bullshit isn't it?"

"No … yes, … Jaril!"

"What d'ya need Jaril for?"

"Jaril's smart, knows what to say."

"Like Cox, he knows what to say and he can say it in ten different ways and use words you never heard of."

"Yeah, like Cox."

"Or we could just talk about this ourselves and hope we don't fuck everything up."

"What if we do fuck it up?"

"Then it will be fuckin funny … I hope. It's funny anyway cause … cause we stole the feathers from other soldiers in Perth called the light horse who use the feathers to decorate their hats. Now how did you know where we were?"

The lead of honesty was compelling and Jarli wanted to respond.

"The spirits, stone country spirits ... fuckin hell ... no spirits, the boss and his mates used wheat to make the emus follow them, they followed you so the emus would run through your camp and then away into the stone country. But then the Major come up behind them, for a minute they think they're caught but there's lots of dust and they get out of the way and Major drives emus full speed into your camp.

"I think the spirits are more believable, why the fuck would they do that?

"Boss Bill says it's Polo Ticks but I don't know about that kind of tick."

"They're the fuckin deadliest sort mate."

The guileless Jarli had triggered something truly amazing and he had done it without the help of either brains trust. Down felt love built on honesty and trust, he was probably going to cop it from his mates but he didn't care.

d'Camry made the safety of his tent and sat at his makeshift desk to think. Telling the truth was more difficult than he had imagined. In his other life he had burbled endlessly about inconsequential nonsense trying to promote himself as a man of some importance who should be worshipped for his expertise and experience and be a sort after consultant on matters military. Now it seemed that at last he had something really important to say and he had no audience at all.

As he pondered this conundrum it became clear that honesty, truth and decency were qualities that could not be forced on others, they had to be experienced and validated over time by consistency. He realised that so much of his life had been self aggrandising propaganda and indeed that the human condition in the age of large institutions and corporations was riddled with this useless and counterproductive activity. Where had it all gone wrong?

Gold Rush

Robert was anxious that he had not been able to get to the Lands Office to register the claim. Keeping up the emu pretence had required his presence 'at the front' and now d'Camry had just informed him that Canberra wanted a phone conversation at 1000 hours with both of them present. He could delay no longer. He would have to send Janet. He had subconsciously resisted the idea and now it burst upon him as inspired. Janet was competent, intelligent, and had the benefit of local knowledge. The word sexist had not been invented in 1932 but the seemingly innate demeaning of female ability was alive and well in Robert's culture and forever clamouring for expression in his psyche.

Janet was much loved and respected by her parents, the farm hands and the local community. As such she was still an oddity, for even as Sigmund Freud travelled the world spruiking his ideas that would lead inexorably to the sexual revolution and as Albert Einstein troubled the minds of many with theories both 'general' and 'special' that, by extension, undermined belief systems that were built on thin air, women were still an underclass, under educated, underappreciated, overworked and overlooked.

"Of course I'll go."

"You know where to go?" She rolled her eyes.

"Here's the company details, we'll work out the shares later."

"I know!"

"It's just a mining lease, we're not buying any property." She put her hands around his neck and mocked throttling him.

"All right I get it … now one last thing, don't get lost …ouch … joking!" Robert had his back to the horse trough.

"And don't forget to get petrol. ...Joking" Janet made to kiss him goodbye, but at the last minute ... Robert found himself in the horse trough.

Janet ran for her Father's truck expecting retaliation but Robert lay there laughing. Janet turned and blew him a kiss and knew this match would last.

While Janet and Robert played, Maurie had arrived with Ted for a meeting with Bill. They walked toward the house over the maze of trenches surveying the damage that d'Camry's scheme had wreaked on the farmyard; trying to take the shortest route Ted jumped a trench, unfortunately the other bank was soft from the deluge and as Ted landed it gave way and he slid backwards into the muddy bottom. More dirt came showering down on top of him as Maurie, already lurching forward collapsed the bank as he jumped over Ted and made the other side unscathed. It was vintage Laurel and Hardy but Ted had not the wit to state, 'well here's another fine mess you've gotten me into.'

Maurie reached down a hand to help Ted out, but only succeeded in sending more loose dirt down on him and eventually overbalanced and fell headlong on top of him. There was a good deal of recrimination, Ted blamed Maurie for the whole catastrophe and then recounted all his previous blunders. When they finally scrambled out Maurie tried to brush the dirt off Ted's back as if to make amends for his continuing incompetence but Ted pushed him aside and continued to the house.

Once on the verandah Ted started to clean himself up, he slapped his clothes and dug into his pockets to remove the dirt. He carelessly dropped the dirt where he stood as if making a statement that this undeserved indignity was not his fault and that he was therefore entitled to behave like a spoilt child; leaving his mess for someone else to clean up. Maurie looked on with embarrassment. If Ted hadn't been such a prat he would never have seen the sparkle, it would have fallen into the garden or been lost in the grass but there it was reflecting the sunlight as if screaming to be seen.

Ted heard it.

"Look at this Maurie!" he said as he picked up the little nugget and wiped it on his shirt and then gave it the 'bite' test. The gold compressed obligingly between his teeth. "This Maurie, is gold."

It was at that point that d'Camry and Robert came up the verandah steps on their way to the telephone and their Canberra conference. Ted hurriedly closed his fist and thrust it into his pocket.

"I see you have been in the trenches, my humble apologies old man, I am most dreadfully sorry, we'll be filling them in today and restoring the garden," said d'Camry.

"I'm fine Major," said Ted tersely as he turned and marched into the house.

"Ted's just found …,"

"Maurie!"

Like a kelpie hearing his master's voice, Maurie bolted inside.

Robert was immediately suspicious and followed close on their heels making offers of help to Ted which were summarily rejected.

d'Camry reminded Robert that they needed to stay by the telephone and Ted slipped away from his scrutiny into the kitchen and out the back door.

"Maurie this is gold we've got to register a claim and I think that lieutenant has the same idea. I want you to register a claim at the office while I keep an eye on this shifty soldier. Make it as big an area as you can and put it in our names, you and me ..., ..., ... and yeah you and me"

"You can count on me Ted. I know just what to do." Maurie took off in the direction of the Chevrolet, determined to impress Ted ...

Register a claim at the office, what could possibly go wrong?

Maurie drove out the gate following Janet's trail of dust.

Go to the office
Register the claim
Maurie and Ted, what about Bill, he must have meant... Bill, Maurie and Ted?

What was the order? He must get it absolutely right.

Ted knows about these things, must concentrate on the detail.

Maurie concentrated.
He concentrated very, very hard.
He concentrated so hard that he began to feel as if he was outside his body observing all these goings on. He heard his own voice and the drumming of the tyres on the road but it sounded disconnected and strange.

Janet was way ahead, in blissful ignorance of any threat to the plan. But at that moment the truck began to splutter and she realised to her horror that she had not refuelled the vehicle Janet was not used to making mistakes. Mistakes were not on her agenda. Janet had no time for mistakes. Her verbal response to this catastrophe was unprintable and loud; she yelled it to the truck, the road, the bush, the sky and everything beyond. It was

155

beyond embarrassment, it was an assault on her person, with no-one to blame but herself. She banged on the steering wheel, blew the horn and generally behaved in a completely irrational manner; she was after all a human being. She flung the door open, got out of the truck and stomped around in the dust. In one of her many furious stomps she looked back towards the farm and saw a distant car approaching. Perhaps she could retrieve the situation; get to town, get a lift back with petrol and make the next leg of the journey to the larger town of Cunderong and the Land Titles Office before closing time.

She stood in the middle of the road and waved for the approaching car to stop. As the Chevrolet emerged from the dust and Maurie was visible at the wheel her heart sank, she contemplated explaining her situation to Maurie and then sitting next to him for hours on end listening to the halting conversation of a lovesick fool, who would be basking in the afterglow of playing the white knight who had rescued his one true love from deadly peril. She wanted to vomit.

Janet was made of stronger stuff and knew that she would just suffer through the indignity and … get the fucking job done. *Janet, really, what would mother say?*

Maurie pulled up, leapt from the car and perceiving that Janet would be distressed *(wrong)* tried to comfort her. *(stupid)*

"Janet, crikey, you're here," *(thinking very fast, must say the right thing … 'distressed' no wrong, quick say something, anything)* Janet you're here in … a.... dress. *(anything but that, what an idiot)*

"Hello Maurie, ran out of petrol, can I get a lift to town?

"I'd take you anywhere Janet, and back again." *(quick open the door for her)*

In his chivalrous rush he managed to knock Janet aside and tread on her foot.

"Ouch!"

"What? Oh sorry, let me see. Is it bruised?"

Janet managed to open the door, flop onto the seat and swing her legs inside as Maurie gallantly tried to inspect her foot. Not expecting her legs to disappear Maurie overbalanced and lurched forward; his head landed in Janet's lap. Maurie was certainly where he wanted to be but the erotic moment dissolved as Janet shoved him back outside and advised him to, "Just drive Maurie."

Her subsequent sigh was only just subsiding as Maurie managed to get back into the driver's seat.

Maurie's mind was racing. He pulled the Chev into first and headed down the road. Janet's mind was ticking along at its usual galloping pace, hatching a plan to complete her task.

"Thanks for this Maurie." Her tone was friendly and inviting, after all she needed Maurie on side at this moment. "Just the regular weekly trip for supplies Maurie?"

"No, yes, no, ... it's a pretty ..." (at that moment Ted's voice came thundering into Maurie's consciousness ... *"MAURIE!"*

"What's pretty Maurie?"

"Your dress ... it's pretty, very pretty.

"The dress isn't the reason you're going to town, Maurie, ... what are you going to do in town?"

"It's Ted." Maurie's brain was stuck back in Janet's lap and Ted's voice was having trouble getting his complete attention.

"Ted's in town? I don't think that's right Maurie."

"Oh no, not in town, Ted, no, he's watching the shifty soldi ... sol, so, son, son of a gun. He's watching that.."

"And what is that, Maurie, 'the shifty son of a gun'?"

"MAURIE MASON IF YOU WRECK THIS I WILL KILL YOU"

Ted's disembodied voice made his skull vibrate.

"Please Ted don't be mad I'm just ..."

"Maurie, Ted's not here, now what shifty son of a gun is Ted watching?"

"It's a ... cat, no dog ...yes, dingo."

"But we don't have a dingo problem."

"It's a film, 'The Shifty Son of A Gun', ... it's about a dingo."

"And Ted's watching it."

"That's right." Maurie breathed a sigh of relief.

"So Ted has a movie projector and he's watching 'The Shifty Son Of A Gun'?"

"That's right."

"Maurie, Ted doesn't have a movie projector. Nobody has a movie projector and there is no such film as 'The Shifty Son Of A Gun' is there Maurie?"

"Well, there might be."

"Why are you going to town?"

Maurie was completely swamped in hopelessness, a slough of despond entirely of his own making. His resolve was completely destroyed and he blurted, "Ted told me to register a mining lease at the office, it's a secret, you won't tell I told you will you, please Janet, Ted'll, ... you know ..."

Having confirmed his intention Maurie was getting back on track. It was just one more minute of travel agony and they came into Dencubbin. Maurie looked up to see a freshly painted, though still misspelled sign that was meant to make the State Grain Authority a bit more farmer friendly. The sign now read 'WA Golden Gain Authority'. Maurie knew he was right on the money.

"I won't be long Janet, I'll just register the claim and we'll get you some petrol and maybe you'll come and have dinner with me."

"That would be lovely, Maurie."

Janet had only one objective and it wasn't dinner with Maurie. As soon as the hapless yokel disappeared into the 'Golden Gain Authority' she slid into the driver's seat, started the engine and left Dencubbin in a cloud of dust as she headed for the Lands Titles Office in Cunderong.

Maurie meanwhile made a valiant attempt with the bemused Anthony Carlisle to 'register the claim'.

"I'd like to register a mining claim."

"Wouldn't we all."

"Ted told me to come here and register a mining claim."

"Ted Wainwright told you?"

"Yes"

"Has Ted been drinking?"

"No, Ted's at Bill's place and the gold is there too."

"There's gold at Bills and Ted is there. Sober?

"Yes."

"Maurie, I don't know quite how to tell you this but Ted Wainwright is an idiot, there's no gold at Bill's place and this is not the Lands Titles Office."

"But it says Golden..."

"It says or should say, Golden <u>Grain</u> Authority, the sign writer is an illiterate idiot."

Maurie was feeling a little sick in the stomach, a feeling that would explode into a bilious emergency when he went outside.

The People Vote April 1933

You must number all the squares for the Lower House, start by placing a 1 in the box next to your first choice a 2 in the box next to your second choice and so on until you have numbered all the squares.

Carlisle, Anthony

Beyersdorf, Herman

O'Connor, Margaret

You must number all the squares for the Upper House, start by placing a 1 in the box next to your first choice a 2 in the box next to your second choice and so on until you have numbered all the squares.

Murat, Andrew

Murray, Simon

Richardson, Robert

You must indicate your choice in the referendum by placing an X in only one box.
Mark the Yes box to vote for secession from Australia.
Mark the No box to vote against secession from Australia.

Maurie emerged from the booth at the Dencubbin School sweating profusely and ran straight into Ted.

"All done mate?"

"Yep, I voted for Carlisle."

"And who was second?"

"I didn't know the others, so I just voted for Carlisle."

"No 2 or 3?"

"No."

"Maurie, you just voted informal."

"No, I voted for Carlisle."

"You're an idiot ..."

"Carlisle said you're an ..."

"What did Carlisle say?"

"He said ... Hello Bill."

Bill's arrival saved Maurie from what he perceived as deadly conflict but the day was definitely coming when he would no longer be Ted's whipping boy.

"Ted, Maurie, just going in to vote. I'll see you on the way out." Bill disappeared into the school.

Ted and Maurie waited in stifling silence.

o-o-o-o-o-o-o-o-o

In Perth the results from a few exit polls were dribbling in as Nationalist and Labor candidates took their seats at their appointed election night haunts.

"Any news?" said Premier Mitchell as he sat down at the bar alongside John Scaddan.

"Only things that don't make sense, the referendum Yes vote is very strong but our performance is ... well ,,, it's too early for meaningful figures James."

"Meaning?"

"It's too early for meaningful figures."

"John, you were Labor premier 20 years ago, before you saw

161

the light. Since then you've been Minister for Railways, Mines, Police, Forests and Industry, you're the most experienced man in this room, just give me your opinion."

"Let's just say the numbers are not in our favour but it can turn around very quickly and probably will, the great majority of secession supporters are also our supporters. Drink?"

"Thanks."

On the other side of town.

"What's the news gents?" said Phillip Collier as he took a seat with the senior members of the Labor opposition.

It's too early to tell but the 'Yes' vote for the referendum is very strong which, ... you know ... doesn't look good for us." said Alex MacCallum.

"Shit, we decided to oppose it and now we're getting punished."

"Well that's the funny thing, when you compare these early numbers with the 1924 election; they're very similar."

"Alex I know you argued for secession in caucus and that privately you still support it; obviously it's a cause that resonates with more of the electorate than we figured ...in 1924 ... we won in a landslide. God almighty, if we win, what do we do with the referendum result, we can't institute something we so publicly opposed."

But this was politics and by 1934 Collier and MacCallum had worked it out quite nicely. Secession was suddenly a valuable weapon with which to attack the Commonwealth Government. At successive Premiers conferences Western Australia threatened to secede if the Commonwealth did not act to redress the financial problems that beset the smaller states after Federation. In fact Western Australia, Tasmania and South Australia all threatened to secede and mercilessly pounded the

Commonwealth at the 1934 Premier's Conference for six days on the subject of their economic woes.

Still outraged by Commonwealth intransigence Collier put through a bill to send a delegation to London to act with the Agent General to put the case for secession before the Imperial Parliament.

The British Government declined to accept the petition and the matter was never formally resolved.

Back at The National Country Party Coalition, the mood was funereal as news of Labor's victory in seat after seat, descended on the gathering. "Your seat's gone Davy and yours Parker, James and I are hanging by our fingernails," announced Scaddan. The consoling pale ale filled glass after glass as members drowned their sorrows.

Premier Mitchell retired to a quiet corner trying to think through what was happening, hadn't he accurately predicted the mood of the electorate on becoming a self governing dominion? Hadn't he and Scaddan hatched the Emu fear campaign and goaded the Commonwealth into undertaking a moronic military mission against the hapless birds? Where did they go wrong? He stubbed out his cigarette, closed his eyes and pushed back in his chair. Sleep came easily after such a frenetic campaign and assisted by ample quantities of beer his mind constructed a dream from random fragments of the last six months.

The familiar face of Mitchell's private secretary entered the room exuding her usual calm and announced that a delegation had arrived to see him. "Show them in Mary."

"There is rather a lot of them Sir and they are … a bit ruffled."

"Don't worry lass I'll calm them down."

"I'm sure you know best Sir."

Mitchell was startled to see Maurie Mason who had vigorously pumped his arm at Edith Cowan's funeral and declared his admiration for Donald Bradman. Mitchell once again felt his natural instinct to flee but his car was gone and he was left without an escape route.

"Mr Mitchell"

"Yes"

"Crikey it's really you"

"To be sure"

"Crikey, I'm Maurie, Maurie Mason" He grabbed Mitchell's hand and pumped his arm vigorously.

"Pleased to meet you Maurie"

"Crikey ... I mean crikey ... lovely day for a funeral."

"We're very fortunate."

"I'm Maurie, Maurie Mason"

"Without doubt"

"What do you think of Bradman?"

"Fine Batsman"

"I've got a bit of a problem Jim."

"A bit of a problem?"

"Yes, it's Ted, well not really Ted, he just started it, you know to help you to become independent and that."

"Ted?"

"That's right Ted and the emus, we used the emus to fool the army so you could be the new king."

"Very gratifying."

"I know some people call you Moo Cow Mitchell, I don't, neither does Ted or Bill."

"Bill?"

"Janet's father."

"Of course."

"So anyway now that we've run out of wheat to feed them we don't know what to do, so ..."

"Run out of wheat?"

"That's right so I brought them with me, can you look after them?"

At that moment a horde *(actually a flock but surely a horde is bigger)* flooded into Mitchell's office, pecking at his clothes, pulling at his papers, helping themselves to the drinks cabinet and PECKING AT HIS CLOTHES until he was naked as a newt. The scene changed to a movie version of the emu attack on the soldiers mess that he'd read about in the papers, he saw the sausages disappearing one after the other and in a sexual panic tried to protect his manhood from disappearing down the same tunnel. Unfortunately his arms had shortened and he couldn't reach, Maurie continued to explain the whole saga, yelling, to rise above the noise of the birds. Mitchell yelled for Scaddan but his voice wouldn't work, Mary came in with a morning tea tray and stared fixedly, she threw him the tray to defend himself but his shortened arms missed it which Mary thought quite amusing and she smiled at him while calmly drinking tea from a Wedgewood cup, the Ranunculus design, a set that she had purchased for the office in 1930. Mitchell felt failure and embarrassment beyond belief.

"James, James wake up." Scaddan shook him, Mitchell, still in his dream state grabbed Scaddan's hat to cover his perceived nakedness.

"James, we all have dreams like that, now straighten your tie and give me my hat, the next Governor of the State must demonstrate the decorum of the office."

"Governor?"

"Collier just rang to pay his respects and gloat, just a little, over winning the election butmthr job ismon offer if you want it."

"If I want it!"

"Did I mention they can't pay you until the State's back in the black?"

"No you didn't."

Mitchell, still emerging from his dream, made a ham fisted apology to Mary who, while completely dismayed but being used to the regular incoherence of politicians, thanked him for being so considerate.

"First Australian born Governor, too right!"

Putting Things Right

d'Camry had had time to think, to observe the world around him, to see people as they really were.

As he saw clearly that things were not as they first appeared he gave a wry smile. He had failed with Robert, because ... Robert was distracted by something, God knows what, maybe that feisty girl, maybe his own family induced expectations, maybe the obvious damage to his career from this farce of a mission. d'Camry freely admitted he didn't know, he would have to wait for things to become clear. In the meantime he could pursue his agenda of reconciliation with just about anyone given that he had alienated just about everyone.

Beginning proved to be the greatest difficulty, just opening the dialogue required a whole change in mindset for the listener. He tried to engage Cox, but Cox was too wary given his recent and complete lampooning of the hapless Major. Sgt Wilkins was equally standoffish having just broken every rule in the book on the recent 'Horse-feather Mission' and then of course there was the ever present Officer/NCO divide. Perhaps one of the women? Janet? too threatening. Elizabeth? a quick mental replay of the scene in the garden made him cringe. Perhaps one of the farm hands? but he had never spoken to them and the cultural divide was a yawning void. And so it was that Major d'Camry, seconded from the British Army, artillery expert and, more recently converted human being, wandered past several kelpies on chains each with its own hollow log to escape the summer sun and the winter cold. These naturally shy working dogs barked as he approached and then retreated to their respective logs as he came threateningly nearer. He asked their permission to visit and perhaps spend a little time talking. He took their reticence as a 'maybe' and sat on one of the log kennels. He began at the beginning and kelpie 1 whose name was Canute (Bill had a bit an interest in early British History) eventually crawled forward as if to listen more attentively. d'Camry ranged over his many trials, his gaffs, his faux pas, his rudeness, his arrogance, his lifelong alienation and his general unhappiness, Canute rested his head on d'Camry's boot and d'Camry scratched him behind the ear. The conversation was going well; d'Camry explained his need to make a universal apology for his bombastic behaviour and as he momentarily stopped the scratching and gestured to indicate the breadth of his feeling, he found a paw on his knee requesting further interaction, he happily obliged.

"I'm talking to a dog … everyone has to start somewhere."

d'Camry was unaware that Canute was Canute and therefore of royal lineage, this one would not rule Denmark, England, Norway and parts of Sweden but he sure could put the wind up a mob of sheep.

d'Camry thanked his regal companion and promised to return. Canute licked his hand.

In the days that followed d'Camry did return and encountered Jarli feeding the dogs one evening. He asked him if he thought it would be alright to take Canute for a walk. Going for a walk is not what working dogs do and for Jarli this didn't make any sense, so before he got into too much hot water he decided to show the Major what working dogs did. He let Canute off the chain and as he did so all the other dogs jumped and barked and generally expressed their fervent desire to go to work

Canute did a quick lap of the yard and returned ready for action. Jarli told Canute to sit then said, "get the chooks." Canute raced away to where the chooks were scratching and pecking and stealthily dropped to the ground. d'Camry had fully expected to see a melee of blood and feathers but this was a regular bit of sport for Canute. Canute crept forward on his belly until the chooks turned in the right direction, he then wheeled them gently on the left wing, taking care not to get too close and cause a panic and then on the right wing. Canute exhibited ultimate patience as he moved the chooks bit by bit to their fox proof night shelter. As the last chook passed safely inside Canute returned to Jarli's side but Jarli simply said, "lock up," and Canute pushed the door closed with his nose and thanks to one of Bill's pieces of farm engineering a latch dropped into place.

"Good boy!" said Jarli as Canute dropped at his side.

"That's amazing!" said d'Camry as he looked down on Canute full of admiration. He turned to Jarli and said "... and, .. I'm sorry, I don't know your name."

"Fred." Said Jarli.

"Peter," said Peter, extending his hand.

Jarli was not expecting this particular response from a white man who he thought to be both stupid and unpleasant. Jarli tentatively extended his hand and Peter shook it warmly, "I've never seen, how do you?, I mean, I don't, I mean, well done, very well done." d'Camry's perseverant speech was incomprehensible to Jarli but he did catch the appreciative tone and smiled in return.

Jarli said, "on the chain," and Canute tore away and lay down beside his log ready to be chained up.

d'Camry's spirits lifted a little. It had been a good day.

o-o-o-o-o-o-o-o-o

Robert knew he had to get on with the business of business and stop this military façade, he had to meet with the men, he had to resign his commission but most of all he had to talk a whole lot of things through with Janet.

They needed to be alone but then at this stage of their relationship they were ... well ... quite easily distracted ... he was willing to take the risk. They had of course seen each other since the 'great race' and he had taken her in his arms, managed to say, "done?". She replied, "done." Whence they found themselves naked on a camp bed in the shearing shed. Despite their libertarian views it was still 1932 and for the sake of everyone else's sensibilities, their private encounters needed to remain secret until they were well away from Janet's parents and the all seeing eyes of the people of Dencubbin.

Janet helped her mother clear away the remains of the evening meal, wash up, dry up and put everything away. She then announced that she would go for a walk.

"You can ask Robert here for the evening you know."

"Thanks mum, I know, but we need a bit of time to ..."

"I know dear," she said with a smile, giving her implicit blessing to the hoped for union.

Robert and Janet met as arranged under the white flowering prunus, Janet said, "shearer's quarters?"

Robert, showing ultimate restraint said, "let's walk first."

"What, are you trying to make an honest woman of me?"

They laughed and walked arm in arm around the house paddock.

"I have a plan," said Robert

"So do I," said Janet, "but you first."

"I asked myself what I really want out of all this "

"And?"

"And I want more than this mine has to offer, I want to leverage the asset to launch a takeover of WA Gold and then, ..."

"So starting small? WA Gold? The biggest Australian miner?"

170

"That's the one, but to do that I need to control the asset, unfortunately, at the moment we have about 30 partners including your parents and the farm hands."

"If there was a company and if you were the Managing Director and the others didn't have a vote and if, if ,if..."

"The voting, I think you're onto it, have you heard of non voting shares?

"Who would want non-voting shares?

"I am guessing people who might like a better share of the dividends."

"So non-voting shares get a guaranteed extra percentage more than the voting shares?"

"Yep."

"And we would hold all the voting shares?"

"Yep."

"And you would be the MD and I would be Chairwoman of the board, which would be made up of, us?"

"Yep."

"I think you should say something more corporate than yep."

"Certainly, absolutely, positively, assuredly, exactly … yep."

"We need to have a meeting as soon as possible, there's just one problem ..."

"d'Camry?"

"d'Camry. If he were to tell Canberra that we'd been gold mining instead of Emu hunting, all hell would break loose and they might even claim the asset. The Commonwealth of Australia is not known to be a good sport where money is concerned."

Of course d'Camy was not a problem but that was only known to Canute and possibly Jarli.

"If d'Camry is a problem then we have to bring him on board."

Robert shuddered, "Is that your first official decision as Chair?"

"Yep! And my second decision is to show you the shearing

shed."

"I've seen the shearing shed."

"There might be something new if you close your eyes and be a very good boy," Janet led Robert away.

o-o-o-o-o-o-o-o-o

Robert knew, or thought he knew that d'Camry would be a tough nut to crack. He would have to work up to it, gradually talk him around, find some way of making it all acceptable. Robert had guessed that d'Camry was probably independently wealthy so he could not use greed as a motivator. He knew he liked to be right and bask in the reflected glory of his own ideas but how on earth … that would require puerile propositions, ludicrous logic and crazy cognition, Robert would leave all that alone. He momentarily considered telling the truth but quickly dismissed it as the worst of all possible options. That left homicide, accidental death (which would also be homicide or perhaps the result of fervent prayer, not something Robert was good at) or … d'Camry could be recalled, Robert could then quickly pack up the mission and remove all trace of their intrusion. It wouldn't be hard to leak evidence of insane behaviour and wait for the call telling him to relieve d'Camry of his command and then send him packing back to Canberra and hopefully back to England. The plan started to take root in Robert's mind, he told himself that d'Camry certainly deserved these consequences, that he was more than just an irritating nuisance, he was incompetent, dangerous and an embarrassment to the professional army.

d'Camry's previously untouchable status could actually work in Robert's favour, the brass wouldn't want to take any formal action that would cause ructions back in England and the English brass would be approached quietly, there would be an implicit understanding that the whole messy affair would be hushed up at both ends with d'Camry assigned to a new desk somewhere out of harm's way. Brilliant, Robert smirked at his own guile and set about to document a comprehensive leak. He could leak it to Janet who could send it to Canberra asking defence for official confirmation of this extraordinary indictment before going to press. Better and better.

o-o-o-o-o-o-o-o-o

Bill, Ted and Maurie met up at the Dencubbin pub and ordered the usual. Molly brought the beers to a fairly subdued little group.

"No smiles for the best Barmaid in Western Australia, not even from you Teddy Bear?"

Ted was still smarting over losing out on the gold find and given his less than noble attempt to register the claim himself had decided that the whole sordid series of events was best forgotten, he had already made Maurie promise to keep the details a secret and opened the conversation as if he knew nothing of the gold.

"Does any of us understand what the hell happened in politics this week?" said Ted

"Nope," said Bill.

"Nope," said Maurie.

"I mean, how in the dingy dong could we lose the election and win the referendum," said Ted

"After all we've done, all that effort, all that wheat," said Bill.

"And we've still got the emus, what'll we do with them? We can't eat them," said Maurie.

Ted finally gave Maurie his attention. "Eat them," he mused.

"We've learned a lot about these birds, we know how to move them around, we know they don't need a lot of water, the

173

feathers must be worth something, the hides are tough enough to make good leather and if the meat tastes good, well, you might be onto something."

Bill maintained a stony silence, the last thing he wanted was to get drawn into another of Ted's hair brained scheme. And having been fully briefed by Janet on the gold and the attempt by Maurie to register a claim, he was less than impressed by Ted's disingenuous avoidance of the subject.

"How about I talk to an abattoir about the prospect of slaughtering a thousand a week?"

Maurie was nursing his beer and looking decidedly uncomfortable and then -

"I'm really sorry Bill."

"Sorry? What about?"

"He's sorry that things didn't turn out as we planned! Aren't you Maurie?" interjected Ted.

"Yes, ... No ..."

"And he's sorry that he mucked up the meeting with Mitchell."

"No I'm not, well I am but that's not ..."

"Exactly, not worth talking about! Another round?" Ted got up and started toward the bar.

"I haven't finished this one yet."

"You always need one in reserve."

"No I don't, ... I don't want another beer, I want to ..."

"Have something different? How about a port? I'll get you a port."

"I don't like port and I don't like you talking over the top of me."

"Sorry, what would you like?"

Bill considered intervening but held back and let the scene play out.

"Nothing, I want nothing, alright, I just want you to sit down and listen."

Ted sat down.

Bill smiled at Maurie.

Maurie drew breath.

Ted stared at Maurie till beads of sweat formed on his top lip.

Maurie was well and truly intimidated but he had been there before and had resolved not to be there again, he knew he wasn't bright but he wanted to be treated with a bit of respect; it was time.

"Bill, I think you ought to know that there's gold on your place and I tried to make a claim on it."

Ted swallowed hard as Maurie seemingly took the blame.

"I'm really sorry Bill, I should have told you as soon as I knew, I just...." he tapered off.

Bill looked expectantly at Ted.

Ted blew air through his mouth and shook his head. "Gold, well, who would've thought it."

Bill leaned into the table and made eye contact with Maurie, "I know mate, Janet told me all about it, but I really appreciate your being man enough to tell me and you know what? Your friendship is worth more than all the gold in that seam."

Maurie had been teased mercilessly at school as an easy object of derision, his social life was minimal, his only skill, breeding livestock, was always overlooked but he had a keen sense of justice, he knew what was right and at last he was vindicated; he sat back in his chair and said, "Thanks, Bill."

Ted knew he had been exposed and leapt to his own defence, "I was going to tell you Bill, I thought,"

"Tell me what Ted?"

"That the gold was ... was ... there, and ,,, and needed to be protected from that sleazy lieutenant."

"That sleazy lieutenant is my future son-in-law and he has acted in the best interests of all concerned."

Ted fell silent but could not utter the words that would make things right.

Bill and Maurie left without a second round of drinks.

o-o-o-o-o-o-o-o-o

Robert and Janet had indeed had an evening with Bill and Elizabeth; they explained about the gold, discussed company structures and boldly announced their engagement. Elizabeth was overwhelmed with emotion, she hugged Janet with tears of joy rolling down her cheeks, wetting Janet's neck, Bill took Robert's hand and pumped his arm almost to exhaustion. Robert was again overcome with emotion in the presence of his future in-laws and blathered endlessly about Janet's extraordinary abilities, so much so that when he started on her brilliant but scandalously deceitful scheme to involve the newsreels in the Emu War story, Janet had to intervene with, "Robert, you are too kind, I think it might be time for that bottle of Champagne that Dad has hidden on top of the wardrobe."

"How did you know about that?"

"Childish curiosity ... sorry"

"You know, I bought it when you were born, seems like yesterday."

Elizabeth produced their treasured Stuart Crystal glasses, Bill retrieved a very dusty bottle of Veuve Clicquot yellow label, while Janet told Robert that some exploits were better left unsung.

Ice to chill the bottle was a little hard to come by at Clovelly Farm and while across the country in the Sydney suburb of Willoughby, Edward Hallstrom was making that refrigeration wonder, the electric Silent Knight, Bill and Elizabeth still relied on the 'kero' model which was more of a cooler really and certainly couldn't freeze water. Hallstrom made millions from refrigeration and generously poured his money into the development of Sydney's Taronga Park Zoo.

The Champagne was a little warm but quickly quaffed and the convivial group made a credible start on Bill's well guarded supply of Johnnie Walker.

There was a good deal of reminiscing and future gazing as the family considered not only their past but also the oncoming and unavoidable collision with wealth and power.

It was somewhat ironic that at that moment the world's first cyclotron was turned on.

The invention, credited to Ernest Lawrence accelerated charged particle beams through a spiral until they emerged to hit a target where NEW PARTICLES were produced and all that stuff we thought we knew about atoms and electrons, protons and neutrons got turned on its head.

In this extraordinary age when even the nature of change was changing, the coming collision of Robert, Janet, Elizabeth and Bill with the future world would be just as powerful, with the springs and cogs of their lives exploding like new particles as they accelerated from personal obscurity into events that they could in no way foresee or comprehend.

Throwing The Switch

In 1932 just outside Moscow a passenger train hit a man who was walking on the tracks. The driver stopped so the body could be retrieved but failed to have flares and other warning indicators put out. A second train coming up behind slammed into the stationary train crushing 6 carriages. As the injured were being helped from the wreckage and laid on the adjacent track, a third train ploughed into them. There were 68 fatalities. Robert expected a collision.

Robert contrived to get d'Camry out of the way while he had a meeting with the men, Janet and her parents. He had asked Janet to ask her editor to invite d'Camry to town for an interview for a human interest piece, 'A British Artillery Major in WA's wheatbelt', that sort of thing. d'Camry almost declined but then he thought that since his attempts to explain himself had been so thwarted, except for his conversation with Canute, then perhaps it might be a good vehicle to present his enlightened self to the world and so in line with his new persona he drove himself to Dencubbin and settled into conversation with Chris Manly: Editor, Senior Journalist, Head Reporter, Linotype Operator and Letterpress Machinist. Manly was convinced of a bright future with an expanding population and he was ready to move to daily editions as soon as the readership demanded more timely and penetrating news. The problem with Dencubbin and surrounds was that the big news was the two headed calf born on Harry McGrath's spread or the winner of the rhubarb wine prize at the Dencubbin show. Chris Manly knew he was doing Janet a favour by interviewing d'Camry but a British Major chasing emus through the wheatbelt was bigger news than he had seen or heard in quite a while.

"Major, thanks for coming in, I afraid we're a bit short on space. Do you mind sitting here in the print room?"

"Not at all Mr Manly ..."

"Please, just Chris is fine."

"Thank you Chris, very impressive machinery you have here."

"Yes, well it's probably more than I need at present and of course the last few years have been a struggle but I am convinced that Western Australia will expand rapidly from now on and I will be ready."

"I'm glad to hear it, have you always been a newspaper man?"

"Yes, ink in the veins, so they say, four generations of the family in the industry, journo's, printers and reporters, I've never wanted to do anything else. My great grandfather reported on the first Anglo - Afghan War."

"How extraordinary, my great grandfather was one of the few survivors but I didn't think they had war correspondents back then."

"My great grandfather was actually the chaplain during the campaign and subsequently published a defamatory, not to say inflammatory account. I have it here, it's part of the family history I'm compiling." Chris reached for a pile of galley proofs, flicked over some 20 or so pages and handed the page with the extract to d'Camy. "Third paragraph about halfway down."

d'Camry read in silence. 'The first Anglo-Afghan War was begun for no wise purpose, carried on with a strange mixture of rashness and timidity, brought to a close after suffering and disaster, without much glory attached either to the government which directed, or the great body of troops which waged it. Not one benefit, political or military, was acquired with this war. Our eventual evacuation of the country resembled the retreat of an army defeated. '

As d'Camry read, his mind flew back to his family home and that library of belligerence that was the background to his childhood. He knew just how bloody the war had been with more than 4,000 British and Indian troops slaughtered along with 12,000 camp followers. He railed against this immoral waste of human life that had come about because of naked imperial ambition and flawed intelligence about a Russian invasion of India. He knew that there was a second Anglo Afghan War and a third, that the Afghans were eventually humiliated as Britain took charge of their foreign policy and paid them for their subservience. He mused that nothing had been learned from Alexander the Great, Genghis Khan, the Timurid Empire, and a host of other empire builders, all of whom came to Afghanistan, created havoc and eventually faded away.

"Tea time, I think." Chris Manly's voice seemed far away and d'Camry struggled to extract himself from the mire of Afghanistan's unfortunate history.

"Yes, tea, yes, thank you ... just black and as it comes."

Manly filled the jug from a tap over the wash-up sink where the grime from the hands that had set and printed many editions was well ingrained in the raw hardwood planks of the bench. He boiled the jug, added the tea and filled a large teapot; enough to provide multiple cups of refreshment. The cups were well stained and had not seen a cleansing hand since he had opened the doors of the Dencubbin Times.

d'Camry was a stickler for cleanliness and felt an immediate revulsion at the insanitary cups and surroundings, but he found Manly interesting and as he forced himself to relax he found the revulsion diminished as his interest in Manly increased. This was so new to him, the connection with people, the exhilaration of relationship. These simple pleasures that had been denied him as the institution always took precedence over the personal. He hesitated when Manly offered biscuits from a particularly grimy jar but he slapped his obsession down and plunged his hand in. This was a new kind of triumph so different to the humiliation of the Afghans, the subjugation of the Indians, the defeat of the French, the destruction of the Russian Black Sea Fleet and the eventual victory at Sevastopol. All this history was suddenly recast from glorious, righteous nationalism into the vicious, grimy, selfish struggle for power that it most certainly was. Concurrently, d'Camry was experiencing dominion over himself, the only morally justifiable dominion and he liked the feeling, he felt genuinely powerful even dangerous and subversive as he challenged such entrenched, long held and well reinforced views of the world.

"So, tell me about this campaign against the emus."

d'Camry was definitely caught on the hop, his brain scrambled to assemble some answer that would rationally align with his new world view. He processed what seemed like hundreds of possible answers, all of which he rejected and finally blurted a response that was more autonomic than reasoned.

"It's a bit like Afghanistan, we shouldn't have been there and we shouldn't be here, it's a complete waste of everyone's time. Plagues, politicians, parties, revolutions and empires they all have their time and then fade away. When I came here I called these birds the enemy but they are just a blip in nature's cycle and I was a rambunctious idiot trying to please my superiors or my family or God or, well, no one of any consequence, by chasing hapless birds around when the locals probably had a much better way of dealing with them."

Manly stopped writing, put his pencil behind his ear, sat back in his chair and said,

"do you really want me to print that?"

"Yes. Yes I do. It's time. I've been looking for a way to end all this nonsense and I think I owe it to the men and to that long suffering family at Clovelly to apologise for my arrogant behaviour. Printable?"

"Start the presses!"

They talked on for hours as d'Camry revised all his life scripts and elevated the meaning of 'candour' to new heights of openness and transparency.

"This will probably end your military career."

No, I will end that, as soon as I can telegraph my resignation, effective immediately.

"Do you mind if I syndicate this story?"

"Not at all."

"Major?"

"Please, Peter, just Peter."

"Peter, I hope you don't regret this. It won't appear for 2 days and if you change your mind I'll pull the story."

"That is very decent of you but no, my course is set."

"Peter?"

"Yes."

"I'm going to take a couple of days off during the wildflower season, do a bit of walking and camp overnight just south west of here, would you like to come?"

"Thank you, I would like that very much."

"This is the most unexpected ... well you see your reputation has preceded you and I ..."

"I can imagine, and it's quite likely all true, but something extraordinary has occurred and I feel like the luckiest man alive. I'll bore you with that around the campfire."

d'Camry left the office knowing that he had put in train *(poor choice of words)* a train wreck of similar proportions to the Moscow catastrophe of that year.

Bonanza

Robert had quickly gathered everyone together to discuss the gold bonanza. True to the selfish nature of humans he had toyed with various ideas that would increase his own share of the gold. He eventually returned to the compromise he had discussed with Janet of a company structure that gave him the lion's share of the power and and a slightly lesser share of the loot. Power, to be in charge, to control, to wheel and deal, to manipulate, to hold the fate of others in his hand; this excited him above all else.

"Men, Mr and Mrs Cole, Janet, Steve and Fred. We have stumbled into extraordinary wealth ..."
Robert laid out his plans, where he would be the Managing Director, Janet would chair the board and together they would control 85% of the voting shares and everyone else would have an equal split of the more profitable non-voting shares and an equal split of the remaining voting shares. There were questions mostly of an inane nature like, "How much gold is there sir?" and "When do we get the first cheque?"
It was only Cox, after the explanation of the company structure, who ventured, "Are you sure you want to do that Sir?"
Robert looked puzzled by the question, of course he wanted to do it, he had no hesitation, Cox might just as well have asked "Do you want to continue breathing?" Cox reflected on one of his favourite quotes from the infamous Lenny Lower, journalist, author and drunkard, "Things that are done cannot be undone."
But even Cox was not immune to the lure of wealth and power but at least he thought about it and in the end decided to stay and share rather than cut and run. Jaril and Jarli seemed the

least interested, their lives were tied to family, land and horses; the concept of capital, enough to provide life long support and extraordinary comfort didn't make any sense, after all they didn't work for money, for even though they were paid, they worked because they loved it. Their situation was a rarity, they knew most of their mob had no choice, were not paid and lived in abject poverty.

Robert advised his men not to resign from the army immediately as the money would take a little while to flow and to keep quiet about their new found wealth so as to avoid any possible conflict with the Defence Forces and their political masters.

It was then that Cox raised the issue of d'Camry. "It seems to me sir that he could cause a lot of trouble with the top brass, if he told them that we discovered the gold while on duty."

There was a stir amongst the men. "Fuck Coxy, let it be." "Always gotta put a damper on things." "Gloom and doom Cox."

"And that Corporal is precisely why we all need to remain quiet until we are well away from here and d'Camry has been sent packing back to England."

"But Sir, surely it would be better to include him, I know it's a risk but it seems like the right thing to do and ..."

The murmuring returned: "Why would that fuckwit get a share?" "Fuckin moron toff."

"Let him speak ... Corporal?"

"He's been different this week Sir, not such a di ... "

"Thank you Corporal, remember we're all still in the Army at this point. If you're all happy for me to handle this I'll sound him out before saying anything rash."

The meeting ended with a unanimous vote for Robert's plan and a great deal of back slapping and excitement about the future.

Amidst all the rejoicing, Down caught Jarli's eye and indicated that he should come up to the shearing shed.

They both quietly slipped away and met at the shearing shed yards. Down leaned on the palings of the counting out race, and smiled at Jarli.

"How does it feel to be rich mate?"

"Dunno, Jaril doesn't know either he's just gone quiet, he gets like that, always tries to make sense of things, he won't talk for days, til he's got it figured out."

"But what about you? No more work, no more bosses, no more shit kickin."

"We're different, a rich black fella is still a black fella, can't go some places, can't talk to white women."

"I'm not so good at that anyway."

They laughed and knew that despite the money they would still be who they were, who they had always been.

"What about buying a place on the coast, get some good broodmares and breed stock horses?"

"My mother's country's on the coast, I like it there, good fishin' too."

"Jarli..."

"Yes."

"Are we gonna see each other again after this, maybe do something together somewhere?"

"You and me? It's dangerous. With my people it's dangerous, with your people, it's dangerous."

"Yeah, dangerous."

They stared at the ground hoping for a magical resolution but none came.

0-0-0-0-0-0-0-0-0

Robert knew Cox was right, he had to resolve things with

d'Camry, it was the singular vulnerability that could destroy all the carefully laid plans. He was expecting d'Camry to return about now but time dragged on and Robert became more nervous. Even this small lack of control, d'Camry not complying with Robert's schedule, was enough to cause a major anxiety. d'Camry of course was busy making his first friend (second if you count Canute) and so, unknown to Robert, couldn't have cared less about Robert's grand agenda.

Robert had morning tea with the Coles and despite all the talk of future happiness he was clearly agitated and when he saw the dust from d'Camry's Model A , he quickly excused himself and went to face the first of many finely balanced negotiations.

d'Camry was in his tent by the time Robert made his excuses to the Coles and crossed the house paddock.

"Excuse me Sir, could I have a word?"

"Certainly Robert, come in." This abundance of congenial human contact was making Peter d'Camry quiet effusive."Come in, have a seat, I'll order some tea." Robert's bladder was already under considerable pressure from multiple cups with the Coles plus the 'anxious constriction' of waiting, but he put politics before comfort and accepted the offer.

"We were interrupted when we tried to catch up last time I think, so what's on your mind?"

"Quite a lot really Sir, but could I put a hypothetical to you?"

"Of course Robert."

"Well … Sir, if you had the opportunity to ensure the wellbeing of your men and I don't just mean keeping them out of harm's way but really look after them, even set them up for life but you had to break some minor rules to do it, nothing illegal you understand, well … would you do it?"

d'Camry took a long pause, Robert's anxiety levels ramped up several notches but his face gave nothing away.

"You know Robert, I grew up under a strict family regime, so strict in fact that when I entered military service, I noticed very little difference between home and the Army. I had been taught by rule, lived under rule, ordered my life and emotions by rule. I was taught not to compromise, that the rules were absolute and once broken could only lead to complete disorder, to chaos even anarchy."

Robert began to sweat, but maintained his professional composure.

"Well perhaps I should put it a different way Sir."

"Not at all Robert, your proposition is a good one and one that we should all wrestle with, you say minor rules what do you consider minor rules."

d'Camry was being quite friendly but Robert increasingly felt that he was being set up for huge disappointment.

"Minor rules Sir, rules that have their place, rules that are based on reason and in most circumstances rules that it is advisable to keep." Robert felt he was clutching at straws even blathering. "Rules sir, that are good rules but ..."

"Yes Robert?"

"...goods rules Sir, that if broken," and here he took a very great chance, " if broken Sir they do not cause any great harm." Robert waited for the expected avalanche of abuse.

"There was a time Robert when I would have reacted automatically without recourse to reason or common sense, when I would have rejected the proposition, but that time has recently passed."

At this point Robert was certain of complete failure and misheard the final phrase as "that time has arrived at last." *Lesson one in negotiating, listen to the other guy.*

"Sorry to waste your time Sir."

"Pardon?"

"Sorry Sir I shouldn't have brought it up."

"I'm not following Robert."

"Major d'Camry, Sir, I'm sorry I should have known better."

"Robert, take a deep breath and listen carefully:

I am no longer Major d'Camry, I telegraphed my resignation on the way back here.

I have been a complete arse and I offer you my humblest apology, you can read the full account in the Dencubbin Times on Wednesday.

You are now the acting CO.

In response to your hypothetical, I would now put the welfare of the men ahead of some ridiculous rule or puerile procedure. Are we clear?"

Robert was speechless, his attempts to communicate resulted in an open mouth and an unnerving joggling of the head. All his cunning and guile had been trumped by an honest, open and unpretentious human being whose sudden appearance had taken him completely by surprise.

"Sir, there is something I have to tell you."

The Empire Begins *and ...they get married*

Bill and Elizabeth staked Robert as Managing Director so he could get things started as soon as Operation Emu had been wound up and as if to preempt the coming corporate culture they managed to secure the promise of a church wedding in exchange.

Robert acted swiftly, raising the necessary operating capital by the sale of 5% of his voting shares to Gold Mining Australia *(keep your enemies close).* The commencement of the gold extraction was almost immediate with the abundance of alluvial gold providing a handsome and speedy return which not only paid for the processing plant needed in Stage 2 and a substantial payment of 'prospecting fees' (a thinly disguised dividend so as not to spook the market) but also allowed for an initial investment in Gold Mining Australia, step one completed.

A proper geological assessment revealed an extensive deposit with associated silver, lead, zinc and copper. The estimate of mine life was at least 35 years with an estimated annual production of 25 tons of gold. Robert showed the report to Janet, placed it in an envelope marked SECRET and kept it under lock and key; after all he didn't want a sudden spike in Emu Resources shares to inflate the price of Gold Mining Australia shares before he had acquired the company. One year of production, a substantial war chest and a cautious dividend would launch Robert onto the world stage of entrepreneurs. The 'cautious' dividend was still more money than any of the individual shareholders had ever seen and gave them life choices beyond their immediate comprehension.

Robert was biding his time on a raid on Gold Resources

Australia, he had to make sure that he struck at the right time and that he could fund the share acquisition and carry his shareholders with him in contributing personal investment. In the meantime he turned his attention to the embattled US miner Basarco. This company, like so many before, was not only carrying too much debt but also too much hubris and as such was incapable of even thinking that a corporate raid was possible. They were big, really big, they were technologically at the top of their game, they were digging up seemingly inexhaustible wealth, everyone on the board was a millionaire and they completely neglected their vulnerabilities. Robert calculated every scenario he could think of, he planned every stage of the takeover, the loans spread over six lenders and the quick asset sales that would more than repay them. He knew who the likely buyers would be, how much they could pay and how much they wanted the prizes. In his passion to start the process he was even tempted to delay his own wedding but the Coles would not entertain a postponement and on September 20th 1933 Robert and Janet walked down the aisle of St Lawrence's Church of England, Dalkeith, Perth. On the morning of the wedding Robert was busy buying Basarco stock and had to be dragged away from his stock ticker to be on time. On the way to the church he told his best man that Basarco would fold within days, that its poor returns over the last six quarters had left stockholders edgy and weary, he told him that this poor performance was completely inverse to its glittering assets, mountains of extracted material and mammoth sales; "But you know Peter, I know just how to turn it around. It's my kind of company."

Robert and Janet were not given to displays of personal wealth which even now was substantial, their wedding was a simple affair and more for Janet's parents than for themselves, though

Janet did look stunning in a copy of an Adrian creation with a Chantilly lace bodice and skirt and a small train. The reception was at their new home overlooking the Swan River with a guest list of family, close friends and quite a lot of stockholders. The guests were treated to drinks and Devils on Horseback (the pitted date and mango chutney wrapped in bacon variety) *(possibly allegorical)* on the lawns before being seated in the marquee.

"Ladies and Gentlemen, the bride and groom." The MC who also ran the catering company led the applause as Robert and Janet took their places at the bridal table. Robert's parents along with his sisters and 'baby' brother had flown in from Sydney. The long slow flight and lack of creature comforts had left them completely wrung out, a condition etched on their ashen faces, as they found their shared table with Bill and Elizabeth.

The wedding breakfast was punctuated by Robert's employees not so cleverly disguised as waiters, delivering fragments of ticker tape while refilling water glasses, offering Champagne and removing empty bread baskets. One notable wit came in with emu feathers arranged to resemble the company logo to adorn the bridal table; on the side facing the bride and groom was a note saying Basarco closed down 10% on Wall St - nervous investors are cashing in their chips. Robert and Janet read the note and beamed their approval. To the casual observer it looked like like lovebird chit chat.

"Congratulations clever boy."

"Congratulations yourself, it was you who got most of our shareholders to buy stock to disguise the raid until it was too late."

"And your idea to use brokers in a variety of countries to slow down any tracking of where the money was coming from."

They kissed and returned to the meal.

In due course the MC introduced the father of the Bride.

"Ladies and Gentlemen the father of the bride, Mr William Cole."

"Dear family and friends, first of all welcome and a special thanks to all those who have travelled so far to share this day with us. It falls to me to wish Robert and Janet a lifetime of happiness. Elizabeth and I have wondered over the years whether Janet would ever find someone who matched her talents and ambitions, someone she respected, enjoyed and indeed loved. Sometimes, darling, we wondered if you were even looking. Her life was always so full and her independent spirit meant that she had to master everything herself and excel at everything she did. I suppose you can see that we think Janet to be rather special but special is not easy; special can be turbulent and headstrong and wilful and opinionated and ...",

"That will do dad."

"Well you can see what I mean, but we love Janet more than our lives, she was often our inspiration and always a foil to our old fashioned ideas. Then, just when she was showing us how to turn state politics on its head, along came Robert and we knew from the first, well Elizabeth knew, that something magical was happening; they turned each other to quivering jellies any time they were in close proximity. Two people who had never been lost for words suddenly reverted to monosyllabic speech while their eyes locked together and ... well, I should stop there. We are so happy to welcome Robert to our family. Robert and Janet make a formidable team and we know they will achieve great things, certainly beyond **my** wildest dreams. I wish I could give you both the gift of happiness but it is beyond my power, because my dear ones, happiness is hard earned. It takes time and patience, tolerance and compromise and yes love and passion. So to my daughter who, and I must say this darling, looks absolutely stunning this evening, and to my new son Robert, who seems to have scrubbed up alright, the world is at your feet. Ladies and gentlemen the bride and groom."

There was quite literally thunderous applause that swelled from many fountains: admiration, gratitude, respect, friendship and pride. It seemed that this was the only way to convey the depth of feeling in the room and it would take Robert to rise and quell the freely given tribute before the room was silent once more.

The MC was quite stunned by the effusive reaction of the guests and the honesty of Bill's speech. While he, off in an absent dream, wondering who on earth these people were, received a subtle jab from a waiter prompting him to introduce Robert.
"Ouch. Ladies and gentlemen, the bridegroom."
Robert rose slowly to his feet, he smiled at Janet and then slowly scanned the room from side to side, with smiling recognition of each guest. In any other circumstances this lengthy silent recognition would have felt uncomfortable but this group of people had shared a great deal, each one knew the part they had played and there was nodding approval as Robert's eyes moved from one to the next. Robert's parents were dismayed at first but they too caught the moment and when Robert's eyes lit on their familiar faces they felt a racing catharsis of every event of their shared family life and failed miserably to retain their composure. Tired from the flight but elated by their son's love and gratitude they wept quietly, drenching first their handkerchiefs and then their serviettes. They had had very little time with Janet but their observation of Robert and Janet together quickly confirmed the mutual understanding, respect and enjoyment that would blossom into love. They nodded their complete faith in the union to both of them.

Robert finally spoke.

"Janet and I,"

"He speaks," interjected Sgt Wilkins to much laughter and applause.

"... neither of us are great speechmakers and left to our own devices we would have shied away from a formal wedding but thanks to Janet's wonderful parents here we are and we wouldn't have missed it for the world."

"Not for the world," interjected Janet.

Robert walked to her took her hand and brought her to the microphone and together they said :

Robert: "We welcome all of you."

Janet: "You all know us, you know all, well most, of our faults and idiosyncrasies ..."

Robert: "You know too damned much to be perfectly frank."

Janet: "Full transparency was never the plan."

Robert: "We thought we would be the shadowy figures moving behind the scenes."

Janet: "But here we are under the spotlight."

Robert: "And with all of you here it feels quite passably good".

Janet: "And it seems like... like ..."

Robert: "Like there is a special bond ?"

Janet: "Yes a special bond with all of you in this room, does that mean we will visit often? Probably not. Live in each others pockets? I hope not. We are quite private people after all, but be there in time of need? I hope so."

Robert: "We are so aware that this adventure has forged strong bonds, we have chosen to cement ours in marriage, to love honour, support and vote for each other in the boardroom."

"To have children?!" interjected Bill with a hopeful inflection.

Robert: "As of today, you bet."

Janet: "How will you cement your special ties?"

Robert: "Our advice is don't leave it undone."

After 10 seconds of silence the applause started slowly and built hand on hand to a thunderous crescendo.

As the applause continued there were many glances exchanged but when Down looked at Jarli a tear ran down his cheek. Jarli looked at Down but took a nervous step backwards so that Jaril blocked his view.

Maurie looked at Janet and smiled for her happiness.

Ted turned to Molly, the barmaid from Dencubbin, and smiled nervously.

Molly smiled and sighed inside.

Chris Manly and Peter d'Camry couldn't wait for the stewards and starting popping the champagne corks and made numerous toasts to the Bride and Groom.

The MC once again overcome with emotion had to be prompted by one of the stewards to move things along.

Wiping his face with a serviette he stepped to the microphone once more.

"Ladies and gentlemen, the best man Major Peter d'Camry."

Despite having been told not to refer to d'Camry as 'Major' the MC had spent a lifetime magnifying everyone's importance and here was a real Major, it was autonomic, he couldn't leave it out.

"Ladies and gentlemen I am honoured to be here for Robert and Janet, and as most of you know I am now just 'plain Peter' and all the trappings of military prestige and all that piffle about titles and protocols seems a world away.

But this is definitely not about me.

My only duty now is to extol the virtue and beauty of the bridesmaids and then Bevin and I will read the telegrams.

I am a bit of a, I believe the Australian expression is, a bit of a dill, as far as women are concerned; complementing beautiful women is not my forte or even my piano, ... and ... I'm obviously hopeless with jokes ... but I'll do my best.

Janet told me that she only had two friends at school but that they were intensely loyal to each other and were a circle of steel as far as any boys were concerned. You know 'Lord help the mister that comes between me and my sister ...' ah ... and singing is another thing I am not good at. Anyway here they are Rebecca and Margaret, loyal as ever, virtue intact, though I didn't actually ask, and quite stunning in every respect.

Ladies and gentlemen, please raise your glasses and toast Rebecca and Margaret."

"Rebecca and Margaret!"

"Bevin could you join me for the telegrams please? For those of you who don't know Bevin Brown, he was what we call the HQ Liaison Officer for our 'emu mission' and a close friend of Robert."

"Thank you Peter. Hearty congratulations from all here at HQ. General Alan Morefield."

"News of a very happy end to the Great Emu War has reached us in Canberra, we wish you all the happiness in the world. Joseph and Enid Lyons."

"Congratulation my dear ones, getting a bit frail to travel but with you in spirit. Joan. Joan is Janet's Grandmother who lives in Dorset."

"May the bluebird of happiness refrain from defecating on your front veranda. ... No signature ... hardly surprising."

"Thanks for the emu's. Robert is a lucky guy. Pierce Strong, Movietone News."

And so it went on, telegrams, speeches, stock movements, dancing ... until the last guest said goodnight and Robert carried Janet to bed.

It was not a good time for a honeymoon with so many deals on the boil, and so they forewent that tradition, vowing that they would have plenty of trips, luxury hotels, haute cuisine and time in the world's great museums. In fact they lived fairly simple lives but were always embroiled together in the cut and thrust of business with the occasional indulgence in art and always museum visits when they were in London, Paris, Amsterdam, Berlin, Tokyo or New York to close a deal.

o-o-o-o-o-o-o-o-o

While in London negotiating the sale of some of the Basarco assets, Robert had met the Managing Director of Stage Door, a British media group with a string of West End theatres, radio stations and some significant regional newspapers. The MD had heard the buzz that Robert was creating in the City and invited him to advise the company on its future direction in high end theatres and other venues. After a quick analysis of the company accounts Robert took advantage of Stage Door's financial vulnerabilities and staged a successful raid on the company. He quickly sacked the MD that had brought him in, sold off the more glamorous assets that he perceived had peaked, and rejuvenated the capital starved assets with modern equipment, mostly from suppliers keen to enter the UK market who heavily discounted their goods for the high profile entrée and chance to display their wares at iconic London venues.

For Robert every post was a winning post, he thrived on new challenges but drifted into a reclusive lifestyle. The business of business was his breakfast, lunch and dinner, he had few friends, hated small talk and knew that his lust for planning and strategy made him more and more a social isolate as the years rolled by. The parade of mergers, takeovers and raids, sometimes unsuccessful but always intensely profitable saw their fortune balloon, they were multi millionaires when ordinary millionaires were a rarity. Robert was no impulsive gambler he did his sums on every venture, planned every move, put contingency measures in place and set aside the blue chip family assets clearly marked 'not for sale'.

Ted ll

Ted had not expected an invitation to Robert and Janet's wedding. He had considered excusing himself with some lie about the demands of the farm but in the end he summoned a modicum of courage and mailed his acceptance. He had not expected to see Molly there, let alone to be seated beside her and he spoke tentatively to her. He thought that he had completely destroyed his friendship with Bill and Maurie but managed to speak to them about the weather and the wool prices. At one point he felt such discomfort that he escaped to the veranda and as he looked out over the river he realised that the only thing that had been destroyed was his farcical masquerade as the aristocratic landholder.

Back home in his kitchen surrounded by growing piles of dirty crockery he reflected on that fateful meeting at the pub when Maurie established his honourable independence and his façade was shattered by Bill's insightful, albeit brief reprimand. Ted had sat at the table long after Bill and Maurie had left staring into his froth lined glass. He'd sat there till all the other patrons had left, when Molly, that rough diamond who had always seen the person behind the masque, sat at the table and looked directly into his soul.
"Really fucked it up this time Teddy Bear."
The voice seemed to reach him from beyond a galactic void. There was static and it echoed; it frightened him.
"What? Who?" Said Ted as he jumped up ready for combat with the forces of evil.
"It's me dickhead." Said Molly calm and composed, "Sit down and have this." She pushed a shot of her best single malt Scotch

towards the crumpled Ted as he slumped back into his seat. Alcohol has no healing properties, it dulls the brain and opens the door to bad behaviour, but Molly's gesture had remarkable powers of communication.

"No one calls me that," said Ted

"What, dickhead?"

"No, 'Teddy Bear'. Not since school, I hated it then and I hate it now … "

"You really are a dickhead Ted, you're so busy trying to impress everyone that you don't even recognise the people that like you, … some of us have liked you from when we were kids, even though you treated us like shit cause we weren't on the land or we weren't pretty or we wouldn't be be impressed by a stupid snob."

"I …"

"Shut up and listen. I hated you for a long time. Remember when you forced a kiss on me as a dare and I kneed you in the balls?"

"Yes."

"I wanted to pay you back cause you were so mean to me, and leaving you crying on the ground in front of your stupid friends seemed pretty good at the time. You always avoided me after that and told lies about me, you told those farmer's sons that I was a slut and that anyone could have me anytime they wanted. That really hurt Ted, I began to hate you more and more and I wanted to hurt you, really hurt you so that you could see what you had done. I rode all the way out to your place on my bike, that's two hours of pedalling, I was going to take a lump of wood and beat you stupid with it.

"I didn't know …."

"SHUT UP! I was there, I had the timber in my hand, but your father beat me to it. I heard the screaming Ted, I heard the pleading for him to stop, I heard your mother trying to intervene and getting walloped for her trouble, I heard it all Ted and I was the only one who knew and suddenly all my anger drained away and all I could see was the little boy that had been tortured until he was turning out to be as big a monster as his father.

"I ..."

"NOT YET. I always tried to help you after that, noticed the bruises, always said hello, tried to dance with you once, but you rejected me, me, the only one that knew and cared and forgave and I watched you Ted, watched you become an arrogant stupid prick that used his friends as pawns in his own game until they'd finally had enough of the abuse and just walked. This might sound cruel Ted but I feel like this is your last chance; Bill and Maurie are two of the most decent men I know so, ... fix it fuckwit ... and next time I call you Teddy Bear, know that it's because I loved that little boy in Kindergarten and I hope he's in there somewhere in the darkness.

By this time Ted knew that this wasn't conversation, this was like truth coming out of a fire hose and pummelling him till he couldn't stand, till all his energy was gone and he had not a tear nor glimmer of remorse or fear or ... he had nothing, he was naked and red raw. His entire stock of emotion had been expended years before in the lonely farmhouse where his torturer relentlessly bashed his body and cruelled his spirit, showing more care for the farm machinery than his only son.

Molly stopped, she was feeling exhaustion for the first time in her life. This whirlwind of human energy, this thick skinned barmaid who never tired of the verbal jousting with her customers, this brilliant business woman was exhausted as she released thirty years of pent up emotion.

Molly reached out a hand to Ted and led him to a vacant room, she sat him down on the bed, pulled back the covers, kissed him on the forehead, breathed out heavily and left the room, gently closing the door behind her.

The final sound of the door latching brought him back from his catharsis, the dirty dishes looked on, awaiting the scrubbing that they both needed.

pGoGordon Cope

Cox, Ford and Down

The three mates could all have resigned from the Army and returned to a very comfortable civilian life but had agreed that they would wait and just let things settle before making any rash decisions.

They reasoned that the Army was a pretty safe bet, guaranteed job, minimal chance of getting shot with no wars going on. After all Hindenburg beat Herr Hitler in the German presidential election and, sure, Japan was flexing its muscles, though invading Manchuria in 1931 was a bit more than a flex. Manchuria is a long way from Western Australia and the West Australian didn't print a word on the issue. After all Japan was a member of the League of Nations. It had supported the French, Russian and British alliance against Germany, Austria-Hungary and Italy. They were on our side, they kept the shipping lanes open and who really cared that the Japanese Navy happily took over German colonial possessions in the North Pacific at the beginning of WW1 and then turned its attention to the German sphere of influence in China. As world history went, things looked pretty good to the casual observer. Add to that good mates and plenty of time to pursue their hobbies, what was not to like. Pity it all went to hell in a handcar in 1933 when the Nazi Revolution began to unfold.

Cox wrote some memorised Shakespeare in his notebook as he waited for Ford and Down.

It was a game he played with himself; writing down poignant lines that had stuck with him and then forcing himself to comment ... honestly.

'When shall we three meet again' – *fairly obvious, in about 30 seconds*

'We few, we happy few, we band of brothers' – *bit sentimental but then I'm a bit sentimental*
'Gather ye rosebuds while ye may' – *no rosebuds but plenty of gold*
'Alas poor Yorick' – *always amusing but in the circumstances; is it treasure or mouldering bones*
'To turn me out on such a night as this' – *the old King rejected, what will the new King or Queen be like?*
'I think we should leave the killing out' – *an epithet to pass on to my superiors*
'The quality of mercy is not strained' – *alright, ... I'm mean ... sometimes*
'Draws his sword cries a rat and kills the good old man' – *but I was sure, so sure, always so damned clever*

Ford and Down ambled in.
"Still writing mate?"
"Can't stop, me old china."

"What a wedding, I don't think I've ever been with so many happy people," said Ford.
"You remember that night around the campfire at Clovelly Farm with Jaril and Jarli," said Down
"I remember my total embarrassment when I insulted those guys with my Umba Jumba remark," said Cox.
"I caught up with Jarli at the wedding, he's thinking about buying a cattle station for his mob, he's not sure if he can own land but Jaril'll give him a hand to work it out," said Down. "I said I'd take some leave and come and look around with him."
Cox raised an eyebrow and said "I spent some time talking to Jaril, asked how Uncle Umba Jumba was going and whether he had any future plans. He told me that he'd heard about this bloke called Doug Nicholls, a Yorta Yorta man, who has a

reputation as an athlete and was starting to work with Aboriginal people who had problems with alcohol and was pretty outspoken on Aboriginal rights. He's going to go see him and thinks maybe they can work together. I'd like to write that story."

"That's brilliant," said Ford. "You know, I haven't got a clue, I mean, I'm going to buy Mum a house but after that, I mean I can't go fishin for the rest of my life."
"You hate fishing". Said Cox.
"Yeah I know ..." said Ford "... what's on your mind Coxy?"
"I think a house for my Mum and Dad and I'll set up a fund so they can retire. They actually like fishing so somewhere on the coast. I think Dad needs that solitude, a kind of healing sleep after the tortures of the Great War, yeah he's still carrying all that with him. He's not the talking kind so peace and quiet is the best thing I can give him, and Mum ... she'll be able to read and read and read and hopefully find some friends with similar interests."

"A retirement fund," replied Ford. "I wouldn't have thought of that, my mum can stop washing and ironing other people's clothes and put her feet up for a change. Thanks Coxy. It's funny isn't it that we never expected to do anything but stay in the army, keep our heads down, avoid getting killed and maybe retire on the age pension. I never thought of anything big you know, nothing grand, and all this has taken me by surprise. The thinkin's hurtin' me brain."

"I'm having a bit of brain strain myself, but it doesn't really matter where I am, I just write down what I see in front of me and there's a lot to see in the Army and a bloody lot to write down mate. You know I wrote to Mildred about the gold and the money, a really long letter with every possible scenario, every possibility, every detail of every possibility, every slant, every take, every everything. She wrote back and said that if I ever write anything like that again she will come for me ... with a cricket bat."

Down listened but was wistful - look after his parents?- of course he would, he loved them and loved to visit, they were always happy when the family was together, always interested in his doings in the army - the story of the The Great Emu War had them laughing till their sides hurt - but he wanted to see Jarli again and soon.

Wild Flowers

Manly and d'Camry packed some camping gear, a few steaks, some eggs, sausages and enough canned food to sustain them for a few days after the fresh food was consumed. They left Dencubbin for the Stirling Ranges early on Friday afternoon and made their first camp a whisker before sunset. Manly's pup tent was just big enough for two so all the supplies had to be kept in the possum proof box strapped to the luggage rack of the car. d'Camry had never experienced the ravages of a hungry possum and thought that Manly might have been 'having a lend' of him as Australians often do, with endless stories of venomous snakes and spiders, ravenous alligators and poisonous plants.

Manly hadn't overplayed the magnificence of the wild flowers and d'Camry was expecting something like an English country garden, Manly was hoping for a jaw dropping surprise. He told d'Camry that there were about a thousand species of wild flowers in the area and that about eighty percent of those were unique to Western Australia.

Peter d'Camry and Chris Manly worked well together, each seemingly knowing when the other required help and sharing implicit agreement on what needed to be done and in what order. As the light dimmed, d'Camry set a fire and Manly produced a homemade hot plate on legs and a couple of camp chairs, they cooked the steaks and ate them sandwich style between two thick slices of crusty bread dripping with butter and tomato sauce.

"I'm afraid the greens are a bit thin on the ground, my mother would not be pleased," said Manly with a grin.

"My mother would be asking, 'where are the footpaths Peter?

What a ghastly place dear!' I'm afraid my family thinks that nature needs to be subdued, manicured and laid out to accommodate a pleasant stroll with a suitable companion and a parasol."

"How did your family respond to your resignation?"

"I sent a telegram and followed up with a detailed letter but to date 'stony silence has been the stern reply'. I am expecting that any minute my father will appear with a psychiatrist in tow, have me scheduled, cart me back to England and keep me incarcerated until I come to my senses."

"I wonder about sanity, I wonder about human beings, I wonder about civilisation, sometimes I feel so out of touch with the rest of the world that I think I'm from another planet."

"Do you think reporting the news has influenced your worldview?"

"Good point, for most of my colleagues, it's either finding relief in the ravages of alcohol or like me wrestling with a brain that won't stop contemplating the crimes of humanity and the manifest suffering it causes. You see if I was from Mars at least I wouldn't be complicit in this madness."

"Popular dinner guest are you?"

"Afraid not old chap and you?"

"A complete failure I'm afraid, in the old days, as in last month, I was a war bore of towering proportions. I relied on my knowledge of military history rather than any personal experience or passion; the ladies were quick to politely excuse themselves and the gentlemen drifted off to drink more port, smoke cigars and play billiards. Once, I just kept talking into the air while the servants cleared the table, one of the maids asked if I was finished so she could clear my plate and still I kept going as if completely engrossed in my own superior knowledge. It was a defence against the 'real people', a fence that kept them locked out but at the same time I was locked in and a complete mystery to myself. It was that experience on the rock that broke the nexus of ego and status.

They talked long into the night, two old chums that didn't fit in; it was a seminal moment for them both. Retiring to the tent they slept on the hard ground in deep satisfaction, a sleep so refreshing that they woke with the sun, ready to explore a new world.

As they walked in silence over a gentle rise that gave entrée to a meadow of flowers. d'Camry's jaw did indeed drop as he took in the floral splendour that rolled to forever. He tried to speak but couldn't, he stopped and stood stock still just staring at the eternal beauty, feeling that he was going to cry with joy. Manly waited, understanding exactly what was going on, knowing that nature was deafening him with silence, caressing him with colour, seducing him with simplicity while confounding him with complexity.
d'Camry remained speechless, his brain was firing so rapidly that he was stuck in a kind of sublime limbo; how could a man be so thoroughly redeemed without punishment for his former bombastic self, how could he be treated to such a glorious effusion that surely was meant only for the gods. He was dumbfounded and silence seemed the only way to convey his gratitude.

The next few days created something between the two men that they found hard to come to terms with, something that didn't quite fit the social norms, something odd, something exceptionally different. It grew inside them as they hiked through the ranges and absorbed its treasures. It was on the journey home in the car that they finally found some words to aid their understanding of what was happening.

"How will it be for us, Chris?"

"How will it be?"

"What happens next, after an experience like this, do we simply say, see the Stirling Ranges and die?"

"I think that this is only the beginning, a baffling beginning, it's taken me by surprise, I mean who are we, I don't think we are, forgive me, I don't think we are homosexual. Are we?"

"I am so internally bamboozled that nothing would surprise me but I don't think so – I mean it goes against what we know about the world but is it possible that love and sex can be different things, is it possible that the affection that we all crave can be just that, just affection not confirmed by sex?"

"Go on."

"God it's hard to talk about this stuff but if we, in a shared moment hugged each other would that lead to a sexual tryst that goes against our natural inclinations?"

"Or would it be a sign of enduring friendship, would we be like two 19th century gentlemen sharing a house like Holmes and Watson or Higgins and Pickering or even the ancient David and Jonathan, though I think they were kidding themselves, randy buggers."

"That was always my reading of it; two very handsome oversexed young men, one standing stark naked while he gives the other his clothes, I'd put money on it. I mean; 'I tasted a little honey with the tip of the staff that was in my hand' 1 Samuel 14:43, has to be the greatest biblical euphemism of all time."

"And you know that quote because?"

"A brief religious period ... and did I mention my photographic memory?"

"No ... you didn't ... any other little surprises?"

"Very few I suspect."

"Does it mean that you can always remember the punchlines to jokes?"

"Oh, I can remember them, I just can't deliver them. And I tend to have so many obscure facts stored away that I can be really boring; you know sometimes I get things completely arse about, when I remember fragments and I think I know how they fit together and of course they don't and if anyone bothered to check the facts I would look like a complete idiot."

They laughed at themselves for at least a couple of miles, like school boys who once tickled by something funny just cannot stop laughing; they might hold it in for 5 seconds or so and then it bursts out again to the annoyance of teachers and the dismay of uninformed onlookers.

Finally Manly spoke, "Shall we give it a try, you know share a house, I have one and you must find it a bit constraining living at the Dencubbin Hotel."

"It's been alright, catching up on what real people think and what they laugh at, quite an education really. But well … yes."

"Good, it feels like the right thing but there'll be the usual gossip, will it wear you down?"

"At the moment I'm hungry for any life experience, I've got a lot of catching up to do. You know at the hotel, there's this one chap, I know he can't read, but he's obviously very bright and very funny, intentional howlers and malapropisms just pour out of him and he doesn't even know Sheridan or Dickens. He's quite fond of saying, 'he's tall for his size' and the other night he offered me a sweet and said 'they're good mate but they make your teeth feel like they've got socks on', such a character, the kind of person that can really lift your spirits. Jolly good company and I would never have met him stuck inside that uniform."

They drove on.

The Great Emu War

A Rich Man's World

Janet was Robert's lover, friend, counsellor and gatekeeper. It was she who kept the world at bay while he worked tirelessly. It was she who planned all family matters and shouldered the responsibilities of wealth in Perth society.

They both wanted children and Janet was pregnant in their first year of marriage and sick as a dog for all nine months.

They walked every evening that they were home together. In summer they waited for the Fremantle Doctor before heading out, but in the cooler months they rambled along the river bank, usually on dusk. Jarli had brought Janet some wild raspberry leaves from his mother and told Janet where to find more. He said his people had used them for morning sickness since the white fellas had brought them from Eastern Australia. She chopped them and made a tea as instructed and it did seem to take the edge off the vomiting; some days she was vomit free.

The long awaited birth of Peter came on July 22nd 1934. A perfect 8lbs 4 oz, after a long labour. Robert had organised his schedule to make sure he was home. Elizabeth and Bill came up from their new home in Fremantle and there was much celebrating. Jaril, d'Camry, Jarli and Manly all arrived at once only to be ordered out minutes later by the dragonesque maternity sister who rigidly enforced rest periods and visiting hours.

Robert knew it was useless to argue with the all powerful sister so he suggested they retire to the Golden West Club. "We can walk down there, it's only a couple of blocks."

"Four blocks," corrected Manly.

"All right, four blocks but we can't get back in here for another 3 hours."

Jaril discretely took Robert aside and said, "Mr Robert, we just wait here. I don't think they let us in."

"Jaril, I would never want to embarrass you and I'll understand if you choose not to come but believe me it will be alright. The Golden West Club needs you and Jarli, much more than you need a snobby white fella's club, so if you can stand just a little bit of fireworks I'd love you to come."

"Just a little bit?"

"Just a little bit."

The half hour stroll from Royal Perth Hospital to St Georges Terrace on a balmy Perth afternoon was like a school boys outing with plenty of stories about Janet, a lot of backslapping and even a bit of horseplay when Jaril and Jarli lifted Robert shoulder high and carried him up the steps of the club. They set him down at the door, Robert straightened his tie, inhaled deeply, took a lighter from his pocket, flicked the flint wheel and said, "light blue torch paper, run like hell." And with that he snapped the lighter shut, pushed through the swing doors and prepared to educate George the concierge.

"Good afternoon George, I would like to sign my friends in."

"Certainly sir," said George as he turned the book toward Robert.

Robert wrote the four names and signed them all in.

"Ah, sir?" said George.

"Yes George."

"These men, sir they're, you know, black fellas"

"Well spotted George, glad you're on the job"

"Well sir, … we don't allow, that is it's against the rules … of the club for, you know, them to come..."

"You know George, I read the rule book before I joined and there is nothing about 'black fellas', 'abos', 'boongs' 'korris' or indeed any mention at all of the original owners of the

Australian land mass, so it can't be against the rules now can it?"

"But everybody knows that ...," (George was now sweating profusely) "we don't allow you know … them … aw Christ Mr Robert I'll get the … sack."

"You will certainly not get the sack George because you are a decent, hardworking and honest employee, now I am taking my friends through to the lounge and, I was hoping it wouldn't come to this, but when you bring this to the manager's attention, which you must do to cover your delicate arse, don't forget to mention that my cheque which he is counting on for some urgent repairs can still be cancelled."

"He don't respond well to threats sir." George was now sweating even more heavily and his usual posh accent and strained grammar which he thought added an air of dignity to the club had completely deserted him.

"No I'm sure he doesn't, but these are my friends and they will be treated as the decent, hardworking and honest men that they most certainly are. Thank you George."

"Ah, Mr. Robert you'll need these sir," said George producing the obligatory ties and jackets for Jaril and Jarli

The friends followed Robert through to the bar where they were greeted by raised eyebrows and cautious murmurs. As they seated themselves in the leather club chairs, Manly said, "delicate arse?"

"Well shall we say I am aware of certain predilections and now that he knows that I know, I am sure that his approach to the manager will be much more favourable."

It was then that George entered the lounge and had a furtive conversation with the barman.

The service was brilliant.

The Great Emu War

Molly

Months after Molly had left Ted sitting on the side of one of her hotel beds and after an awkward encounter at Janet and Robert's wedding, she felt a stultifying nagging void. Running the hotel was as easy as right foot, left foot. She had her routine and it saved her from sliding into the kind of introspection and possible depression that follows the exposure of deep emotions. She had risked it all on speaking the truth and now she felt … she felt …. she felt … she felt a lot of contradictory, confusing, irritating things that refused to be ordered into a coherent whole with a satisfying conclusion.

Every attempt to reconcile her emotional inventory ended with more questions:

Who am I after all? A forty year old publican built like a brick shit house.

Where are my friends? Not applicable

What is my future? Live alone, die alone.

Where is my family? Dead.

Molly's ruminations neglected all her great attributes and like most humans in distress, focussed on the deficits.

And where's fucking Teddy Bear? Not fucking here, that's for fucking sure.

Teddy Bear was in much the same condition; wounded and vulnerable and surrounded by dirty dishes.

Someone needed to move. Someone needed to be courageous. Someone needed to risk more hurt, wounding and embarrassment or fade into oblivion nursing their overpowering grief. A tough call for those that have already suffered more than most.

It was a bright sunny day that penetrated even the dark recesses of the main bar, it was the same light that lifted Molly a sixteenth of an inch higher on the emotional happiness index.
It was the same light that penetrated Ted's kitchen and thawed his emotional log jam.

They resolved to act.

Ted, still a bit zomboid walked slowly to the Model A, sat in the driver's seat, turned the key and drove slowly toward Dencubbin. It was like watching the starting of a large diesel engine; open the decompression valves, close the diesel fuel cock, open the petrol cock, crank the monstrous machine slowly until the spark plugs ignite the petrol, wait till everything is hot, close the petrol cock, open the diesel cock, listen for the rich thud of exploding diesel, close off the spark plug chambers, close the decompression valves and hear the great heaving as the leviathan turns the flywheel faster and faster until the governor finally tames the beast and it settles into the powerful rhythm that will labour faithfully hour after hour.
As Ted's flywheel finally reached its operating speed he felt somewhat younger, more powerful and able to look at the world around him and smile.

Molly's happiness index rose like her favourite sourdough, she left the pub, locked the door and walked to the local mechanic. In line with their long standing arrangement she borrowed a car and drove towards Ted's place.

Ted was now starting to feel like time was of the essence and took a shortcut through the rough track on Baker's place.

Molly, drove faster than usual wondering how this would turn out but increasing in expectation as the odometer clicked over the miles.

Ted arrived in Town.

Molly arrived at the farm.

Ted found the pub locked.

Molly found the house open.

Ted consulted the mechanic and headed home.

Molly looked around the kitchen and saw Ted's state of mind reflected in the growing mountain of crockery.

Ted drove furiously and with serious intent he did after all have a double helix brimming with serious intent but this time it was for something real.

Molly wandered through the house and shivered. Had Ted been hit with this fire poker? She remembered a serious gash on the forehead of 'her' 14 year old boy, she had reached out to touch the scar but he had pushed her away.

Ted hurtled on.

Molly found a family photo; Ted had cut his father's head out of the picture.

Ted was driving but his sinews hurt as if he was running a marathon, his heart pounded, he doubted his ability.

Molly wondered what it was like to live in this torture chamber, surely it should be destroyed.

Ted drove over the front grid, past the car shed and right up to the front door.

Molly heard the car and rushed outside.

Ted met Molly on the verandah. They stopped stock still, unable to move. A tear rolled down Ted's cheek. He had shed many tears caused by pain, this, was not one of those. Molly reached up to wipe the tear away but Ted caught her hand and held it gently as the tear continued its journey of healing.

"I want you to see it Molly, I want you to see that something is happening, something real, not a plan not a scheme, nothing to do with Ted Wainwright but everything to do with you. The beautiful Molly Ryan."

Molly led Ted down the front steps and into the overgrown garden; there was no way she could re-enter the house of horrors. They found the garden seat and sat, still holding hands and both of them crying and laughing and crying and laughing and crying and laughing. The end of torture and grief and disappointment is beyond words. Ted pulled the tail of his shirt out of his pants, wiped Molly's face, gently held her nose and said, "blow."

He turned away to blow his own nose when Molly said, "no, I want to see."

Ted obliged and they embraced each other while time stood still. The past heaved and fought for its premier place, every blow, every insult, every shred of hate, every careless word, every cutting look punched them in its death throes. Still they hugged and withstood the onslaught together. As their demons gradually faded, they relaxed and let their arms slide down each other's bodies.

"Do you want to … ?" said Molly.

"More than anything," said Ted, "but not here, not in this place and not today. Today is something special, something different."

Molly nodded and said, "what should we do with this place, burn it down?"

"It should be wiped off the face of the earth but my romantic conversion is not quite complete so … let's just sell it."

"Not a great time to be selling wheat properties, Teddy Bear."

"Don't care, don't care. Can you hear me actually saying that, I DON'T CARE."

And Ted sang for the first time in his life. ʻI don't care, I don't care, what they may think of me. I'm happy go lucky, girls say I am plucky cos I don't care.ʼ

"Living here, being a farmer, that was my father. I've hated it all my life and clung to it so I wouldn't be punished. I'll be a good boy, a good boy, I promise. Well fuck you dad, fuck you!"

At the height of Ted's declaration of freedom Molly suddenly screamed, "and fuck you Father O'Brien! Fuck you, you bastard!"

"Father O'Brien?"

"My God, I thought that was gone."

"Molly?"

"That miserable arse wipe priest, fingered me in the confessional."

"Oh Molly."

They hugged again for another round of tears and marauding memories.

"Did you tell your parents?"

"No, Dad would've killed the mongrel and then he wouldn't have had the sense to lie about it so he would have got himself hung, the dopey bugger."

"Molly, do we have any more, I wonder, things we've forgotten or … Jesus what a day … the sun's still shining."

"I hope that's it. Time to go home Teddy Bear?"

"Time to go home. Do you think I could get a job in the pub."

"Strong possibility, I know the publican quite well. Actually it appears that I know the publican better than I thought."

"Molly can we both go in your car, I don't want to leave you right now?"

"Hop in Teddy Bear."

The Dark Clouds

Robert's research was broad in the extreme, it wasn't just capitalisation, market trends and balance sheets, he wanted to know the bigger picture as well. He listened to the dire predictions of Marshall Foch, who had led the allied forces at the end of the Great War and felt that the Germans were let off too lightly. Meanwhile Winston Churchill was rattling his sabre and supporting British rearmament to counter German aggression. Mostly these doomsayers were written off by the commentators as warmongering fanatics who just couldn't enjoy the peace but Robert took it all in. He knew that Churchill's position was ambiguous even confused since he had previously supported deep cuts to the defence budget but Robert was developing a holistic approach to planning an empire. This approach was amoral, it didn't care about good or bad, left or right or right or wrong; it was all about managing risk, predicting outcomes and protecting assets. It was the prediction of another war looming in Europe that Marshall Foch said would be highly mechanised and wreak unspeakable havoc on the population of the entire world that caught Robert's attention.

Robert was a distant father, it was always business and not enough time for childish fun and games. Always a new venture, a new conquest, more research, more cunning, more guile, more profit. He was happy to talk business with the children and Peter made an effort to be interested but never quite caught the fascination of money, power and control. The twins couldn't bear it and made any excuse to escape … bath time, homework, gotta feed the dog … they became quite good at it.
If Robert didn't have a new project he was, not unbearable,

violent or ill tempered, but rather dull and reclusive. It was at these times that he withdrew from any social life and Janet could not persuade, cajole or even drag him out of the house.

Janet kept up all her commitments and tried to engage Robert with the latest gossip or happenings in the cultural world but it was hard work and she began to worry.

Robert lived mostly in his head, he made endless propositions and worked through multiple scenarios, it didn't actually make him happy but it pleased him, gave him a kind of obscure pleasure and defended him against his greatest fear. He had long ago laughed in the face of regular fears like death, embarrassment, failure … he had not laughed at boredom, it genuinely scared him and now he was running from it to save his life, he had not the slightest doubt that it wanted to kill him in the most excruciatingly painful way imaginable. Every merger held it back, every raid bought him time, every acquisition gave temporary relief; the cure was at hand but he couldn't see it. "The thing which I greatly feared has come upon me," said the doleful Job of old. But this was not some demented high stakes game between God and the Devil, there was no unseen force, no hand of righteousness or retribution; just a man obsessed who had wandered away from the tribe and become lost in his own high stakes game where he was drowning in adrenalin and ordering more.

Janet was at her wit's end, she could not penetrate the isolating shell that sealed Robert off from his family, his malaise was foreign to her. She consulted a physician who recommended a psychiatrist but Robert refused to see him. Her pleading fell on deaf ears and she could only cry at her failure and rail at the refusal of the universe to help. Casting around for answers she fell asleep, still alone with Robert ensconced in his study, she saw the dreaming rock. She climbed as she did all those years ago but this time it was more than the inquisitiveness of a brash young woman that drove her on. This time she sensed that, with every step she was treading on history. The rock was an archive, every action every memory, every thought of everyone catalogued in granite crystals. Her expectation grew as she expected to meet Robert at the top and regain the exhilaration that had confirmed their lives together and launched them on the journey.

Robert was not on the rock. She saw a body and knew it was not Robert, not his trim torso or his army uniform. She approached the body with all the confidence of the younger Janet, as the invulnerable mistress of the world. She knelt, rolled the body over and looked into the ashen grey face of Peter d'Camry. Peter wasn't dead but he wasn't exactly alive either, his eyes were open but locked as if in some suspended state, as if his being was elsewhere on important business and he couldn't be disturbed.

Janet sat beside him and watched him twitch occasionally. Last time the rock had showed her things, surely it would show her now. The sun was hot, she wanted to go. If there was no ecstatic revelation, no tingling, no embrace from Robert only this half dead twitching man then, she definitely wanted to go. But the rock holds you, she could see it was holding d'Camry, she tried to get up and couldn't, this would only end when the rock was finished.

Janet woke with the sunrise, Robert was sleeping beside her, she kissed him on the forehead, slipped out of bed, closed the curtains and wandered to her study to ring Peter d'Camry.

"Peter, it's Janet, sorry to ring you so early ... I dreamt about you ..."

"Well that is extremely gratifying, did I behave myself?"

"Peter I need to ask you something, when you ... when things changed, I mean when you seemed to be different, all those years ago, on my parent's farm."

"Yes, it was pretty sudden."

"This might sound weird but did you climb a large rock?

"Yes I did."

"And what happened?"

d'Camry's mind went hurtling backward with the kind of speed that is uncomfortable and then unbearable and then deadly, it stopped at the edge of an abyss when he gasped as if he had been holding his breath for days and in a supreme effort he sucked in the life giving air. Assured that he was still alive he said, "your dream, what did you see?"

"I saw you on the rock, you were somewhere between alive and dead. I wanted the rock to tell me things but there was nothing but silence and I couldn't leave, couldn't wake up."

"I didn't know that you had been ..."

"Yes, I convinced Jaril and Jarli to take me and then I took Robert. It was wonderful, we saw our future selves, not everything but enough to whet our appetites. This time, I was so worried about Robert and I wanted answers but all I saw was you, as if you were dying."

"Well yes, I think I was, it certainly felt that way, I tried desperately to escape but the more I struggled, the tighter the grip of the rock became. Plunging into that blackness I saw what a moronic self centred prig I had become, and you would think that it would be easy to let that go, like shedding dirt in the shower, but it wasn't, I hung onto it because it was mine, it was me and at the end I had to be prepared to die before I could get out of that place and there was no guarantee of anything, maybe there was life at the other end or maybe death. In the end I decided that my life had been a misery and that death would be better, only then did it release me."

"Wow."

"Wow, indeed. So you see what you dreamt actually happened. I didn't tell anyone at the time because it sounded so crazy but it was an unspeakable gift. Now, why the worry over Robert?"

"He is so remote, I mean he's always lived in his head but this is different, he has withdrawn from me, from the children and he seems to run the business like a …. like a I don't know..."

"Like a Cadmus Soldier?"

"Sorry…?"

"No, I'm sorry, just more of my useless accumulated knowledge of things military. Cadmus was the first king of Thebes and legend has it that he planted dragon's teeth which sprouted and turned into soldiers."

"Well, yes, a bit like that, except for the dragons and the teeth."

"Janet, I don't know, all I can say for sure is that the rock is concerned with life and death issues and that's probably not much help."

"Thanks Peter, at least it's not just some random piece of nonsense."

"Perhaps we should think about a plan to get Robert interested in something other than business."

Jaril and Cox

Jaril had become disillusioned with the 'missionary' work in South Australia. The problem of alcohol in Aboriginal communities distressed him to the point of despair. The work they did was like emptying the Simpson Desert with a teaspoon. How do you persuade someone, anyone, of the evils of alcohol, when alcohol, is their only momentary escape from a life sentence for a crime that they didn't commit or even know about? How is it that you are segregated, maligned, disparaged, deprived of your land, your supply of food and your system of justice and if you try to do something about it you'll be arrested, jailed and then maybe hung? The nagging "how did this fuckin' happen?" taunts you, but alcohol lets you escape - then makes you too dopey to do anything about it. Just as Shakespeare had said on what strong drink provokes: "Lechery, sir, ... It provokes the desire, but it takes away the performance."

Jaril was determined to 'do something about it'. Pastor Nicholls had told him about the Aboriginal Progressive Association, a group more inclined to action than handouts. He travelled to Sydney and found a group that knocked his socks off. The Association had just declared a Day of Mourning and had scheduled a conference/protest against inequality, injustice, dispossession of land and protectionist policies. This was where Jaril wanted to be but he would do it among his own people.

Jaril fumed over the 1936 amendments that the WA Government made to the **Western Australia Aborigines Act** which permitted Aboriginal people to be taken into custody without trial or appeal and prevented them from entering prescribed towns without a permit.

It was a sudden awakening for Jaril that not only were

Aboriginal people deprived of basic human rights but when they could enter the labour market they were badly exploited by employers.

Jaril had loved his work on the Coles farm, he loved horses and stock and knew that the Coles respected him and that Janet especially regarded both he and Jarli as family members. It was true that he was underpaid but then the work had more meaning than the money and he didn't actually feel exploited - but he also knew that he was 'lucky.' So many of his mob were treated inhumanely, grossly underpaid, if they were paid at all, and totally excluded from white society. The more he thought about it, the more he knew that change just had to happen.

Home is always the best place to start and Jaril started. He travelled from farm to farm pretending to be a visiting relative. He told his people what he had seen in Sydney. He told them about William Cooper, an Aboriginal man in his 70s who led a delegation of the Australian Aboriginal League to the German Consulate in Melbourne and delivered a petition which condemned the 'cruel persecution of the Jewish people by the Nazi government of Germany'. He told them how many farmers and graziers depended on Aboriginal labour to run their properties – he told them that they could be powerful. Jaril was sowing dissent without a plan of action, he had heard a preacher talk of 'sowing the wind and reaping the whirlwind' but he wasn't quite sure how to get to the whirlwind bit.

His first experience of increased turbulence was more like a willy willy; the graziers had cottoned on to his real purpose and arranged a State Reception, a police state reception. Jaril was summarily arrested and gaoled without charge or trial.

The bush telegraph erupted with the news of Jaril's arrest, from campfire to campfire, from humpy to church meetings.

Jarli had been travelling looking at grazing properties when the news came, he had no idea what to do but hurried back to Perth to get help from Cox and Robert and Janet.

Cox immediately took leave and went to visit Jaril. At first the prison authorities denied him access, but a man in uniform has a few tricks up his sleeve.

"I suppose you are aware that Steve served gallantly with the Australian forces at Gallipoli," said Cox.

"No mate, I had no idea I just thought, you know, a trouble makin' Abo."

"No mate, just an Abo that has served his country and thought he'd get a hero's welcome."

"Well I s'pose seein' him won't do no harm, just 10 minutes though."

"Thanks cobber." Cox almost choked on 'cobber' as he hid his derisive look from the feckless guard.

Cox was taken to the cells, where Jaril, head down, looked like a man ready to die. Accompanied by last night's drunk and disorderly cellmates he was ashen grey and clearly agitated.

Cox spoke to him through the bars.

"Jaril, it's Cox."

Jaril raised his head, looked at Cox and sank back with his head in his hands.

"We've gotta get you out of here mate, talk to me."

Jaril rose and came to the cell gate, gripping the bars, he recoiled as if he was going to head butt the steel.

"Jaril, no!" yelled Cox as he placed his hands to prevent Jaril's head from connecting with the deadly metal.

Forehead met fingers with an almighty crash and yells of pain from Cox.

"Fuck that hurt," said Cox, instinctively putting his bleeding fingers in his mouth. The pain and yelling seemed to bring Jaril back from wherever he had been and there was a look of surprised recognition on his face.

"Coxy, what you doin' here?"

"Smashing my fingers and … bleeding."

"You done a good job."

"You don't remember do you?"

"Remember what?"

"Trying to smash your head into the bars."

"It was dark, I thought I was dyin'… "

"Yeah, well you're not and we gotta talk about getting you out of here. You know there's going to be a riot if anything happens to you and a lot of good people will get hurt, so try to stay alive, that's number one. Jarli's already talking to Robert and Janet; their lawyers'll be able to figure something out."

"It's not just me you know, it's all the farm workers that aren't bein' paid and livin' under sheets of tin."

"OK, listen we're going to find a smarter way to do this, one that doesn't get you killed."

They talked on until Cox felt sure that Jaril was out of danger and that his message of hope and reason had been received.

Friends and Power

Jaril didn't have long to wait but the enclosure and isolation still took its toll. A free man suddenly confined is a terrible thing. Despair set its appetite on his soul and tortured him with endless fear of the eternal night, to never again see the sunlight or smell the forests or the plains. Never again to ride a horse, to canter, perchance to gallop – *not for you my man, you are mine, I own you and I will do whatever I like to you and you will fade into oblivion and no one will care.*

Robert heard the news from Jarli and Cox and shrugged. It took Janet to say, "Robert, this is Jaril this is our friend who's in gaol because he tried to do the right thing. Friends help each other, friends ..."

"Alright, alright." He lifted the phone and called the Western Australian Attorney General.

"Doug, Robert here, I need you to do something."

"Anything for you Robert, you know that."

"Your wallopers are holding an Aboriginal man without charge and I want him released with an apology and a guarantee that this will not happen again."

"Ah yes the seditious little Abo, it's a little bit sensitive, quite a lot of farmers with their knickers in a twist, it would help if you would place a good behaviour bond and undertake to keep him out of trouble."

"Doug, please listen carefully. There will be no bond, this man has committed no crime and it is only your appalling Western Australia Aborigines Act, which drags us all closer to legal slavery, that has enabled his arrest in the first place. So if you are serious about being the next Premier you could demonstrate some leadership, release Steven Smith and hint at some overdue reforms."

"You're asking more than you know..."

"I know exactly what I'm asking!"

"I will need some guarantee of support from the popular press."

"Done, we will pick Steve up from the prison at 3.00pm this afternoon. Thanks Doug, it's good to see justice triumph isn't it." There was no reply.

As Robert put down the phone Janet could see a spark of his former self, the man she had so readily loved was still in there somewhere.

"Next Premier, my arse, the man is a snivelling, self serving sack of shit."

"Thanks darling, if you do the press I'll organise the pick up."

There was a short lived lightness about Robert, he smiled, he took Jarli's hand to reassure him that everything would be OK.

Cox

Cox wrote again to Mildred. He rambled on about his mates, the fortunes of Robert and Janet, the surprising partnership of d'Camry and Manly, of Jarli's search for property and Jaril's activism.

He finally came to what was on his mind. Without any formal qualifications and with no portfolio except a largish box of notebooks he wanted to write the stories of the age; he wanted to be a journalist. He had talked it over with Janet and she agreed to use what influence she had with the press 'fraternity' in Perth. He discussed the idea with his C.O. but with no previous experience and without a war going on, the chances of being an official war correspondent were remote.

Cox had read about Banjo Paterson's coverage of the Boer War and of course Charles Bean and the courageous rogue exploits of Keith Murdoch in WWI. Like Robert he reasoned that there would be another European war and he wanted to tell the story and who better than an actual soldier.

Janet found that her influence with the Perth Press was greater than she thought; it's always hard to say no to money and power. Cox would write some local stories and subject to approval would join the press gallery in London, concentrating on European affairs.

His next letter to Mildred was effusively excited, he was writing for real, his first story, an anniversary reflection on the Conniston Massacre of 1928 in the Northern Territory, when Europeans shot 32 Aboriginal people in reprisal for the killing of a white Dingo trapper, and a station holder. He underlined the injustice of the court and the total disregard of the principle of measured response. His editor toned down some of the hyperbole and finally put it to press, relying on the small but growing awareness of his readers on the Aboriginal question.

Cox was cocksure he would be in London before the year was out.

Mildred wrote back.

June 4th 1939
Dear John,

Wonderful news, I know it's what you were born to do.

But the thought of you being far away in a dangerous world fills me with dread. I know it will be brimming with excitement and that compared to my life as a teacher here on the mission at Yirrkala, it will be like the emperor and the ant. I am variously disillusioned, distraught, angry and sometimes happy here, the conditions are terrible, we are living in tents, stifling hot in the dry season and damp and acridly mouldy in the great wet summer. The community is filled with people from different language groups so it's hard for any natural leadership to emerge and any potential leaders have been so destroyed by threatened and actual brutality that they keep to themselves. The children are so loveable, many are half-casts that have been rounded up so we can 'assimilate' them. They are sometimes spurned by their own and in any case many have been ripped away from the only family they have ever known.

The overcrowding is unbelievable, cattle are treated better than these people. I am in constant turmoil as to whether to stay and do my best or flee and try to tell this appalling story. Does anyone really care? Will anyone listen?

I tell them that learning English and maths is important to get on in life, find a job, help your people. They smile and laugh at me and say come swimming with us missus. I say, what about the crocodiles? They say, "we go different places every time and one boy watches from up a tree."

I say, "I'm too scared."

They say, "you're crazy missus and run off to the beach." I hope they're right.

I had to lie about my 'Christian values' just to get a position here, I'm sure that if anyone discovers the truth I will be accused of poisoning their young minds with my atheistic socialist propaganda. And that is just slightly ironic when you stop to think that these are tribal people who are natural socialists anyway and so superstitious that they easily swallow the Christian dogma that has its roots in ritual sacrifice and the terrifying all powerful murderous and loving God; my atheism doesn't stand a chance against such a spectacular being. I will give this letter directly to a pilot that I trust, I may be paranoid but I wouldn't be surprised if the mail is censored.

What I really want to say is, <u>don't go</u>, you are my only real friend and perhaps I should have said something before now but it's pretty hard to say that, you think you're in love with your 'brother'.

So there, and as soon as I can organise some leave and a flight, I'm coming to see you. Don't you dare go before I get there, remember I still have that cricket bat.

Love

Mildred Carter

As always Cox eagerly opened the letter … he smiled at Mildred's desire to do good in the world, it made him feel small. He knew she could endure the conditions, after all being the daughter of a shearer's cook she knew all about privation and at least she would be in the same place for a while and have the opportunity to make friends and develop a sense of belonging.

God I'm a condescending prick, should I tell her that? - naw she'll find out soon enough.

He finally came to the 'in love' part and his 'mile a minute brain' came to a screeching halt. He read the sentence over and over and tried to reconcile their platonic friendship with what was apparently turning into something else. He thought about his sexuality – who the hell was he? - he flogged the log as much as any bloke - why had this not occurred to him before? - where was his natural desire to have sex, to reproduce, to be a husband, and a father? His considerable intellect had long suppressed any thought of sexual relations with his 'sister'; he really did think of her that way. Perhaps some reassessment was needed.

Between Fremantle and Perth

Bill and Elizabeth had sold Clovelly to Maurie Mason and moved to Fremantle to be closer to family and easily slipped into the role of the proud grandparents of Peter, and after 12 months the twins, William and Elizabeth. They had considered Perth for a while but the beauty of the coast north of Fremantle won out, as did the whales and dolphins that passed their western windows. The merciless afternoon sun was kept at bay by storm shutters and they never tired of walking on the beach as the sun set. Bill took to swimming and snorkelling in the warmer months, discovering the pristine world beneath the waves while Elizabeth tended her new garden. Her attempts at dahlias in the sandy soil were disappointing so she had the grounds excavated and garden loam brought in from further east. The results were stunning but the salty wind often caused a total flattening of the blooms. Never daunted she had a brick wall built to provide shelter and managed credible and sometimes prize winning entries at the Perth Show.

Janet meanwhile was invited to sit on the board of the Art Gallery of Western Australia, she became a very effective member and enjoyed the company of the Gallery Director who in turn valued her advice and assistance with significant acquisitions. Janet started her own collection just as she had foreseen on the dreaming rock; a collection that both she and Robert enjoyed immensely. They discussed the merits of contemporary painters both aesthetically and economically Who would make a lasting impression on the art world? Which works actually moved them emotionally? Which ones were technically unique, which were profound, which were complete rubbish and which were simply a good investment? Their pontifications were ever so slightly pretentious but at least they shared the interest.

Robert and Janet bought a horse stud and engaged an architect to design their own rambling Australian farmhouse. Ironically, preliminary sketches from Australian firms were cast in the mould of English manor houses until a friend suggested Wilson, a proponent of the Colonial Revival Movement in Australia. Wilson was reluctant to come to the West but eventually succumbed and captured the essence of the WA bush with a long low design with just a hint of grandeur at the entrance. He also designed a complimentary guest house, that was always available to their loved ones and close friends. Jaril and Jarli were regular visitors and lovingly put in endless hours handling, breaking and training the young mares and colts.

Janet felt herself the luckiest woman alive to have her love of country life restored and revelled in taking the children to Bellebury on school holidays. She and Jarli taught the children to ride and they passed on the love of the natural world that they shared. It wasn't all plain sailing; there was a warning flash when she detected a hint of snobbishness starting to infect her beautiful children. Her eldest remarked that Jaril didn't seem to know his place. Janet quietly explained the pivotal role that Jaril had played in her life and that as far as she was concerned, his place, was with them as part of their family. She remembered her time as a border in Perth; the dominance and snobbishness of the children of the landed aristocracy and now her own dear ones were those children. She would have to work hard to ensure their humanity, to teach them the real value of friends and the natural world. It was here that she found such terrible and sometimes terrifying internal contradictions. She loved her life in the top echelon of Perth society, the intellectual stimulation of the world of art and culture and the planning, scheming, buying, selling, raiding, financing and managing that produced the rivers of cash that enlarged their fortune hour by hour. Janet juxtaposed all of this against her hankering for simplicity and sincere relationships. The two things would just not coalesce.

The time from Peter's joyous birth to the day that Elizabeth (the younger) started school, raced by as Elizabeth fussed over her little treasures showing them the same love and kindness that had filled her own childhood. She introduced them to soft soil, earthworms, bees and blossoms, she gave them little trowels, watering cans and packets of seeds.

Elizabeth and Bill divided their time between Fremantle and Perth taking every opportunity to visit or have their grandchildren stay with them. Bill bought an open 16 foot fishing boat with the revolutionary Evinrude outboard motor; a staggering 8.5 horsepower with electric start. It was a quick trip up the Swan River to Janet and Robert's jetty, especially if the tide was running in. The children loved the salt spray in their faces and the unlimited attention from Bill and Elizabeth. In some ways they felt like child stealers as they regularly filled the role of parents, with Janet and Robert so busy and often absent. They worried for their beloved little ones that somehow they weren't getting enough parental nurture that would allow them to be confident adults and decent human beings, but they did their best and revelled in the doing of it.

They listened in stunned silence on the evening that Robert and Janet announced that for their secondary schooling, the boys would go to The King's School, Parramatta and Elizabeth to Kambala, Rose Bay. The reality that their beloved grandchildren would be nearly 2,500 miles away slowly seeped into their hearts, the chill made them shiver as they sat speechless in the solarium that overlooked the river. The tide was running out and it seemed to them that the children were adrift in the current that would carry them into the vast void of the Indian Ocean.

Robert explained; "both schools have excellent reputations, they accept young borders and provide opportunities that simply do not exist here in Perth. Our children will enter a world of wealth and sophistication and they need to meet other children that are facing the same challenges. It may sound harsh but they need to develop a circle of friends where they fit in. Janet and I have thought about his very deeply and we feel it is the only way to prevent them from being ostracised as the poor little rich kids."

Bill and Elizabeth were speechless, they felt that at the very least they should have been consulted, they who had invested so much, they who had provided the nurture, the warmth and care and guidance that had borne the fruit of open hearted, trusting children who would take their gift of essential goodness into the adult world. As these thoughts whirled in their minds their emotional temperatures rose, they felt anger, disappointment and rejection. They knew that this was not the time to voice this volatile frustration, it might wreck everything and send them into some kind of emotional Coventry. They hastily made very stilted goodbyes and Elizabeth managed to contain her emotions until she reached the safety of the car, it was there that the flood gates opened, "how could they, how could she, Janet, my Janet, to Sydney, the other side of the world, how will we see them, will they even come home on holidays, it's cruel is what it is, I mean we sent Janet to school in Perth but we saw her all the time and that was hard enough. Bill drove on with his heart in his mouth, he could not speak and eventually his stoicism was overruled by grief and he pulled over. He reached his arms out to Elizabeth and held her tightly as they both sobbed, their chests heaving in great synchronised waves.

In the days that followed, Bill and Elizabeth could speak of nothing else – Sydney, it's the other side of the world – it takes days even to fly there - when will we see them? – should we move to Sydney? – would that be over protective? - little Elizabeth seems grown up but I know she feels frightened – and she won't have anyone – at least Peter and William will have each other.

And so it went on until they resolved to create as many happy childhood memories before the fateful day arrived. Even with departure still a good way off they hastily organised a camping trip in the Swan River Valley. They would go all the way by boat, sleep in tents, cook damper in the coals of the campfire, swim and catch fish.

Came the day, Bill and Elizabeth took the boat to Robert and Janet's jetty for the nine o'clock rendezvous. Peter looked glum and refused to be cheered up while William played the larrikin, pestering Bill for a turn on the Evinrude tiller while Elizabeth the younger, somehow feeling her elder brother's pain, as well as her own trepidation, lay wistfully in the bough of the boat gazing into the water and letting her hand trail through the gentle wake of the boat.

"Shark," shouted William.

Elizabeth jerked her hand out of the water, felt a rush of fear and then as she turned to face her 'saviour' a rush of anger fuelled by feelings of stupidity overtook her. The only object at hand of any substance was a landing net which she seized and brought it down on William's head, which would have been funny if the net had covered William's head, unfortunately it came down sideways and unfortunately William instinctively leaned backwards and very unfortunately copped the full force of the metal frame on his nose which began to violently spurt blood.

Elizabeth the younger then burst into tears at the sight of her bleeding brother. Peter grabbed William, held him tight and pinched his nostrils together as he'd seen his kindergarten teacher do many times for a boy they called the bleeder. William instinctively pulled away but Peter held him firmly and calmly told him, "everything'll be alright mate, just sit still and let me do this". Elizabeth the elder stumbled forward to comfort her crying granddaughter. "I didn't mean to ..." "I know darling, I know." Bill had no choice but to keep control of the boat and look on with pride at the way everyone responded. "Hey," he yelled over the roar of the motor, "have you ever been on a picnic as good as this?" There was a moment of silence and then rolling laughter which carried the tension away as if on the wind. Peter released William after about 5 minutes and they sat bonded together.

Elizabeth looked up at her brother and William smiled while letting his head rest on Peter's arm.

Bill and Elizabeth had silent communion, their spirits buoyed by the family ties that would sustain their precious ones when they were thousands of miles away.

In another half an hour they pulled alongside a grassy bank, Peter feeling very much the man grabbed the mooring rope, took a giant step onto the bank and secured the boat to a tree. Tents, food, sleeping bags and Bill's homemade camping tripod with hot plate and kettle hanger all followed and a campsite progressively sprang up among the gum trees.

As they sat back against the trees with cups of tea and Elizabeth's chocolate slice William delivered a carefully crafted line. "I don't think that outboard's vulgar, I don't think it's even rude."

"Americans have a lot of trouble with spelling mate," said Bill. And then because adults like to show off just as much as kids, he launched into a diatribe about what a genius Ole Evinrude was and how he had read about him in Scientific American. He was well into "And of course the technical brilliance of the design ..." when Elizabeth plugged him up with more slice and declared it time for a swim.

The grandchildren raced each other to the riverbank, Bill stood up and swallowing the last of the slice, said "I was just saying, you know, kids need to ... know things."

"Little and often, my beautiful man - concentrate on the little."

They joined hands and wandered down to join the children.

The Whirlwind Visit of Mildred Carter

Flying from the Northern Territory to Perth was a gruelling experience. The first leg to Darwin in a modified mail plane made many stops at remote communities before the final dash to Darwin. The noise was deafening, the flight time eternal and the creature comforts non-existent.

It was then Darwin to Alice Springs, Alice Springs to Adelaide, Adelaide to Kalgoorlie and finally Kalgoorlie to Perth.

In a sleepless stupor Mildred contemplated all other forms of transport including hot air balloon, motorcycle, bullock dray and camel and vowed never again to fly anywhere at any time for any reason.

Having no way of knowing even an approximate arrival time she had brought a stash of pennies so as to ring Cox from the airport.

He found Mildred looking like a vagrant, asleep on a bench outside the Perth terminal; Cox woke her gently, picked up her suitcase and led her to the car.

Cox had never contemplated the need for accommodation until he left the Army and discovered that he had nowhere to sleep. Having no interest in lawns or gardens he bought a block of flats in the city and moved into one of them. Fortunately they were furnished so he was quite happy with the aging furniture that bore the marks of many previous tenants, the idiosyncratic refrigerator that could pick up Perth radio and a dining table that accommodated his new Underwood typewriter.

Mildred surveyed the Spartan surroundings and smiled, this was definitely the home of John Cox.

"The bedroom is through here, I'll sleep on the couch."

"Will you indeed?"

"Well I thought..."

"You're not so bright are you? I didn't come all this way to ... I want to do what we should have done years ago ... do you remember? We were 16 and went swimming in the billabong, it was all terribly decent we got changed behind some boulders and ran into the water, you picked me up and threw me, I pushed you over in the shallows and when you stood up your very erect penis tried to escape from your trunks. I laughed and you were embarrassed and you turned around to make some adjustments."

"Yes, I do remember that, I had no idea what to do or what to say."

"It would have been the most natural thing in the world to strip off and have sex right there but we were so restrained by the threat of pregnancy and the likely disappointment of our parents that we dried off and ate our sandwiches and went home."

"So tonight, you and me, in the bed ...?"

"NO, NOW YOU IDIOT, you and me in the bed!"

"You never did waste any time, do you remember ..."

Cox was cut short by Mildred dragging him to the bedroom.

"If it was left to you, the human race would have died out by now."

A shirt flew through the air, a belt unbuckled, pants and jocks ripped down, top, bra, skirt and knickers made a Hansel and Gretel trail to their destination but there would be no going back. Finally two naked bodies fell onto the unmade bed and a pent up torrent of passion yelped and writhed, hugged and screamed rolled and laughed until the two were joined and sperm searched for ovum in a long overdue conjunction.

"Do you know, I write about everything, but not this, this belongs to us."

"You can tell the world if you like and if you did I would be the happiest and proudest woman alive, though I'd have to look for another job. You know you can be as cruel as you like to the Aboriginal kids but don't show any sexual impropriety in your private life or you'll be out on your ear. The hypocrisy is breathtaking."

"Come with me to London."

"What?"

"London, with me, Friday."

"But I'm not ready."

"You, not ready for adventure?"

"I was thinking more about packing and you know, things."

"You're already packed and what … things?"

"A passport?"

"We can fix it at the other end."

"And what would I do in London? Write fashion articles for the Times or maybe a modelling career. I hear there's a huge demand for brick shit houses."

"Mildred bloody Carter you'll do what you always do, find the neediest human beings and try to be helpful and the rest of the time ... we have lot of sex to catch up on.

"Again?"

"You bet."

The afternoon drifted into the evening when the two finally emerged showing signs of exhaustion and wandered off to find something to eat, later they walked down Hay St and were drawn to the Ambassadors theatre where they saw 'Goodbye Mr Chips' which they thought an apt introduction to British culture.

Robert and d'Camry

Peter did not know the cause of Robert's darkness but he understood the power of stupid ambition; something that could drive you like a slave to achieve something that will certainly kill you. He had read about heroin and its horrible addictive power but also that addicts would say that it was their purpose for living, that it filled every corner and crevice of their being and that they loved nothing but the needle. He understood, he knew those feelings, the ambition that had haunted him since early childhood, and he hoped that he could help.

d'Camry and Manly came unannounced to see Robert. Janet greeted them and brought them into the spacious lounge that overlooked the river. The northern aspect soaked up the sun and it seemed that its blasting rays could never be quenched. Janet called for Robert as she went to prepare some refreshments. Robert came in looking like he had just rolled out of bed, glasses in hand and a sheaf of papers, which said, "I'm busy so make it quick."

Janet came in with a tray of tea and cake.

She poured for everyone and cut slices of cake without asking, she served everyone and sat down next to Robert on the two seater lounge.

d'Camry spoke first. "Robert, how good to see you. I'll come straight to the point. We've noticed that you're driving yourself very hard, it's like you are a corporate athlete, your achievements are amazing but it's clearly not good for you, shut up here like an emperor in his castle. So this is a case of 'your best friends will tell you'. I know it's not about the money, ... am I right in saying it's never been about the money?" Robert nodded.

"Robert, this is not about me but my life might serve as a metaphor. I trust you remember what a bombastic imbecile I was when we first met? No need to respond, I'm just stating the obvious. I've never told you what brought about the change. There was no flash of rational insight, I was on the rock, what I now understand is the dreaming rock. I know you've been there, the rock shows you things, for you, I'm guessing it was your future, you and Janet and success but that's where it stopped. I was fortunate, I saw my past, my hideous family, my ludicrous military career, my obnoxiousness; the rock seemed to be giving me a choice, complete escape or certain death. Now you might think that was an easy choice – it wasn't. I would not let go because it was the very core of my being, I had no idea who I would be, what I would become; the unknown is terrifying and even more so when death is snapping at your heels. But enough of that, the question before us is will you let go of this obsession and face an unknown future? It will certainly take courage but also desperation. You could of course go back to the rock but I suspect nothing will happen because you already know everything that is to be known."

They sat in silence for a social eternity, only broken by the call of the crested terns.

Robert was quick, astute, rational, he tried to speak but had no words. He had been king hit and left gasping for air, he wanted to hit back but the ambush had been so complete that any response seemed facile.

Janet took Robert's hand in hers and said, "I think they're right, it's decision time."

Robert nodded and finally spoke.

"There's a lot I could say but it would all be complete shit, I think that translates to 'bollocks' in the King's English, Peter."

"Quite so," said d'Camry.

"Chris, I think we should go and let Robert and Janet take it from here."

d'Camry and Manly both shook hands with Robert,they each pulled him close and hugged him before they slipped out.

Robert was still reeling, his immediate thought was to escape, simply to go back to his endless research, but he stayed still, holding tight to Janet.

"They really have no right you know."

"No they don't but they were very courageous, they took a huge chance; you could have thrown them out and never spoken to them again.

"They brought it all back, the way Peter spoke to me in his tent, that day at Clovelly, he was like some kind of living saint, guileless, completely honest and transparent. I knew then that something extraordinary had happened to him and there was I, ready to throw him to the wolves."

"And now?"

"Now I think I am the wolf. Perhaps it's too late, I don't have another script. If I should die ..."

"You're not going to die."

"But if I should, I have nothing to leave you, nothing to leave the children, I'm devoid of happy memories, the sum total of my legacy is a succession of plundered companies and defeated adversaries who loathe me."

"You're being very hard on yourself."

"Am I?"

"You've been very generous."

"You can't cuddle up to money. The power that it brings pushes people away, no one should have that much power. Look at d'Camry, he finally stood up and spat power in the eye. Look at Manly he actually prints the truth. He doesn't dissemble, he'll end up a pauper. I've never told you this but all those years ago in Canberra, when I was pretending to be a soldier - but actually just waiting for an opportunity to pounce on some poor unsuspecting enterprise, Bevin Brown, my Captain, tried to enthuse me about a military career, tried to convince me that the path my father had taken in military service was honourable and good and fulfilling but I wasn't having it, not a bar of it. I wanted what I thought was the top of the tree, the pinnacle of success, the holy grail, it has turned out to be the unholy chamber pot. I have tried not to reflect on the trail of destruction that has followed my entrepreneurship, all those jobs lost, all those people that had families and homes and mortgages. They were just collateral damage in a just crusade, now their faces haunt me, the faces of their children terrify me, I have no excuse. d'Camry has destroyed my last bastion, he has demolished the vault where I thought I could lock it all away and hope that it would decay into dust but it has putrefied, it stinks and it sticks in my nostrils and rips at my throat. Janet I have have hurt you with my neglect and the children, will they be damaged beyond repair? Even now there is a voice inside that says; don't be weak don't give in to these milksops who have no stomach for conflict, no courage and no ambition; jelly-backs the lot of them."

"And so?"

"And so, I have a lot do in a short time but I think the first thing to do is cancel the enrolments at Kings and Kambala and I think the second thing to do is take everyone on a picnic. Will you come?"

"Of course I'll come you silly head."

"Janet if I wake up tomorrow and revert to locking myself in the office, could you please shoot me – no reasoning, cajoling or jollying, just shoot me. People don't change, at least that's what I've always thought, people are on a fixed path and if they do think about change they soon revert to their old ways."

"Shoot you?'

"Mmm."

"Choice of weapon?"
"Hey, it's alright for me to be serious."

Jarli and Corporal Michael Down

Down was restless, he couldn't settle to the humdrum routine of the barracks. Ford was on furlough, buying his mother a house and Cox consumed every second of free time writing a fulsome account of the last three months. Down tried to interrupt but Cox was in a world of his own and could only manage incoherent replies. After three or maybe four interruption he did look up, apologised and said, "sorry mate, what do you need," but Down was gone.

Down was double timing it across the parade ground to see the C.O. and request leave. By the time he got there he had decided to resign. He knew what he wanted, there would be no more waiting. His future did not lie in the Army and as much as he loved his mates, his future was not with them. Uncertainty had ruled his life since his early teens, there was nothing that really anchored him, he had been completely adrift until the Army gave him structure, routine and good mates.

Good mates, for the first time ever, friends that could talk about real things, not just their sexual prowess, the size of their dicks or how much they could drink on a Saturday night. And Cox, God almighty, Cox, who took the trouble to learn and remember and know things and share it with his mates without being a smartarse, well mostly. And Ford, who seemed to rise above the indignity of a violent and then absent father. Ford, who loved his mother so dearly because he knew what it had cost her to have him, to love him. He loved Cox and Ford and had much to thank them for but they were not his future.

Down hitched a ride to Perth, bought a new Rover and drove to

Clovelly Farm. He would eventually tell Cox and Ford but only if this worked and only if ... Jesus he thought he knew them but there were things he didn't know, things he hadn't asked - it just never came up, well except for that one time around the campfire when Jaril had playfully accused them of being a bunch of bum fuckers. Bum fucker? He wasn't, he never had, he didn't want to, he was sure that that was just a bit of fun, they laughed, he laughed, they had all definitely laughed. So he had no idea, how things would pan out, it might be the end of the section, it might end everything.

As he drove, the torrent of thoughts kept on coming, what about his parents, his beautiful loving parents who goaded him about girlfriends and grandchildren and urged him to hurry up. *Not getting any younger mate.* What about Jarli, did he have parents, what would they think, what do Aboriginal people think about buggers, poofters, queers and queens . . . what do they even call men who love men? Down was becoming increasingly anxious, what if ... what if ... what if he had misread Jarli!

Down was approaching panic as the new Clovelly water tank poked its shiny galvanised head above the horizon. He was poised to cut and run when the Clovelly farm truck loomed up in the distance. Single lane dirt road - nowhere to turn - nothing to be done - it seemed like slow motion as each vehicle veered to the left so that both could safely pass, the drivers acknowledged each other with a lifted hand and Down saw the smiling face of Jarli. Jarli who? *Christ, I don't even know if Aboriginal people have surnames.*

"Hey Michael Down, what you doin here?"
"Good question Jarli ...."

They both got out of the vehicles and met in the middle of the road.

After an excruciating silence Down finally found his voice. "I've come to see you."

"Here I am."

"So I see. You're looking well."

"Thanks."

"How's Jaril?"

"Good. How's Ford and Coxy?"

"Yeah good. What's it like working for Maurie?"

"Yeah good."

The conversation was grinding along but no one wanted to finish it, no one wanted to say well better be off, so much to do today. Two people who had so much to say to each other just stood there like a couple of house bricks. 'Stony silence'? You bet.

The meeting was so unbearably stilted that the Universe decided to intervene and mercifully sent a wool truck down the road blowing its horn.

"We better get out of the way," said Jarli.

"Yeah," said Down.

"Follow me," said Jarli.

Back in their vehicles they pulled forward, one in each direction, to make room for the wool truck to pass. Down backed and filled with the Rover and eventually managed to turn around and follow Jarli down the road. Jarli drove off the road at the first side track and stopped in a spot shaded by Jam trees and a few Sandalwoods that had escaped the axe.

"Michael, come and sit under this tree," called Jarli. As Michael approached Jarli picked up a rock, using it like a hatchet he knocked some bark off the Jam tree.

"Smell." Said Jarli. Michael sniffed at the wounded wattle.

"Raspberry Jam," said Down.

"Yeah," said Jarli.

They sat with their backs against the trunk.

With the initial tension fading Down confessed. "You probably noticed I'm a bit nervous."

"I was so happy that you come here but when we stood in the road ... lucky we didn't get run over."

"That'd be right, finally find someone you like and you both get run down by a loaded wool truck."

"You mean that Michael Down?"

"Well it could've been any kind of truck."

"You're a funny man . . . I like you."

"After we talked at the wedding I wanted to see you again straight away, but we'd all agreed to stay in the Army for a while. I was just walking around going crazy and yesterday I resigned, went to Perth, bought this car and came straight here."

"I been hopin that you would come. I couldn't talk about this to Jaril so I been a bit crazy too.

"I was hoping that we could spend some time together, go looking for a property that might suit your people."

"I'd like that Michael. But we gotta be real careful."

"Careful?"

"If you and me love each other, no one can know, not even Jaril.

"You mean ..."

"With my people, mainly the younger ones, if a man touch another man's cock, they kill him."

"With my people if a man touch another man's cock, they put em both in gaol."

"You can come back from gaol but you can't come back from bein killed."

"No. So all this cock touching, it's a bit serious."

"It's fuckin terrifyin."

"So what are we going to do, live like priests."

"Naw, them priests they touch everyone's cock and everyone's cunt.

"And they're the ones that reckon that men who love men are evil. So we run away?"

"I can't leave my family or my country – not forever."

"So its gotta be a secret from everyone forever.

"Yeah."

"Jarli, do you want me to touch your cock?"

"Yeah, but it's dangerous!"

"Is it that big?"

"No, it's mostly pretty small, other boys used to make fun of me."

"Sorry."

"No need to be sorry, just get on with the touching."

They both stood up and embraced each other. It was like coming home, like finding your place, like being a real part of the world. They took off their clothes and made a blanket on the ground. They lay down and gently touched each other, hand on hand, till they screamed and came and left their seed on the ground of that good country.

"Hey Jarli, do Aboriginal people have surnames?"

"You're a nutcase Michael Down."

"Just askin."

"Yeah well I got my name, a tribe name an a language name. I'm Jarli a Whadjuk man and I talk Noongar. It gets more complicated, cause there's a group you belong to depending on your mother, so I'm Wardungmaat, that mean crow and Jaril's Manitjmaat, that's cockatoo."

"I've got a bit to learn."

"I'll teach you if you want."

"I do want."

Jarli's Mob

If it wasn't governments passing racist legislation to restrict aboriginal people from freedom of travel and association or repossessing land already granted to them, as happened with Coranderrk Station, Victoria in 1924 or forcefully separating half caste from full blood as happened just about everywhere, then it was powerful squatters pressuring governments to open land that was 'too valuable for Aboriginals'. How strange that squatters who had grown wealthy on the back of free or near free agricultural or grazing land not to mention the slave labour that underpinned their success should want even more at the expense of the unrecognised traditional owners.

Jarli met with his elders and talked about establishing a pastoral company that could not be taken away from them, a place to live and work and preserve their culture. Michael Down came with him, as an advisor. Michael knew nothing of agriculture or grazing but he and Jarli had talked with Robert and Janet about how to structure the enterprise so that it would exist in perpetuity. The Elders talked for many days, slowly planning how it could be done and who had the skills to make the project a success.

Could it be on their traditional lands? Would they have to go elsewhere? Could their children be educated their way? How could they combat state sanctioned kidnapping? A number of younger men thought they could defend their country by arming themselves but the elders reminded them of Jandamarra's efforts fifty years before. Jandamarra had armed himself and knew the ways of the white police from the time he spent with them as a tracker. He perpetrated many payback killings of settlers and stock and evaded the police many times but was eventually gunned down by the superior forces of white society. The wisdom of the elders was that armed resistance always turned into outright war and that was never going to succeed.

Robert had described to Michael how to get round some of the legal impediments but still ensure that Jarli and his people would always have control. Michael in turn tried to describe to the elders how a proprietary company could be used to safeguard their interests. It was a harrowing task; what was a proprietary company, what was a company director, why did they need at least one white director, why was the government involved, why did the elders have to be directors what did being elected mean, what were shareholders, who were shareholders and how did that happen, and … 'fucking hell', thought Michael Down.

Jarli and Michael made sure to keep their secret, they slept with different families and avoided the time with each other that they craved so much. Aboriginal culture was a steep learning curve for Michael, sometimes he thought that the possibility of sustaining both Aboriginal and white culture on the same planet might be impossible. While Aboriginal people had a strong sense of ownership around their lands and hunting grounds, it was nothing like the individualistic ownership in white society. The white idea that land was a commodity that could be bought, exploited and sold was incomprehensible to Jarli's people. They clearly understood the results; dispossession, slavery and hunger but the system that supported these crimes was impenetrable to them. They had seen their children taken away, their relatives arrested and chained never to return, their hunting grounds fenced off and then heavy retribution if they killed the settler's stock for food. Michael slowly realised that there was no trust and very little optimism. Why should they trust him and why on earth would they trust the advice provided by Robert, someone they didn't know and if they did he would simply embody all the things that seemed poised to throttle their existence. His own life had been utopian by comparison, his happy family, a house to live in, good mates, good food and good fun. How could it be like this? Of course he knew exactly how, he had just shut it out and joined the chorus of: lazy abo's, dirty, stupid, subhuman. Now he was in love with one, with Jarli. His head was like a bag filled with smashed fragments of stained glass, the likelihood of shaking the bag so that all the fragments fell into place to form a coherent picture was an absurd proposition – he shook his head anyway – it didn't help. He had never really experienced depression, didn't even know what it was but the black dog made him feel hopeless and helpless. He had come with a great sense of purpose, to help Jarli's people but it wasn't help they needed it was liberation and in Michael's limited experience that meant war. He walked out of the camp hoping to find Jarli and praying that he wouldn't. In the years with Cox, he had been educated about the Romans and their cruel empire and the Spanish, French, British and American slavery in the new world. Cox had spent some time recounting the only successful black slave rebellion in Saint Domingue which after unparalleled violence resulted in the destruction of the slavery system and the establishment of the new state of Haiti in 1804. The French endeared themselves to the fledgling nation in 1825 by demanding 150 million gold francs to compensate French ex-slave-owners. This extortion was enforced by the French as the price of official recognition. Michael had epiphany after epiphany, what had been a rare event in a far away place, a century and a half ago suddenly snapped into focus as he contemplated the dilemma of Jarli's people.

Michael had vacantly wandered several miles down the road when he saw Jarli sitting on a rock, looking out over the vast expanse of his country. He wondered if they had been thinking the same thoughts; tortured with the prospect of failure and tormented with the anxiety of discovery. His conflict was unbearable, should he turn back or go on, wave in recognition or pretend not to see. What was he, a simpering child? He was, or had been a soldier, he had faced the emu menace – he ... he gave up on that line of thought and waved to Jarli. He motioned to him to come up. Michael climbed the rock and sat beside his mate, his real mate.

There is much beauty in silence when silence is the absence of words rather that the absence of sound. On this particularly still day they could hear the sound of bird wings cutting through the air.

Jarli took Michael's hand and still they sat until Jarli ventured, "is this harder than you thought?"

"I never stopped to think what we were trying to do – it all seemed pretty simple. Sweet Jesus, I wish Cox was here."

"Cox is smart, clever man, but he can't do magic."

"No he can't but he might make us laugh. ... Did you know he's going to England to write stories for the newspaper in Perth?"

"No, maybe when he comes back he can write our story."

"I thought you said our story had to be a secret even from Coxy and Jaril."

"Yeah I did, but somehow I think Cox'll understand."

Jaril At Large

Janet brought Jaril home from Prison, moved him into the guest room and assured him he could stay as long as he liked. That night at dinner with Jarli, Michael Down, Cox, d'Camry, Manly, Elizabeth, and Bill, Robert and Janet struggled to keep everyone buoyant with the celebration of Jaril's release. A cloud hung over the room; the darkest of brewing storms. Jaril was in no mood for celebration, he had no wish to share the horror of his imprisonment or the effect that it had on him. His dinner companions had no way of comprehending the horror – to them it had been a matter of false arrest easily mended with a phone call. To Jaril it was an abrogation of his humanity, an assassination of his spirit, a gauntlet thrown down to his entire race. Was decency too much to ask? Was a simple 'thank-you for sharing your land with us' an unreasonable expectation? Was co-existence even remotely possible? His good manners kept him silent and no one dared broach the obvious. Manly, struggling under the weight of his implicit complicity and racial seclusion ventured at the early conclusion of the evening that Jaril might like to come and see how an insignificant rural newspaper worked. "It can be a lot more than bleeding heart story telling, maybe ... if you want, I don't know, it might help or hinder or both – Christ I'm making it sound attractive." Jaril laughed for the only time that evening and agreed to come.

The guests dispersed and Janet gave Jaril some clean clothes and a towel. Robert took Jaril by the arm and said I want to show you something." Still carrying the clothes and towel Jaril followed Robert down the hallway.

"This is my office," said Robert.

"Big," said Jaril.

"Yes, yes it is, but the reason I wanted you to see it, is that it has also been my prison and my torture chamber. A lot more comfortable for the body than where you've been but I venture to say just as destructive on the mind. Have a seat, and you can put that stuff on the desk. When I first heard about your imprisonment I have to say I didn't care, it took Janet to bully me into action and it was then that my own escape, my own release, started."

"I don't see no bars or overflowing toilet."

"No, and I don't mean to say that your experience was any picnic but comfort is a clever disguise for torture, so clever that the inmates can't even see it. So clever that it tricks you into thinking that everything is just fine when really your comfort blinds you to what is important in the world around you."

"I'd still rather be here."

"Yes, we all find comfort appealing even a dog would rather sleep on a bed than in a hollow log, but there's a cost to everything, pampered dogs get lazy, fat and useless. I started to believe that my life, power and position made me more important than other people, I could determine the fate of hundreds, sometimes thousands of people when I took over a company and made it profitable or sold off the good bits and scrapped the rest. Do you understand what I'm trying to say?"

"Yeah …, … no."

"Sorry, Jaril I know you are pretty smart, probably very smart but we've lived in different worlds and it might sound like I'm speaking a foreign language."

"Yeah, I get that."

"Well, I've done some bad things that I called smart business and now I want to do some good things. I think you want to do good things too but I don't know where to start, maybe you do. My dad taught me a lot about how your people have been mistreated … you know robbed, murdered, cheated … I think I should shut up now."

There followed a very long silence.

"My dad told me some o' the same things but then he couldn't say no more, I kept askin him but he said it made im sad ... sad enough to ... you know ..."

"And did he, ... end his life?"

"No but he got so he couldn't talk to anyone, kept goin off by imself, visitin the sacred places and if a bloke can die o' sadness then I reckon that's what happened.

You wanna do good things, do ya reckon that anyone can do enough good things to wipe out the bad things?"

"No I don't, not even close, the results of the bad things never go away, they just keep rolling on affecting other people like: a dad loses his job because I close down the company he works for, his daughter tries to help the family finances by working as a live in nanny but gets raped by the man of the house, she's so ashamed she doesn't tell anyone and has a backyard abortion and dies from loss of blood. The mother never recovers from the loss and the father takes his old .22, shoots the rapist and gets hung for murder. The mother is committed to a mental institution and dies of grief."

"But you didn't do all those other things, only the first thing."

"That's right, but the point is that other people made bad choices because I took something away, something precious, something that wasn't mine, something I had no right to touch. I would've thought that your story was pretty similar."

Jaril sat silently digesting Robert's confession, he had never put words around his own situation, never tried to explain the burning anger that he felt, always thought that being angry was the same thing as being violent so he ignored the feelings as too hard to deal with because he wasn't a violent man.

"I tried what I thought would be good stuff like working with a group that helps Aboriginal people break free of alcohol but it's hopeless, alcohol isn't the biggest problem; poverty is. And not just the lack of money kind, there's no self respect and they feel like they don't have no future in this country that used to be theirs."

"I'd like to think that we could turn back the clock, all the way back, you know, before Cook and all that …"

"Some of my people have tried to fight but they just end up gettin killed and then white fellas think we're all murderin thieves and … you know how it goes … I tried to organise to get what was fair pay but ended up in gaol. You know, I thought I was strong, thought I could take anything they threw at me but I collapsed in a heap, like a horse that falls at the first hurdle. I don't think I'm up to it … too soft … my mum always said 'you need to toughen up boy' so I'd try and show how strong I was and she'd say, 'your one possum power never gonna lift that' and I'd say I'll be strong when I grow up and she'd say 'some is strong, some is smart, some is wise some is soft like jelly, we'll see which one you are' … I guess I'm the jelly."

"You're smart enough to know what's fair and maybe now you're wise enough to know you can't do anything if you're in prison. And there's another possibility. Some can feel!"

"I'm not sure I like that."

"Hmmm."

Cox and Carter

John Cox and Mildred Carter arrived in London in late June 1940.

After sorting out Mildred's lack of a passport, they made contact with someone called Donald Grey at Australian Associated Press, who, in line with the arrangement with the West Australian, found Cox an empty desk with a phone.

Donald looked the lovers up and down and asked, "got somewhere to stay? ... No? Well it just so happens that I have a friend of a friend who has a vacant flat in Chelsea, not cheap but quite splendid really, four rooms plus kitchen and bath, perfec." Grey was a master organiser and with two telephone calls and a gentleman's agreement to pay the rent John and Mildred were settled.

"I'm thinking you two are not really city types."

"Actually we're barely house trained," said Mildred.

"Yeah, but we're educated," said John.

"I've read your work," said Grey. "You'll do. Come on I'll get you a cab."

It was a short cab ride to 11 Old Church St in Chelsea and the exhausted lovers finally stumbled out of their London cab, paid the cabby, hauled their luggage through the gate, found the key under the designated rock in the garden, breathed a sigh of relief when it turned in the lock, found the bedroom and collapsed onto a very comfy double bed, held hands and went to sleep.

Cox couldn't wait to get started, he wanted all the briefings he could get from the other journalists, and then he wanted to talk to the Poles who had made it to England, anybody from Dunkirk and then ... It was still breakfast time and Mildred was thinking about exploring Chelsea but she knew that was going to be a lonely adventure.

Cox kissed Mildred goodbye, which was an odd feeling because they had not bothered to talk about how a life together would be, who would do what, would they continue to be independent but together at the same time, what? What? Mildred could not quite see herself as the long suffering housekeeping ever supportive spouse, so in the midst of the odd feeling she smiled awkwardly and Cox smiled awkwardly back and said, "Yeah, tonight."

Cox went to work, Mildred went exploring, she discovered it was a short walk to the Chelsea Embankment and the Thames ... she could walk along the Thames! It was a very far cry from the dry season in the Northern Territory, her tent accommodation and her beloved pupils. She had written them a longish letter explaining why she wasn't coming back and sent it to one of her literate pupils via the friendly pilot. It was strange that she had left behind such a completely controlled highly regimented situation and now she and Cox were looking across the channel to a new order that was completely controlled and highly regimented. Were all these power hungry freaks related ... she seriously wondered.

She gazed over the Thames and thought, was this the spot where the Royal Barge floated up river on the incoming tide, while George 1st listened to Handel's Water Music played by 50 floating musicians, just 243 years ago?

Cox supplied his own typewriter and settled into his corner of AAP. He was going to need a lot of help, without contacts, without the experience of how big government worked, without any entree into the military, not even the casual low level contact he had had in Australia.

While John and Mildred had enjoyed the relative comfort of the Queen Mary, the one time luxury liner but now troop carrier, the German Army had rampaged across Western Europe and occupied most of France, The Netherlands, Luxembourg and

Belgium.

News bulletins were minimal at sea and Cox ached for real detail. He had spent time with some of the 5,000 Australian Troops on board but of course they knew less than he did. The early communiques from the British and the Germans put the most positive face on their respective situations. On May 27th when the Dunkirk evacuation was already in full swing, the British did admit the situation was 'grave' but then claimed that all was not lost and that they might reverse their fortunes. They didn't, well not quickly or easily.

Cox started to put some detail together, the French had had an overwhelming superiority in troop numbers, heavy armour, heavy and light artillery and general mobility. They had the British Expeditionary Force to back them up, they had the heavily fortified Maginot Line. What the hell had gone wrong? The Germans had far less armour, fewer troops, longer supply lines and much less mobility; a good percentage of their transport was still horse drawn. Any military boffin would tell you the Germans were as mad as coots and the French as safe as houses. The French had out-spent everyone in Europe on armaments, had collected part of the war reparations from Germany set at 132 billion gold marks and they had controlled the Saar basin with its fabled coal resources until 1935. In short German industry had been starved of resources and the German economy was in ruins. The rebuilding of Germany's armed forces was strictly limited by the Treaty of Versailles; an army limited to 100,000 troops, the Navy limited to six battleships and no submarines and absolutely no air force. The Weimar republic immediately undertook clandestine operations to rearm and even though these efforts were necessarily limited, they laid a foundation for the expansionary program of the Nazis. When they came to power in 1933 and openly defied the allies and rejected the Versailles Treaty, rearmament ramped up astronomically.

Everyone could see that the speed of the German advance even with their inferior tanks was a daring raid that took the unexpected route through the heavily forested Ardenne but against the odds the Germans sustained it, they caught the French and British in a classic pincer movement, they took a staggering, estimated 1.5 million prisoners and inherited the vast amounts of materiel left behind by the fleeing forces.

Cox wanted to answer the big questions, he had seen military hubris first hand, he knew its sound and its smell, he had listened to the stories of the survivors of the ill conceived campaigns in the Dardanelles and later at Gallipoli in 1915; this was the story he would tell.

He put out feelers to the Belgian and Dutch soldiers that had made it to England; they were not hard to find and they were eager to talk.

Mildred tired of sightseeing fairly quickly. After the British Museum of Natural History, The Victoria and Albert Museum and The Army Museum; museum fatigue had peaked. Mildred sought refuge in a tea shop and indulged in a Devonshire Tea. It was here that she noticed a dog eared poster affixed to the wall with sticky tape.

Not to be used before October 3rd
SPECIMEN 3 minute speech No 3
Suitable for women audiences

A.R.P. RECRUITING CAMPAIGN

I am grateful for this opportunity to say a few words about the A.R.P. and the campaign for volunteers that is going forward this week.

The international situation is like the weather we enjoy in this country. We leave the house in the morning for business or shopping, to visit our friends or merely to take a walk. All seems well - the sun is shining and we go out dressed for a fine day. An hour later the outlook changes, a storm comes up and we run for shelter - if there's any to be found - if not, we go home drenched, catch a cold, and blame ourselves for not taking an umbrella or a mackintosh.

So it may very well be in international affairs, but if the cloud overhangs Europe should burst, it won't be rain but bombs that fall and God help us if we are caught unprepared.

It's a nuisance to carry about an umbrella or a mackintosh when it's not raining, though the weather might not look too promising. It is equally trying to give up our spare time to train for the A.R.P., but unless this country is to be at the mercy of any heavily armed aggressor we must take A.R.P. very seriously and get our training while there's time.

What would you do if an air raid warning sounded tonight? Would your ambulance driver's uniform be ready; would you know where to report; would you be ready equipped for warden's duty and know where your warden's post was to be; would you rush to your fire station to take the wheel of one of the new auxiliary pumps?

Would you, ladies, know where your first aid station was placed; would your "communications" car be ready at the door?

Or would you have to say with shame -" I waited to see - I left it to others - and now it's too late to train."

If unhappily the time should ever come, the raiders won't give you time to train, won't even give you warning. Next time if war should come the attack will be from the air, rapid, ruthless and terrifying. Preparedness, complete preparedness is our only protection and our only insurance against attack.

My final word to you is, get your training while there's time.

Women's Voluntary Service for A.R.P will give you any information you require.

Mildred, thought the text a bit condescending but still enquired of the owner who explained that, what was now the Women's Voluntary Service had begun well before the war and that she had read out the official recruiting speech at a local football match and then stuck it to her tea room wall.

"Do they take Australians as volunteers?"

"We take just about anyone luv, interested?"

"We've just arrived in England, seen the sights and ready to help."

"What did you do back in Australia and what the hell are you doing here?"

The answer left Theresa Reckitt, tea room proprietor and WVS volunteer open mouthed. Theresa had no conception of Australia's Northern Territory, thought Sydney was the national capital and that people kept kangaroos and koala bears as pets. Mildred stumbled a bit when it came to Cox, that he was a war correspondent was fine but the marriage thing ... well they weren't married, they might be, one day, but neither of them were religious and Mildred at least thought a church wedding would be hypocritical. She rambled on trying to steer a middle course that would not give offence to her new acquaintance until ...

"Don't worry luv, I'm not one of those stuffy, judgemental Englanders who can't abide free women."

"Don't you mean, 'loose' ?

"No, I mean free. My mother was a Catholic trapped in a loveless and often violent marriage, she named me Teresa after the great 16th century saint, hoping I would follow her into a life of prayer and contemplation and avoid the horrors of marriage."

"And did you?"

"I started, the nuns are always on the lookout for fresh meat, and I swallowed it hook line and sinker. All the way through the War we prayed every day for peace, every day, until the news came of my father's death on the day before the armistice, my mother's brain snapped, it was a twofold answer to prayer but she couldn't rationalise it. The nation had peace from the German menace and she had peace from her husband but she thought she was a murderer who had conned the almighty into a bargain that would send her soul to hell. She saw the pension that came from the government as blood money; it compounded her guilt. The church was no help with their ten 'hail marys' and six 'our fathers'. And nobody ever said, 'the old bastard deserved everything he got, it wasn't your fault, so just like the rest of the country it's time for you to enjoy the peace."

"Did she recover?"

"Never, I nursed her till she died and even at the last she had no peace, she left this world in abject terror about what was to come. And that luv, was the end of my religious experience."

"I don't know what to say, I travel across the world, pretty much on a whim but madly in love with my childhood friend and the first person I meet thinks about life in the way I do."

"Well we better keep in touch then, friends are hard to find for people like us."

"People like us. I thought I was the only one in the Northern Territory."

"Hmm sounds like the Scottish Highlands, London on the other hand has a few that you might get on with."

Mildred had much to tell Cox and John had much to tell Carter, as soon as one drew breath they involuntarily surrendered the talking stick to the other; Mildred's sightseeing, John's morning at the Belgian embassy, Mildred's Devonshire Tea, John's meeting with Belgian refugees, Mildred's new friend, John's discovery of Belgian military intelligence, they 'shuttled the cock' back and forth until they sat in the dark and John sheepishly produced some cold fish and chips that he had forgotten in the intensity of the exchange.

"We need to finish what we started this morning," said John.

"Bugger that," said Mildred, "I'm hungry and I've got beer in the fridge."

The Clouds

As Jarli and Michael sat on the rock trying to come to grips with history and humanity and the ambiguity towards homosexuals in Aboriginal culture their brains began to hurt.

Jarli reached for Michael's hand, there was a second's hesitation until Michael breathed a deep sigh of relief, acceptance, satisfaction and a whole lot of other feelings he didn't know the names of and locked his hand with Jarli's. They lay back on the wind smoothed granite and watched the clouds float across the sky.

"You ever think about floating on a cloud," said Jarli.

"No, but lying here with you I couldn't think of anything better, you and me just floating in that soft cloud, no one else, no problems, no meanness, no shame, no time, just floating."

"Do you remember drinking that stuff at Robert and Janet's wedding, the stuff with the bubbles?"

"Yeah, the Champagne."

"I thought it was, you know lemonade, but it made me float, so I had some more glasses of it and I floated over to you and I talked about everything I could think of which was funny cause I don't talk much, Jaril does all the talkin."

"I know. ... Jarli, I want to run away from here, could we just go ... somewhere where we don't have to pretend and hide."

"But where is there? ... I'm even worried about Jaril ... you know whether he would understand and even if he did we'd be askin him to keep our secret forever."

"Hey, I know somewhere safe, Cox gave me the key to his flat and asked me to keep an eye on it even live there if I want."

"Maybe we could take a break from here while the elders work out what they really want to do. I forgot how long big decisions can take. We could come back in a month, if that's alright with you.

"You'll come with me to Perth?"

"You bet."

And that would have been the perfect time to kiss and hug and hold and feel each other but their restraint was exceptional. Almost completely so until Jaril helped Michael up, turned him around and pulled him in close so that at least he could feel his pent up desire and know the longing that he felt. Michael closed his eyes in bliss and feigned dropping his hat so that he had to bend over to pick it up while Jarli held him by the hips and pulled him closer still. Michael slowly picked up his hat and as he straightened up said, "we're going to get sprung … but it's not far to Perth."

They made their way down the rock feeling the relief of having a plan and the pleasure of being close.

They were not alone.

They had been seen by two eight year olds and a dog. Like most kids the eight year olds found adults pretty fascinating, especially when you can spy on them. The boys had gone out to play their version of Gorri. They tied a fist size rock to some string and tied the other end of the string to a tree branch, then they swung the rock so it moved like a pendulum and then you threw stones at it and if you hit it you scored points.

The string broke pretty early on in the game and the boys decide to rock climb instead. When they saw Jarli from behind they knew he was important cause the men had been meeting a lot since he arrived, they mimed to each other that they would hide behind some smaller boulders and see if he was going to do some magic or talk to spirits or other things they didn't know much about yet. They were pretty sure that Michael Down wasn't a spirit cause they had seen him around the camp.

They were a bit surprised when they held hands and even more surprised when they looked like two dogs making puppies, they had seen plenty of that with so many dogs in camp.

They were left wondering exactly what they had seen. If it was a men's ceremony then they should keep it secret or they'd be in big trouble for being where they shouldn't have been, but if it wasn't then maybe it was alright to ask what is was.

The problem was … they asked an older brother of about 14 who told them that those men were poofters and that they should be speared to death. The missionaries had been amazingly successful in embedding so called Christian values into Aboriginal culture even though they often lacked simple

Christian charity. Before the white invasion there was a wide variety of sexual practices in Aboriginal society, some were universal, others were frowned on or even prohibited in some mobs but condoned in others. The young however were well indoctrinated with the Christian sexual proscriptions and of course the eternal hell fire and brimstone that awaited unrepentant transgressors.

So strange that the Hebrews did not think homosexuality worthy of inclusion in the ten commandments, adultery gets a look in but that just meant, don't fuck with another man's property.

The 14 year old told a 17 year old who was fully initiated and then the trouble really began with lots of murmuring that Jarli must die until it finally came to the elders who wanted to consider the situation more thoroughly and basically told everyone to calm down and leave it to them.

But it didn't calm down the young men were hostile. It was as if it threatened their manhood, their precious hard won painful manhood. This threat must be dealt with before it infected the young and innocent.

It was a cloudless sky that night which made it easy to follow anyone out of camp. Jarli had told the elders that he would go away for a month while they thought over his proposal. He left them and walked beyond the glow of the campfire to look up at the night sky as his ancestors had done for thousands of years as they conceived the dreaming stories and realised that the stars could show you the way to other places. He knew he was headed to another place and as he spread his arms, still looking at the wondrous sky he whispered, "I love you Michael Down."

The spear that killed Jarli was straight and true, it ripped through his neck and severed his jugular.

The spear was removed but Jarli the friend was already dead.

The murderer skulked away but everyone would eventually know who had done it and another cycle of blame and hate and revenge would begin.

The body was discovered within minutes as the dogs barked and ran in the direction of the spilled blood. The uproar was immediate as the whole camp gathered and the incredulous

Michael Down broke down as he embraced Jarli's lifeless body. He could not speak, he could only sob. In time one of the elders came to him and with great gentleness and dignity raised him up and walked him away.

Michael had a sudden surge of emotion and turned to go back to the body but the elder strengthened his grip and said, "this is best." Michael walked with him dazed but comforted.

The Elder's name was Naral, he spoke softly to Michael saying it was hard for him to explain but to keep safe Michael should leave the camp as soon as he could. They would bury Jarli tomorrow and everyone would be stirred up and some might blame him for Jarli's death. "I know you loved this man and that's alright with elders like me but it's not alright with others, especially the young fellas.

You understand what I'm sayin to you?"

Michael nodded and said, "thank you. Can I just go back and be with him for a while?"

"I think it's not safe Michael. Go back to your people, talk to them but don't come back here."

The heartbroken Michael Down drove away in a trance like state. He had no thought of where he was going, his only thoughts were of Jarli, the Whadjuk man who talked Noongar.

The gentle kind man whose name meant friend, ripped away from him.

"Fucking Noongar – fucking why?" Michael yelled as loud as he could, as if to make the universe hear.

His chest convulsed again as he sobbed, has nose ran but he hardly noticed, his tears made his eyes sting, he saw Jarli sitting round the campfire, laughing and slightly drunk at the wedding, then in his arms – never to be so again. Michael wrenched the steering wheel to the left, the Rover left the road, ploughed its way down a steep incline and crashed violently into a tree. Michael sustained fatal head injuries.

Jaril Meets The Press

Jaril's time with Robert had given him a lot to think about. Things were not simple, he had always known that, or he thought he had, but now it was like it snapped into focus and demanded that he pay attention. He knew he was smart but it was never a good idea for a young Aboriginal man to appear too smart, at the very least it invited a flogging.

Without a plan Jaril decided to take up Manly's offer to visit the Dencubbin Times. Manly and d'Camry invited him to stay and he turned up late on a Friday evening with his swag and not much else; it seemed the sudden influx of wealth had not impacted greatly on Jaril's lifestyle.

d'Camry opened the door and welcomed him in.

"Jaril, so good to see you again, let me show you to your room and then we have some supper ready, if it's not too late for you."

"Er yes, ... no um yes."

"My apologies, too many words, follow me."

After Jaril was settled they sat around the table and Manly produced ham and tomato Pudgy Pies with mugs of tea. It was already 11.00pm but everyone found their appetite once the smell of the crusty bread invaded their nostrils. "These are good," said Jaril, "I haven't eaten since breakfast."

"There's more," said Manly, "it'll only take a few minutes. A friend sent me this gadget from America you butter two slices of bread and lay the buttered side on one half of this clamp thing, put in the filling and lay the other piece of bread, buttered side up on top and then close the clamp and cook it over the gas ring, they call them Pudgy Pies."

"More Pudgy Pies'd be ... bloody good," said Jaril.

More Pudgy Pies, more tea and more talk; Jaril recounted his recent story from the incitement of direct action to his arrest and finally his release from gaol.

Manly shook his head in disbelief even though he was a journalist and a historian of sorts and shouldn't have been surprised by anything that involved human beings and their petty sectional interests.

"When I asked you if you wanted an introduction to the world of journalism it was more because I was nervous and looking for some kindly words to fill an embarrassing silence but now that you're here it seems like a happy accident. You see, journalism is all I know, writing stories for people to read, that's what I do and you have just told us what I could only describe as a cracking good story. I don't know what you've got in mind but this stuff needs to be exposed and if you wanted to work with us we could write it together and I can publish it in Dencubbin but more important we might be able to get it published in a Perth Newspaper or even Melbourne or Sydney. What d'ya think?"

d'Camry chimed in, "don't let us push you into something you don't want to do, this has to be your decision and remember you will be putting yourself in the spotlight for everyone to see."

"What's a spotlight?" said Jaril.

"Sorry old man, a spotlight is a powerful electric light that is used in theatres, not motion picture theatres but theatres with people on a stage acting out a story."

"Thanks, there's a lot I don't know about the white fella's world."

"Well there's a lot we don't know about the black fella's world; is it alright to say 'black fella'?" said Manly.

"If you keep servin them Pudgy Pies and tea you can say it as much as you like."

"Fucking brilliant," said d'Camry in his most affected English accent. Jaril and Manly laughed at the irony and d'Camry was well pleased that he had managed his first joke.

"So what do you think?" said Manly.

"Stop badgering the poor man," said d'Camry.

"What's a badgering?" said Jaril.

"Well, just think it over and we can talk about it some more. Would you like to see the newspaper office tomorrow? It's just machines and paper and ink and …"

"I love machines."

"OK a bit of a sleep-in, Peter's cooking Eggs Benedict for breakfast and then we'll make a start."

"I've discovered I really like cooking, my father would have a fit; it's not what d'Camry soldiers do you know."

The aroma of Eggs Benedict drifted through the house, d'Camry had set the table, had toast in rack, made a generous pot of tea and finally called his customers to come and eat. Jaril had never had Eggs Benedict before, his only experience of eggs had been boiled or fried but he found it agreeably different and fronted up for seconds.

The short walk to the printery was filled with chatter about, Eggs Benedict, the stir Manly and d'Camry had created by sharing a house, Robert's amazing transformation and of course Jarli and Michael's trip to visit Jarli's mob.

"I know my people and I think that will be – I dunno - getting everyone to agree on things is like makin water run uphill, I hope they don't end up on the wrong side of the river."

"Would you say it's like putting their own land in a white fella's package and giving it back to them?" said Manly.

"Yeah, I reckon that is real close - but they won't get it in their heads, it won't make sense to them. Jarli and I lived and worked with Bill and Elizabeth Cole for a long time, so we've got more of an idea about how things work in the white fella's world. Bill didn't just tell us what to do but he showed us how he ran the farm and Elizabeth showed us how she kept the accounts and Janet ... she was … just a good mate. The Coles were different to most white fellas."

"I grew up in a family that needed a good war every now and then to fulfil their destinies. It was a crime to think or act differently and I tried ever so hard to fit the mould, until …. well you know that story. I suppose it is the same in all cultures. It is one thing to discover a foreign culture, to study it at at close quarters, to write about it as a curiosity and then go home to the security and warmth of what you know. It is quite another to be the ones that are studied and then overrun, dispossessed, pushed towards extinction while everything your family and tribe told you was ultimately important is suddenly of no value; a worthless currency."

"I like your words but I want everyone to be able to read and understand what we're on about, my people, white fellas everyone."

"That's where I come in," said Manly, "writing for newspapers is all about keeping it simple. Hey you want to see the works?"
Jarli followed Manly to the print room and was impressed by the size and complexity of the machines. Manly sat at the Linotype and typed 'JARIL - The Owl', created the slug and showed it to Jaril, then he inked it with a roller and pressed it by hand onto a clean sheet of paper, he inked and impressed it several times and Jaril suddenly saw first hand what the Gutenberg process meant and how these machines could send his message. Jaril kept looking at the page with his name and title standing out boldly as if it was being announced to the world.
"You can help me do this?' said Jaril.
"You bet," said Manly.
"I can pay you."
"No need, the story will pay for itself and anyway it's what we want to do, isn't it Peter.
"More than you know," said Peter. "And don't think we are just foolish do-gooders. Chris and I have talked about this at length. We both think the world needs to be in balance and that we all need to work as hard as we can to bring that about, as Dostoevsky said, 'we must work only work'".
"Dusty who?"
"Sorry, really good Russian writer."
"I've heard of them Russians, no one seems to like em much. And why 'work'? Doesn't sound like many people agree with him."
"It's complicated really complicated but let me ask you, did you and Jarli enjoy your work for the Coles?"
"Yeah we did, when you see the country between the two ears of a horse that's a good feelin."
"In Dostoevsky's Russia most people were made to work too hard and for too long and other people didn't work at all, 'Dusty' was saying that work, that means something, is good for people and good for the country and yet so many of us try to avoid it. Anyway too much talk from me as usual."
"I like your talk, it makes sense to me."
"Finally, a happy listener, just tell me to shut up when you're sick of it."

As they all moved toward the door the phone rang.

"How peculiar," said Manly someone ringing a newspaper."

As Manly put the receiver to his ear he heard Robert's voice with Janet in the background saying, "this is the worst news ever, how could this happen."

"Hello Robert, this is Chris Manly."

"Chris, I'm afraid I have some terrible news. Is Jaril with you?"

"Yes, he is."

"Could you put him on, I really should speak to him first?"

"Certainly, Jaril, it's Robert."

"Hello."

"Jaril, I'm sorry to have to tell you this especially over the phone but Jarli's been murdered and Michael Down was killed in a car accident. I don't have a lot of details except that they had been visiting Jarli's mob but I expect you knew that already."

Jaril was speechless, he mumbled "yes," and put the receiver on the table, he looked at Chris and Peter and as tears welled up in his eyes he said,"Jarli and Michael are dead."

Peter put his arms around the sobbing Jaril and held him as Jaril's body heaved with grief.

Chris picked up the receiver. "Robert, Chris, how? why?"

"We don't know. The police finally got through to us, our number was in his address book, they'd found Michael in his car wrapped around a tree. They seemed definite that the impact had killed him – I told them he'd been with Jarli visiting Jarli's Noongar mob – they told us, later that day that they had been around the camps and found Jarli about to be buried – they couldn't get anything out of the locals - and they said to me, 'we generally let the Abo's look after this sort of thing themselves' - it's unbelievable. Can you tell Jaril that if he needs anything, anything at all, we are ready to support him to the hilt and don't let him be alone or at least keep an eye on him, he's probably in shock and after his gaol experience. This might all be too much, you understand what I'm saying?"

Manly nodded. After several seconds he realised he had to speak and confirmed that Jaril was safe with them for the time being.

Goodbyes

The funerals of Jarli and Michael Down were not easy. Jarli's people mourned his death and the murderer was punished. The two young boys who had observed his innocence grieved for Jarli and regretted their inquisitive stupidity and their longing to win the approval of the young men. Jaril spoke with the Elders and invited them to Michael's funeral, against the odds they agreed to come, more because of Jaril's persuasive words than any desire to be involved with white people. For the Elders it was another example of how things always go wrong when white people are involved.

Michael's family came and stayed with Robert and Janet who gently explained to them the relationship between Michael and Jarli. They were stunned but in this loving family they understood and reflected on the hints Michael had given over the years and regretted their blithe dismissal of the things that they now realised were of profound importance to him.
"Funny old bugger," said his father as tears streamed down his cheeks, "God I loved that boy."
The Elders stayed with Jaril, Peter and Chris and at the funeral, they brought leafy branches of the Emu Bush, some they put in the grave as if to make a comfortable bed, the rest they kept back for a smoking ceremony which they performed as Michael's body was lowered into the ground. As the smoke swirled around the mourners the chanting and the throbbing of the dance knocked again and again at their bodies as if demanding entrance to the depths of their being. In turn they gave way and allowed their feelings free reign; some screamed for their loss while others stamped in time showing their anger and their sorrow. Peter, Elizabeth and Michael were at their first funeral and were initially stunned by the events but as they put aside their childish reticence and remembered their friend who had taught them to ride and showed them the rudiments of training a dog they let themselves enter into the ethereal connection and the heartbreak of loss.

As the smoke thinned and drifted away to the north west the elders looked knowingly in that same direction, for to them as the smoke drifted toward their home it affirmed the bond between Jarli and Michael. Perhaps in their minds it united them in death, giving them what had been denied them in life. Michael's Mum and Dad thanked them for coming and told them with great sorrow that they had not had the chance to meet Jarli. The words exchanged were few but the depth of emotion was palpable.

Bill and Elizabeth sought out the elders and tried to explain their attachment to Jarli and what an important part he had played in their lives especially when they were so new to the whole farming venture and of Jarli's friendship with Janet that broadened her horizons. Henry Ford, Sergeant Wilkins, Molly, Ted and Maurie paid their respects and that night everyone came and sat round a campfire at Robert and Janet's farm. Jaril told them the story of another campfire where three soldiers and two stockmen had met and become friends and embarrassed themselves with the creation of Uncle Umba Jumba. Most of the white people present had not heard Aboriginal people laugh before and had a sudden realisation that all of humanity laughs but usually in the company of friends and when (and this realisation struck them very hard) when there was something to laugh about.

As evening broke into morning and the campfire had turned logs and stumps to coals, Janet brought out breakfast which drifted on into morning tea and lunch. It seemed no-one wanted to say the words 'goodbye' until finally Molly and Ted heard the call of thirsty patrons and headed home to Dencubbin with Maurie. Over the next few days d'Camry and Manly were surprised that the Aboriginal elders were in no rush to go home. They stayed and talked and Manly asked them if he could write down their stories. With that assent Manly encouraged them and wrote page after page; the seemingly endless story of dispossession. The elders told them of cruelty and massacres, of stolen children and stolen wives, of greedy protectors and illegal alcohol sales that destroyed so many lives. At times

Manly had to stop them because he could take no more. At the end he had to confess that the stories were so horrendous that he wondered what to do with them. In the end all he could promise was that he would somehow publish every detail, he just wasn't sure how.

Manly and d'Camry were now the custodians of what would surely be an unpopular history, who would want their children to know that their forebears had perpetrated such crimes? He could publish it himself, but his readership was small. Perhaps London or New York might be more receptive but there was this minor irritating diversion called The Second World War that looked like it might go on for a while yet.

Robert's War

Robert's war from 1939 to 1945 was not the haunted hiatus or the black and torturous psycho-circus that it was for so many others, for alongside the mining and the corporate takeovers Robert had spotted an opportunity in machine tool manufacture. In 1936 there were only 4 Australian companies producing machine tools, the consequent competition in a small market kept prices and profits low. Within a year of an initial acquisition Robert controlled the sector. His consolidation of the industry delivered considerable economies of scale, consistent quality control, improved logistics and above all, increased profitability. Robert's timing could not have been better. He had reasoned that there would be a war in Europe and that Australia would have to be much more self reliant as the supply of manufactured goods dried up. He had not expected a war in the Pacific nor on such a scale or with the speed that Japan brought the fear of invasion to his homeland. He had expected good profits but the tidal wave of cash that flooded in was a bonanza beyond his wildest dreams. Robert supplied the vital machine tools to every metal manufacturer and fabricator in Australia, and in the parlance of a country at war he was an essential industry. Robert was vital to the war effort, much more useful as a business leader with a natural flare for logistics and economic performance than as a commander in the field. Australia was gearing up in large and small factories across the country to make armaments and munitions and Robert would play his part while building his own empire.

He had reduced his exposure to European assets in 1938 correctly judging that mechanised warfare could destroy tangible assets at a whim. He started negotiations to manufacture British weapons like the Bren Gun under license but found the Federal Government uncooperative, preferring to control their own factories. He settled at last on the booming chemical industry heavily protected by the tariff wall. He managed to buy out a small company called Simbrol, made a significant investment in ICI ANZ, negotiated a seat on the board and a deal to share technology with Simbrol. It was a license to print money and remained so for the next 25 years.

John and Mildred's War

The German Invasion
by John Cox European Correspondent
… So dear readers what more can I say? The Germans cheated. They picked the weakest points in the Belgian French defences, they set up anti aircraft emplacements at all the bridge heads they captured and destroyed the expected aerial attackers. They used too many combat aircraft (there is surely a limit on this sort of thing) and inflicted severe casualties on soldiers retreating on foot. Did I mention that they cut Belgian Telephone communication so Belgian HQ could not tell their soldiers to retreat. And then they used radio communications in all their tanks when the French tank commanders had to stop and dismount in order to communicate. Did the Germans wait for them to converse? They did not. This is so unfair.

This is also the kind of nonsense, hubris and incompetence that got so many of our soldiers killed in the First War and it seems very little has been learned. The loss of materiel and men in the allied retreat can only be described as catastrophic and was completely preventable.

As Cox typed the last of his first article he knew it probably wouldn't get past the censor or would be heavily edited, but channelling Keith Murdoch, someone had to tell the truth.

He took the last sheet and the carbon copy from the typewriter placed the original with the other sheets in an envelope ready for dispatch.

In the following months Cox wrote about the German occupation of the Channel Islands, the USSR invasion of the Baltic States, the German attacks on Channel shipping, the first RAF attack on German munitions factories, the raid on Berlin and the Germans ramping up their bombing campaign, targeting British airfields but suffering significant losses.

Perhaps his best piece before the intensive German bombing of civilian targets was a long article on the expansion of American military capacity and the prospect of America entering the war. With the USSR taking advantage of a trade agreement with Germany, the Italians moving into North Africa and flexing their naval muscles, it seemed like it was Britain and her very few allies against the world with America the only hope of bringing some kind of balance.

As the bombs fell on London Mildred and John like so many other Londoners built an Anderson shelter in their backyard and prepared themselves to use it on an increasingly regular basis. John recalled some 'happy memories' as he dug the trench to the four foot depth required. A second gold strike? Not likely but at least the earth was soft. By October 1940 London was pounded over and over as the Germans, failing to destroy the Royal Air Force, concentrated more fire power on civilian populations to demoralise the British people prior to an invasion. As the bombs fell Mildred and John sheltered in their backyard 'fortress' or when caught away from home as the sirens sounded took shelter in a tube station wondering if they would see each other again after the all clear sounded. In November of that year a high explosive bomb destroyed their house at 11 Old Church St. John spent the night in South Kensington station and emerged with increasing dread as he walked toward Chelsea. He was used to the carnage, the fires, the dead, the weeping and the dispossessed but he agonised over the fear of never seeing Mildred again. As he turned off Fulham Road and into Old Church St he was still five blocks away from home but he could see that the area had been hit. His throat dried and seemed to enlarge as he pushed his aching body to run towards the destruction. As he arrived the volunteers were picking through the rubble looking for survivors. There were no questions to ask, he simply joined the search. As he moved toward a crumbling section of the house, a kindly constable said, "I can't let you go in there sir it's not safe."
"I'm looking for Mildred," blubbered Cox, "we live ... lived here."
"I know matey ... I know."
They continued the search to no avail.
Mildred was asleep in Teresa Reckitt's front room. They had

been out all night driving ambulances, Mildred had wanted to go home but as she sat drinking tea, exhaustion overtook her and as she thought, *"I'll just catch five minutes and then I'll go,"* she slipped into sleep, Teresa rescued the tea cup and covered Mildred with a blanket.

Mildred woke in a panic at about 8 o'clock, wrote Teresa a note of thanks and hurried towards Chelsea. It was a 15 minute walk. Coming from the opposite direction to John she hurried along Cheyne Walk and finally turned left into Old Church St. She could immediately see their ruined house and people searching for survivors. Her heart sank as she ran towards number 11. She stood crying in front of the ruin when a grimy man emerged from behind a wall that was still standing; it was Cox. They came together in a sobbing embrace homeless in a foreign city, knowing next to no-one, like babes cast adrift in a turbulent sea they held each other tight until Mildred ventured, "well at least those weeds are done for."

"I feel an article coming on, 'Extreme Gardening With The Luftwaffe.'"

"Or 'My Mother In Law Was Coming To Visit But The Luftwaffe Saved Us' ?"

"Steady on, my mother's a pretty decent old stick."

"Facts facts facts – facts are not very funny."

"No, no they're not. Shall we go for a picnic or the races, perhaps, a nice Day At The Races."

"Excellent, you will be Hugo Hackenbush and I will be Mrs Upjohn."

It seemed appropriate that they play out the Marx Bros. farce in this inexplicable chaos that surrounded them.

"The Sanitarium is just down the road, I believe we can get breakfast there."

Mildred walked with John back to Teresa Rickett's tea shop masking their shock with more nonsense from Groucho and Chico.

"Tutsi Fruitsy Ice Cream – Tutsi Fruitsy Ice Cream."

"Hey where can I get a Dicodcis Guide – as if I didn't know"

"You gotta buya the set – ones a no good – you needa the set."

"How much for the set?"

"$5 for six books"

"I really just wanted a guide not a public library."

"Here, now you gotta the set."

"Wait a minute what does this mean CQZP …?"

"It's the Jockey's code, you look up the code to find the jockey and then bet on the horse he's riding."

"I look it up in the book?"

"Yeah but not that book."

"This book?"

"You ain't gotta that book, you need this book."

"How much?"

"$5"

"I've only got $10."

"I gotta no change, I takea the ten."

"I got it, the horse is Rosie. Hey my good man, $2 on Rosie."

"I'm sorry sir, that race just finished."

The tea shop was still closed and Teresa was likely still asleep but they banged on the door until a bleary eyed Teresa appeared and opened it.

"What are you two …? Don't tell me you've been bombed out." Mildred and John nodded.

"Oh you poor things, come in, how about a nice cup of tea?"

"That would be tickety boo," said John.

"Tickety boo?"

"I just like saying it; there's something about British nonsense that really appeals to me."

"A bit upper class for me, I don't think I've ever heard a working class person say 'tickety boo'."

"I see," said John slightly embarrassed.

"Don't worry yourself about it. It's funny when Bertie Worcester says it, but that's a whole comedy built on upper middle class stupidity and I … I … get far too serious about it … so … tea?"

"Yes please," said Mildred and John in unison.

Teresa was soon back with the tea and with it came toast with real butter and some jam.

"Oh Teresa thank you, I know how short you must be on everything ... and trying to run the shop and …"

"Just let me worry about that, tuck in. Was it a complete wreck?

The house I mean."

"Yes, everything's gone furniture, clothes, everything."

"The only thing I have left is my typewriter and that's because it's at AAP."

Teresa looked a little sheepish as she poured more tea. "Look you can stay here with me, but there's a problem, ... it's not what you might think and I'll understand if you want to go elsewhere ... it's just that I'm a sort of ... a nudist when I'm at home."

"A naked, don't wear clothes nudist?" said John.

"That's generally what nudist means. I hope you don't think it is all too queer, I'm not alone really. I hear that Enid Blyton plays tennis in the nude and a friend at the Home Office says Winnie often works naked."

"You mean Churchill, Winston Churchill? He doesn't look the type," said Mildred.

"Do I look the type?"

"Point taken," said John.

"Look stay tonight and see how it goes. You can always retreat to your bedroom if it's all too much. God, life is never easy is it. Actually I would have thought there would be a lot of nudists in Australia, all the warmth and sun and endless beaches."

Mildred felt obliged to confess, "we're just as prim as everyone else I'm afraid and then there's sunburn, biting insects and beach inspectors. ... Do you expect us to strip off as well?"

"Of course not, I mean you can if you want to but it takes a lot of getting used to, it's a strange feeling to be naked when it's been drummed into you that it's a sin and will inevitably lead to a lascivious lifestyle."

"The army spends a lot of time naked, open showers and bunk rooms and it pretty lascivious from time to time, of course that's probably the same for any group of young men including the priesthood. But I've got to be honest, naked with two beautiful women I'd be worried that I might ...

"What, become a rapist?"

"No, Jesus, become aroused, it doesn't take much."

"Hmmm I've noticed."

"And would you be embarrassed John?"

"I should bloody well think so."

By this stage the tension was decreasing and the three friends in absurd circumstances were verging on laughter at this uniquely human predicament.

"You know I'm a journalist and I write about everything?"

"Some discretion might be required about my flabby tummy."

"And no telling that I have one breast bigger than the other."

"But it would sell like hot cakes.

Germans scared by suburban Amazons
Luftwaffe forgets to drop bombs while sightseeing in Surrey

It'd all be for the war effort and if Winston would join in I think we'd have Jerry on the run."

"It sounds like we're going to cope," said Teresa standing up and dropping her gown.

"Not bad for my age, what do you think?"

"Rule Britannia," said Mildred.

"Fucking hell," said Cox, "what have I got into?"

Gordon Cope

Naked Warriors

The truly great things about nudism are that no uniforms or special equipment is required, literally anyone can do it and there is no mandatory skill set.

But Teresa was right, it took some getting used to and there were certain drawbacks; hot soup for instance was treated with extra safety precautions and a simple ringing of the doorbell was enough to send Mildred and John sprinting for the bedroom.

Cox's stimulatory concerns were well founded, he frequently had to excuse himself and *retire hurt*; more from a bruised ego than any physical harm. He began to think that the female anatomy had a lot more going for it in terms of convenience but then there were those floppy bits that tended to fly in all directions if one jerked suddenly.

Time passed and they all got on, with laughter the best medicine for any embarrassment. As the cooler months came, clothing seemed like a good idea but Teresa had been stockpiling her coal ration by making do with tepid baths and electric cooking. She was fortunate enough to have a combustion cooker that also heated hot water and now she could extend its hours of operation which made the kitchen the social centre of the house.

As Teresa and Mildred ventured out each night, John lay awake in naked worry until the all clear sounded and later the door creaked as the women came home, exhausted from their mission, they nodded good night and fell into bed, ironically, fully clothed.

Nudism is not like other indulgences, the number of London nudist in 1941 was likely smaller than the membership of the London Society of Patagonian stamp collectors. Consequently nudist friends were quite hard to find in war torn London. It was sheer luck that Teresa met with a volunteer Warden called Albert Guinness, she recognised the name from an article she had read in the Daily Mirror: *Naked Church Organist Hounded From Loft*. The story was sensational with multiple *organ* double entendres like ... *his organ throbbing with contrapuntal invention* – a Bachian illusion that was probably lost on the majority of the Mirror's readership. Albert seemed a quiet gentle soul and Teresa wondered whether his behaviour was simply the joy of playing great music in nothing but his skin rather than the dangerous perverted child molester as implied by the Mirror. She saw him often enough to observe his humanity, courage and compassion and finally asked if he would like to come to her tea shop and meet some of her friends. Albert was reticent, he had suffered greatly after his expulsion from the church. He had been serially bated by indignant parishioners, had hateful slogans nailed to his front door and then was literally beaten by a bunch of marauding teenagers. At that point he decided to move to escape the persecution. As Teresa spoke to him he didn't really hear her, he was in a fog of pernicious memories.

"Do you know who I am?" Albert stammered.

"You would be Albert Guinness, the Fire Warden."

"But who I really am?"

"You mean Albert, the naked organist?"

"So you do. And do you want to make fun of me? Because if you do..."

"I most certainly do not. Albert I am inviting you to meet some like minded people."

"I'm not queer you know or perverted like they said in that article."

"No, I don't think you are."

"Then why?"

"Why do you think, for the same reason that you get carried away playing Bach without any clothes."

"That's it?"

"That's it."

"Can I bring my baby harmonium?"

"Only if you promise to play for us."

"Oh, yes, thank you, thank you very much."

And so it was that a week later in the early afternoon Albert and his baby harmonium on wheels arrived at the tea shop. The tea shop always remained closed on Mondays and Teresa led

Albert through to the residence, introduced him to the already naked Mildred and John, removed her clothes and invited him to do the same.

"I've never done this before, I mean not with other people and even in the church, well, I thought all the doors were locked."

"And yet that is the way you came into the world and there were other people waiting to greet you. I think I'll make some tea and then perhaps a little Bach?"

"Thank you Teresa, John, Mildred, thank you so much."

o-o-o-o-o-o-o-o-o

In the weeks, months and years that followed, Cox had plenty to write about, the slowing of the blitz, the African campaigns, the internment of all Jews, the mandatory wearing of the yellow stars, the devastation inflicted by the U-boats, the German betrayal of the Soviets. Things always seemed to go from bad to worse, punctuated by the occasional allied victory, bringing some cause for hope.

In March 1941 Cox met fellow journalist Jack Hetherington from the Sydney Morning Herald. He was on his way to Africa to join the Australian 6th Division on its way to Greece in an effort to reinforce the Greek Army who had repulsed an initial Italian invasion on their western border with Albania. The Allies reasoned that the Germans would take over the attack and dispatched British, Australian and New Zealand troops.

Hetherington was back six weeks later, lucky to be alive and not a POW. Hetherington explained that the force was woefully inadequate and that when the Germans attacked via Bulgaria, the Greek army was on the other side of the country and the reinforcements were easily over run resulting in the capture of 7,000 allied soldiers. Those who had escaped had done so only due to the valiant effort of those good men who held back the German advance long enough for an evacuation to be planned and executed. They paid; some with their lives and others with their freedom. Jack was furious at the incompetence, calling the campaign, ill-planned, disastrous and short, he showed Cox a quote from a senior commander: 'in almost every Allied campaign so far, the worst mistakes of the politicians and

296

strategists have been moderated by the bravery, fighting qualities and sheer dogged determination of the troops.'
Hetherington's articles were published around the world.
Cox was in awe.
But then the momentous events of December 1941.
The Germans abandoned their campaign to take Moscow, the Soviets launched a counteroffensive, the Japanese bombed Pearl Harbour and at last the United States was in the fight.

John Cox Writes 1942-45

After 1941 Cox could barely keep up, he simply wrote a digest of daily events to be published weekly back home. He felt like a school boy writing a summary rather than a real journalist with real analysis and real opinions.

By 1944 he knew that the Germans were on the run but censorship was tight and there was no point in speculating about a full scale allied invasion of Europe. The allies were already in Italy, Germany was under heavy bombardment and the five million strong Soviet Army was steadily pushing the Germans out of eastern Europe. Then to his eternal amazement he received notice that he could be one of the 558 journalists and photographers to accompany the allied invasion force.

Cox had been an office bound journalist since 1940 but now he could be the real thing, he would be the storyteller for what would surely be the biggest invasion in history.

Being a Journalist of no real reputation Cox was shunted onto a hospital ship with no combat personnel for Cox to interview. Feeling somewhat dejected he had a few beers with the doctors and senior nurses and gathered enough for a piece on these unsung heroes. After more than just a few pints Cox was suddenly in need of a toilet. Others feeling the same urgency had occupied all the units close at hand and Cox was forced to seek out urinal relief on the lower decks.

Just as he was contemplating relief in a dark corner he came to door marked *men* that was leaning slightly open due to a broken latch. Cox pulled it open to discover it was already occupied, by a women. He slammed it shut and nervously said, "sorry madam, I was just looking for an empty ..."

"Well look somewhere else, this berth is taken."

"Yes, of course, just in a bit of a hurry."

"Are you taking the piss?"

"Well, not **the** piss but **a** ... that is I need to ... and they're all taken."

The door opened again.

"Hmm your need sounds greater than mine."

They hurriedly changed places.

"Thanks, ... oh ... what a relief. Are you a nurse?"

"Why? Do you need something amputated?"

"No, Jesus, just trying to be friendly."

"A friendly man, just what I need."

"Well to complete the piss take, you sound a little pissed off."

"Just a little! And who the hell are you, you're not a doctor or a medic."

"I'm a journalist."

"Fuck me, a fucking journalist. Get rid of one and another one turns up."

"Um, sorry?" said Cox. who was not used to hearing women swear so volubly.

"Let's just say that my experience with journalists is not good."

"Are you famous? Sick of the gossip mongers?"

"No, in fact, not famous enough, done over by that misogynist son of a bitch."

"A journalist ... and a man I'm guessing."

"Clever boy, you'll go far, real nose for a story."

"So how come, you ... in the lavatory and no journalist in pursuit?"

"I'm not being pursued you idiot, I got bumped."

"In a crowd ...?"

"You are so thick, who do you write for?"

"The West Australian."

"There are newspapers in Western Australia?"

"Yes! I'm sure it's not as grand as the Times but it does get read before it becomes a fishwrapper."

"Alright, I'm sorry."

"Thank you, now as a clever rejoinder that will demonstrate my journalistic skills, ... who the hell are you?"

"I'm a fucking journalist."

"And you're doing a story, what, on trans channel urinals?"

"Very witty. I'm on my way to cover the invasion?"

"For?"

"For those sycophantic slugs at Colliers magazine."

"Getting on well with the bosses are we?"

At this point, Martha, for that was her name became so angry that Cox took immediate evasive action.

"Sorry, that was unfair."

"Yes, but accurate, piss weak little piss-ants. I risk my life in war zones to give them brilliant copy and then they bump me as their nominated journalist ..."

"For a man?"

"Yes a man! But not just any man. That self proclaimed swashbuckler and subjugator of women Ernest Hemingway."

"Wow!"

"Yes, wow, but that's not the best part!"

"And the best part is …?"

"That little prick is my husband and he demanded my spot from Colliers and they gave it to him."

"Oh, that's not good."

"Manipulating, self obsessed, egoistic, son of a serpent."

"So, you are a stowaway?"

"You fucking bet I am."

"And you are?"

"Martha Gellhorn."

"Bloody hell. I've read your stuff. You're amazing."

"Thank you."

"You covered the disaster in Spain."

"Yes, I couldn't believe that the Western Democracies threw the Spanish Republicans to the wolves. I kept reporting the Franco atrocities. I even wrote personally to Eleanor Roosevelt but there was too much paranoia about the communists in the republican government. The US, British and French preferred that murdering bastard Franco even when he was clearly backed by both the Italian and German fascists."

"Would you like to come up and have a drink?"

"I need to stay hidden, just to make sure I can get off this rust bucket at the other end. I didn't come this far to end up in the brig."

"Of course, can I bring you some food?"

"Thank you, that would be very kind. Is there any booze on board?"

"Just beer I'm afraid."

"I would kill for a beer, even that strange English stuff."

"Done, cabin service will be with you shortly Miss Gellhorn."

"And your name, strange Australian cabin boy journalist

person?"
"John Cox."
"Really, you're John Cox. I read your expose of the debacle in France and Belgium."
"But that didn't get published."
"You'd be surprised what floats around in the better circles. It caused quite a flurry."
"A flurry indeed, not quite a Pulitzer, but good to know that somebody read it."
"OK that's enough mutual admiration, go get the beer!"
That night Cox wrote to Mildred telling her he was safe so far and that he had met Gellhorn. The ship's purser agreed to get it to her on their return.

o-o-o-o-o-o-o-o-o

The D day landing June 6th 1944 was upon them. They were lucky to be with the British forces headed for a beach codenamed Sword. The unsuspecting Americans at 'Omaha Beach' were confronted by strong fortifications and a German division that had been unexpectedly moved to the coast from further inland. Intelligence had wildly underestimated the strength of the resistance, which on top of comprehensive fortifications, included widespread mine placements, plenty of wire and tank traps that were also mined. The naval bombardment at Omaha was completely inadequate and the aerial bombardment had mostly missed its targets and on the morning of the attack they concentrated their efforts further inland so as not to bomb their own forces. The seas were the roughest in 40 years, swamping many of the landing craft and drowning their occupants before they hit the beach. The engineers suffered heavy losses trying to clear safe passages across the beach. Many tanks were destroyed on landing and soldiers that had to wade ashore without being shot then had to clean their weapons before they were operable.
The result was over 4,000 deaths and 10,000 casualties, It was remarkable that small groups still managed to scale the cliffs and stage successful assaults on German positions. At the end of the day the beach was not secured and the second wave of

troops faced many of the same problems that had beset first wave.

The objective of linking the five beach assaults and forming an 80 km front on the Normandy coast on day 1 was not achieved. At Sword beach things were much smoother. While John Cox and Martha Gellhorn ate meat pies and drank beer, paratroopers from the British 6th airborne division successfully landed their gliders secured two strategic bridges and destroyed the menacing Merville Battery with minimal casualties.

Landing at Sword beach was no picnic, but there was nothing like the carnage at Omaha.

Getting off the hospital ship was just as smooth. When a beachhead had been established and there was some cover available to foolhardy journalists, the lighters unloaded the wounded and picked up Cox and Gellhorn for the return trip. They landed 'safely' on Sword beach.

o-o-o-o-o-o-o-o-o

After several days of trying not to get killed they were given the all clear to scale the cliffs and view the wondrous success achieved by the troops. Gellhorn was a seasoned war zone correspondent but even she was in awe of the courage and persistence of these men.

When the linking of the five invading expeditions was finally accomplished Gellhorn hooked up with an American division and learned that Hemingway had arrived much later than she had. A small but sweet victory. They said their goodbyes, promised to keep in touch and Cox went off to find his assigned place with a British tank regiment.

The Sherman tank was the pride of Detroit. The American car giants had applied their mass production technology to turn tanks out almost as quickly as cars, they even used a standard V6 petrol car engine.

The Shermans were light and quick, just the ticket for infantry cover but limited in their armour and fire power. As Operation Overlord gradually spread beyond the beaches progress was slow as the Allies battled the Germans for every bridge and every town.

Cox soon discovered that the Shermans were vulnerable; the Germans had built a tank they called the Tiger.

Tigers were big and heavy with almost twice the armour of a Sherman and an 88mm gun that could destroy a Sherman at a distance well beyond its firing range.

The British tank crews nicknamed the Sherman, *The Ronson* (cigarette lighter) *"Lights up first time every time"*. The crews told him that just like the RAF pilots in the Battle of Britain they knew that every mission could be their last. Their only chance in an engagement with a Tiger was to run and hide and even then the Tiger's range was so superior that they would likely be destroyed. Cox observed first hand a Sherman firing on a Tiger with the shell bouncing off the armoured body and causing only a slight shuddering movement to the massive machine.

Once again Cox was furious, for even when the British managed to fit a gun that could destroy a Tiger, the Americans refused to fit a foreign gun and the Brits only managed to fit what they called the firefly to 25 % of their Shermans. After all, crews were plentiful.

It was not the time for another accusation of hubris in senior ranks, the war was being won and the Sherman's overwhelming numbers were going to prevail. The Americans produced nearly 50,000 Shermans while the Germans produced only 200 Tigers. Cox stored it away with his plethora of inhumane actions.

By 1st July 1944 Cox and the Anglo Canadian forces had not moved very far. It took longer than expected to consolidate the allied dominance of the Normandy Coast. The Germans had put massive resources into building the defensive structures of Hitler's Atlantic Wall and this was backed up by hundreds of thousands in troops and more importantly the West Panzer Group.

Field Marshal Erwin Rommel was in command of the western front and had been arguing strongly that the most effective plan was to stop any invasion on the beaches rather than allowing the invaders further inland before counter attacking using their armoured divisions. Rommel was in Berlin on June 6th which did create some initial confusion and lack of leadership but the final result was never in doubt.

Cox joined the chorus of approval for the meticulously planned invasion, he interviewed some of the unassuming heroes that had scaled the cliffs under enemy fire. They told him they were just plain lucky, not heroes really, after all they only made it because their friends didn't.

The next objective for the Sword invaders was the capture of Caen, a major river city with important road and rail junctions. They faced stiff opposition from the Panzer IVs, for even these tanks had more armour and fire power than the Shermans. Losses were heavy on both sides and civilian casualties were disastrously high; the Allies had bombed Caen seemingly without any strategic objective reducing a town of 60,000 to a mere 17,000. When Cox walked through the streets of this ancient medieval city on July 20th he could not believe the devastation, the streets filled with rubble, the ancient university completely obliterated, it was a horrifying sight. Some of the residents tried to tell him of their plight. His French was non-existent but he could read their faces and see their tears. Most of the population were now living as refugees, many in old tunnels on the outskirts of the city wondering why such carnage was necessary.

But it was the next stage of the war that had Cox shaking his head, it seemed to him like a repeat of WW1 tactics as the Allies moved turgidly through the difficult boggy country to the south west instead of using their air superiority to leapfrog and isolate enemy positions. At the same time that master of surprise tactics General George Patton and the 3rd US Army was effectively sidelined, having been assigned the longest route into Germany.

Patton was his own worst enemy, his public persona being forever characterised by his slapping of a wounded soldier, telling him to get up and return to duty. A year after that event, he was neither penitent nor patient; he moved the third army at a rapid pace by entrusting his flank defence to the US Air Force. His troops leapfrogged over enemy divisions, encircling them, forcing capitulation and moving on. True his supply lines rapidly grew longer but his biggest problem was the diversion of gasoline supplies to Montgomery's disastrous Market Garden campaign. At that point Patton had to sit and wait on the

German border.

This unofficial fragmented news gave Cox hope that someone had learned from the mistakes of the past but he was with the plodders, where every hedgerow could conceal a Tiger tank and losses were accepted as inevitable.

Supplies for a massive push to end the war were simply not available. The Allies had taken what seemed like forever to gain control of critical ports, like Antwerp and then clear them of mines and rebuild damaged infrastructure and only then be able to supply their troops.

Cox had heard the woeful tales of long supply lines using five time as much fuel in transport as they delivered to the front and he heard first hand the dangerous complacency that the Wehrmacht was finished and it was just a matter of time before the complete collapse of Germany. He tried to counter this position in his articles but the good people of Western Australia had much more interest in the war in the Pacific and preferred to believe the complacency rhetoric because that would free up resources in Europe and hasten the end of Japan. Cox sighed as he sent his dispatch which pretty much coincided with the great German Winter Offensive that once again descended from the north on weak American lines and threatened to retake Antwerp. The Allied response was swift and included the redirection of the American Third Army, a move that Patton had anticipated ahead of most of his comrades. Being caught unprepared again inflicted great losses on the Allies but even more devastating losses on the Germans who could never hope to recover from such devastation. When Cox read a newspaper that coined the term 'The Battle Of The Bulge' he smiled at its brilliance and wished he had thought of it.

For the next 6 months Cox was constantly on the move. In March he crossed the Rhine but his elation at nearing the end was dashed as the soldiers that he had spent the last year with opened the gates of the Bergen-Belsen concentration camp. There was no time for reflection or anger or outright disbelief, it was simply a matter of offering whatever help he could to the 60,000 walking and dying skeletons of this hideous place.

It was only later that Cox was stretched to incredulity when the local authorities wanted to negotiate a handover of the camp as if it were some kind of prize that could be bartered; a prize infested with typhus, dysentery, and tuberculosis. Was this the madness that infected Germany? Was this the triumph of process and ideology over reason that the Nazis had inflicted on the epicentre of European culture?

Cox wrote down all of these reflection but the newspapers only wanted news of a new victory every day and that is what he delivered. He crossed the Elbe with the British 21st army group and it seemed that German resistance was crumbling before them, the road to Berlin was open but the city would fall to the Soviets as three Soviet Army Groups simultaneously surrounded and punched through the centre of the city. Germany surrendered unconditionally of May 8th 1945.

It was over, Cox would never go to Berlin or see the treaty signed or even witness the gathering of the four allied commanders (Montgomery, Eisenhower, Zhuchov and Tassigny) there in June. Everyone just wanted to go home, the Canadians were the first to leave, having no desire to be involved in the zoning of Germany. Cox had long decided that despite the lure of post war stories, he had had enough, he wanted to be with Mildred, he wanted to smell the Indian Ocean and feel its cooling evening breeze, he wanted to see Henry Ford, he wanted to visit Michael Down's grave, he wanted to write about home.

It was not easy travelling without the British Army but Cox decided to make his way home by whatever means he could find.

Not being an expert in European geography he had no idea of the most practical route to a channel port but then practicality was not a consideration, it was more a matter of where you could catch a ride. Cox was on a north south main road and he knew he sort of needed to go a bit south and a bit west so he got on the first army vehicle going south. No-one was too worried about security or papers or anything really, they could see even without his journalist pass that he was an alright sort of chap and not an escaping Nazi. When the convoy reached Hanover his new friends pointed him towards another group heading to Dusseldorf as part of the endless supply train to feed the starving civilian population of war torn Europe.

By the time Cox reached Antwerp it was early July 1945, Cox reasoned that he would be able to hitch a ride on a supply ship and at last be back in England but one of his 'truckin buddies' on the Red Ball Express had given him the name of a friend who scheduled flights out of Asch Airfield Y29 North of Zutendaal . After we go through Chemelot, I'll get you on the road east, the base is south of the road just ask for Willy, tell him Charley sent ya.

Armed with these impressive credentials Cox charmed his way onto the base and asked around for Willy.

"Willy, yeah sure he's in the tower, thinks he's a princess, tower - princess get it?"

"Yeah, I get it. Thanks.

Cox went on his way looking for the royal transvestite.

A guard blocked his entry to the tower, Cox sheepishly said he needed to see Willy.

Willy, yeah sure he's in the tower, thinks h..."

Yeah thanks, I'll find him.

Running up the stairs and not knowing what to expect he collided with a US soldier.

"I don't suppose you're Willy?"

"Yeah, I'm Willy, I work in the tower everyone calls me th..."

"Yes, yes I know, very funny. Look Charley sent me."

"Charley, Charley, did he give you the money he owes me?"

"No, I'm sorry he didn't.

"He's a hellava nice guy, Charley, but he's a useless poker player. What can I do for you?"

"Charley said you might be able to get me on a plane to England."

"Friend, I could put an elephant on a plane to Iceland."

"Glad to hear it."

"I can get you on a Douglas at 23:50 if you can do a bit of play actin."

"And that would involve?"

"Well I got this pain in the ass Colonel, you know the type, throws his weight around, everything is real important and real secret. I mean what's his problem, the war's over, right?"

"Right."

"So you'll just tell him you're a navigator that was took sick and has to catch up with his crew or some bullshit and it'll be sweet as a nut. I'll give you a uniform and you get on at the last minute and while he's blowin smoke out his ass the ground crew'll lock the door and the plane will start down the runway. You just apologise take a seat and enjoy the ride. Done and done."

"What's the Colonel's name?"

"Pash, Colonel Pash, pretty funny."

"Yeah it is."

Everything went just as Willy had described including the voluminous ass smoke.

While Colonel Pash ranted about the lack of professionalism and the fact that Cox had no clearance to be on the aeroplane or anywhere near this mission, Cox surveyed the passengers, a US guard and a bunch of civilians that looked like they would rather be somewhere else.

As soon as the Colonel told Cox not to fraternise with the passengers Cox was on high alert his radar was scanning the crowd and looking for some hint as to their identities. He explained to the Colonel that having been taken ill and unable to fly for three days he now had to connect with his regular crew in Wyton.

"Hmm, alright I can see why that idiot scheduler put you on this flight, at least he got your destination right. Brains of a gnat."

"Pardon Colonel?"

"Nothing. Sit there, no talking."

As Cox took the last available seat he bumped his fellow passenger and apologised. The passenger smiled and responded in German.

Clue one, he's German.

"No talking, got it?"

"Yes sir, sorry sir."

Cox observed that the man was well fed, well dressed and had the hands of an office worker. Perhaps he was a high profile Nazi.

But why was he on a plane to England?

Surely anyone facing trial would be interred in a military prison in Europe.

Was this man part of a fifth column and needed to be rescued before he fell foul of an anti Nazi mob.

But why the need for secrecy, it was all over.

Maybe he knows something about allied operations that still needs to be kept secret.

But then he is German so maybe he knows something about Nazi operations that still needs to be kept secret.

Cox decided to feign sleepiness for the first hour of the journey and hoped that others would follow suit.

There was soon snoring that seemed to synchronise with the throbbing of the engines and Cox Stood up, stretched took a quick look around the cabin and sat down again. Colonel Pash was asleep but the guard behind him was awake and alert.

Cox casually took out his notebook and wrote his name on a fresh page and nudged his fellow traveller.

The traveller stirred and Cox pointed to his name and discreetly offered him the pad and pencil.

The German wrote his name, Werner Heisenberg and passed the pad back to Cox.

Cox made a question mark.

Heisenberg wrote 'physicist – contact wife Elisabeth tell - alive'.

At that point their eyes met and Cox nodded and wrote 'anyone else?'

Heisenberg wrote 'Niels Bohr Denmark'

A rustling sound behind them cued them to desist, Cox slipped the note pad under his jacket and let his head drop into a sleeping posture, as the guard casually walked the length of the cabin and back.

Cox remembered that Niels Bohr had won a Nobel Prize some time in the twenties, something to do with atoms. That set his mind racing, this guy was a scientist, he was being smuggled to England to be interrogated about … about … about … science? Genius deduction!

o-o-o-o-o-o-o-o-o

Back in England Cox easily found his way back to London, the Tea Shop and Mildred.

Surprised to see him in uniform and happier to see him without it they fell into bed and held each other as if never to let go again. Explanations seemed irrelevant and it wasn't until the next day that the long story unfolded with each telling the other alternate episodes.

"You'll never guess - sword beach - the V2's – Belsen – dancing in the streets – Martha Gellhorn – rescued a baby - Willy - Theresa – the Labor Party – Heisenberg. It took days and even then a moment of silence would produce another memory, the world was different, again – 1918 – 1929 – 1939 – was the world exhausted? Would it lie down and sleep for a hundred years? Would peace allow a healing of the horror – evidently not.

Mildred and John Cox along with Teresa Rickett were sailing to Australia when the news came of the atomic bombs dropped on Hiroshima and Nagasaki. The unimaginable carnage brought a swift end to the war in the Pacific and a new threat to civilisation. The word 'atomic' set off alarm bells for Cox as he recalled his scribbled conversation with Werner Heisenberg. Was this man the Nazi's scientist for things that go bang, were the Nazis also building the mother of all bombs? Did the allies win by the skin of their teeth?

It hadn't been easy to get in touch with Elisabeth Heisenberg but via various military contacts he successfully sent her a message that Werner was alive and well but probably being interrogated by the Americans and the British in England. He eventually received a reply, expressing her thanks and inviting him to their country retreat at Urfeld if it was still there, if they still owned it, if Werner was ever released.

In the month long voyage Cox put together a longer piece on war time journalism and planned some follow-up stories including one on Heisenberg when he was released. The lazy days were welcome after a frenetic 6 years when every day could be your last, they all took stock and quietly mourned those they had lost and the millions of dead that were unknown to them. Sometimes overwhelmed by sorrow but then buoyed up by the simplicity of feeling the sun on your face they 'passed their time', as the Afghans say.

When an overcast Melbourne came into view they felt a reverence for their country, a strong combination of thankfulness and luck. No ghostly derelict skyline, no streetscapes pock marked with bullet holes, no stench of death; for while Cox was all too well acquainted with the inglorious Australian past, the present was filled with hope and populated in the main by well fed well dressed Australians.

Robert and Janet

"Do you still love me?" Said Robert.

"What a question, after such a life, painted on the broadest canvas, in sickness and health, in riches and more riches, in adversity and triumph … Should I go on?" said Janet.

"I was remembering that day on the rock, the dreaming rock, when I saw that kaleidoscope of all my dreams that burst the seams of my imagination. I know now that I didn't have to take it all, but I was greedy and in a hurry. I could have chosen more wisely perhaps but for some reason I felt compelled as if time was short. Do it now or don't do it at all. And you know - I nearly lost my mind."

"Yes, I know that, it was terrifying, I was on the edge of the abyss, not knowing if you would ever find your way back."

"And then Peter and Chris came and were the truest of friends. I didn't see them on the rock, I wonder why not. A friend shaped hole in the universe, perhaps. What would Einstein say to that?"

"That sounds lovely but I have no idea what it means."

"Lovely? It's profound."

"No it's complete rubbish."

"Just a little profound?"

"No. I'm a journalist, I can spot rubbish at 500 yards."

"Fine. Just trying to explain the inexplicable."

"That's an oxymoron. Another scotch?"

"No thanks. All that I want in the world right now is to hear you say, I love you."

"I love you Robert."

"And I love you Janet Cole. I feel extraordinarily complete and satisfied and, god it's been a big day, …I'm suddenly exhausted, I'll have to go to bed."

Robert pulled himself up by the arms of the chair, kissed Janet good night and wandered down the corridor to sleep.

Janet watched him go and smiled, much as she had when she climbed the Dreaming Rock so many years ago. She wandered through the house picking up pictures of the children in turn. Peter, now all grown up and seeking admission to the West

Australian Bar. Elizabeth, ever the rebel, travelling in India. William, following his brother and at university. The house had been empty all this year, just the two lovers rattling around with Robert finally having time to be a father but all too late and Janet, looking after Robert's mental health and trying to pull him gently into a more active social life.

She didn't feel sleepy, she considered the miraculous entertainment box in the corner of the room, black and white pictures and sound without wires, they called it Television but she took Bruce Gyngell's sage advice and left it off most of the time.

It was early morning when Janet finally fell into bed, she rolled over to stroke Robert's cheek and found it strangely cold, she took his hand to put his arm under the blankets but it was even colder, in a sudden panic she reached for his neck but found no pulse, she listened for sounds of breathing but there were none. Robert had suffered a fatal heart attack. Janet ran to the phone and called their doctor. Five years later CPR would have been known and perhaps then she could have ... but not now, she lay beside him in some vain hope that her warmth would revive him; she lay there sobbing waiting for the doctor.

o-o-o-o-o-o-o-o-o

Robert's funeral was small, just family and close friends. There were hundreds of condolence messages but Janet knew that Robert was only interested in a very few people and would have raged against mourners who turned up just to be seen or because they had some tenuous business connection. The Mayor of Perth used his secretary to ask where he should attend and at what time, the flat refusal was not appreciated.

The elderly Bill and Elizabeth stood by ready to help if Janet could not cope with making the funeral arrangements. She did cope, as staunch as ever she continued her feisty protection of the man she had loved. Elizabeth the younger was already on her way home and joined her brothers in a melee of grief. Robert's aging parents were too frail to make the journey and wept into their respective pillows in their respective nursing homes and raged against the unfairness of untimely death.

Robert was farewelled in a small ceremony at home. Peter d'Camry and Chris Manly gently guided the gathering in a retrospective of Robert's life; the good, the bad, the ugly and the hilarious. Chris Manly had gathered press clippings and together with family photographs and his own notes on many stories, that he had felt obliged not to print but had now published and bound a memorial book for the family and friends near and far. John and Mildred came from Melbourne with Jaril while Sergeant Wilkins and Henry Ford came from Perth, Bevin Brown, now a colonel, came from Canberra, and from Dencubbin; Molly and Ted with the ever guileless Maurie. This rag tag group that came together in the most unlikely circumstances toasted their friend, not only because he made them rich but in the process he had eventually shown them the meaning of decency and fairness. They raised their glasses to their absent friend and stood silent as grief and loss overtook them.

It was Maurie who brought them back with vintage inappropriateness.

"Ted and I tried to steal that gold and you know we would've if I hadn't been so stupid eh Ted? But Robert, he knew just what to do."

There was laughter all round and Janet came to Maurie and simply hugged him, he opened his mouth to respond but she put a gentle finger against his lips and he understood.

John, Mildred and Theresa

John Cox, Mildred Carter and Teresa Ricket had stayed in Melbourne and stayed together. John had been offered a journalist position with The Age almost as soon as they heard he was in town. Teresa fell in love with Melbourne and opened a tea shop in Little Collins Street while Mildred joined a group of feisty Aboriginal Women and together they opened a co-operative that centred on Arts and Culture, with their first retail outlet opening next to Teresa's tea shop.

In September 1946 Mildred gave birth to an 8lb 5oz baby girl, they called her Madelaine.

A wonderfully bright, not so pretty but very precocious child, Madelaine brought the usual mixture of joy, anxiety and pride to Mildred, John and Aunty Teresa, from early teenage she mocked their strange nudist practices and made them dress up when she wanted to invite friends over.

Cox became well known not only for his incisive political commentary but also for his regular articles on Aboriginal Culture and the appalling state of Aboriginal health, education and 'mission life'. He became the conduit for Chris Manley's collected material on injustice to Aboriginal people constantly hounding his editor for more column inches becoming typecast as a bleeding heart for the black fellas.

Jaril came to live close by and brought that extra touch of authenticity to Cox's work.

The rarity of an Aboriginal man having white friends, real friends that he saw often was something that he had to explain constantly to his Aboriginal friends. Despite the clarity and constancy of his explanation they still struggled with the idea and were always alert to any any cracks in the relationship.

Jaril never came to terms with the nudist thing, he thought clothes were pretty damned handy, especially in Melbourne, and had no wish to return to what could be seen as a more primitive lifestyle. He would often tell his friends that he was off to see the natives in their natural habitat.

Molly and Ted

It was never going to be easy for Molly and Ted, they had let too many demons out of the bottle. Naming them had been just the beginning of a much longer journey. They were both targets for the kind of depression that can follow the recognition of traumatic life events. Sometimes one could lift the other up but when they both received a blow from the past at the same time there was a destructive silence followed by doubt about everything including each other. It was only work that saved them. The daily demand to get up, shower and dress and then to serve their customers and in so doing each other.

It was an unlikely customer who helped them the most, a descendant of an Afghan camel driver and an Aboriginal woman. They nearly refused him service; racial prejudice is never far beneath the surface in Australia. Abdullah Mahomet was in his seventies and with his camels, still serviced the smaller remote settlements and stations that were neglected by the trucking companies. Thirst was all that was on Abdullah's mind as he ordered a beer from Ted.

"I thought you Mohammedans didn't drink beer."

"My father taught me from the Qu'ran that beer contains some good and some evil, but that the evil is greater than the good."

"So, you don't want a beer?"

"My mother taught me from the Bible to take a little beer for my stomach's sake."

"So, you do want a beer?"

"Both of them taught me to honour my parents."

"Jesus, make up your mind."

"And Jesus taught me to hang around with publicans and sinners."

"Anything else?"

"Yeah it's 108 in the shade, I'm thirsty and I reckon that beer might do me some good."

"You're a funny bugger, I'm Ted and this is Molly, we're publicans and sinners."

"I'm Abdullah and I'm a camel driver."

"This one's on me. Tell us why do you still do it, you know with the camels, I mean you could buy a truck."

"Yeah, I could but my father taught me .."

"Jees, not this again."

"My father taught me not to exceed the bounds."

"What? What bounds?"

"I could buy a truck but then it would cost too much to go to the places ... the places that are my places, where the people live that need me to come there."

"And I bet your mother taught you ..."

"My mother taught me to treat people the way I want to be treated, so I can't just leave them out there with no one to bring them supplies."

"And what was the most important thing they ever told you?"

"They said, we have raised you for the good of mankind, so do good to everyone you meet."

"Does that make you happy?"

"I don't know, whether it's that or the sun coming up or the warmth of the fire or the faithfulness of the camels, but what I do know is that all those things are like a shield that takes the power away from the bad things."

Molly put her hand on top of Ted's and gently squeezed, Ted looked at her and she made a subtle nod toward the Afghan and uncharacteristically Ted got the message and asked, "would you like to stay the night as our guest, you know on us?"

Little more was said for this was no firebrand preacher or learned imam, it was just a human being who lived well.

Molly and Ted slept peacefully and rose early to bid their guest farewell, this traveller, this servant, this ruler of his own domain.

Maurie and Judith

"Judith, who is Judith?
Janet stood open mouthed as Maurie announced that he was engaged.
"Judith Petrie."
"Yes, excellent, that's her name but when ... how? Details Maurie details!"
As usual Janet's demands put Maurie into a nervous fluster.
"She is, I mean, she works – well not – that is she does but not like before so because ... "
Realising her own overpowering nature Janet took Maurie by the hand, led him to a chair, poured him a drink, sat back and waited. The result was only moderately better.
"Judith?"
"Yes."
"I ... love ... her and that."
"Good."
Janet bit her tongue and waited and waited.
"She's my f i a n c e e."
"Wonderful Maurie."
"You're not upset?"
"No you ding dong, I'm really pleased."
"Oh."
Janet could wait no longer and proceeded with the gentlest calmest voice she could find.
"Her name is Judith and ... ?"
"Yes, Judith."
"Where did you meet?"
"At work."
"I see. ... Her work?"
"Yes."
"And what does she do?"
"She's a waitress."
"In a restaurant?"
"Yes."
"Whose restaurant?"

"My restaurant, well not then but now ..."

"You bought a restaurant?"

"Yes."

"Why? You know nothing about cooking or fine dining or ...."

"I bought it cause she worked there and then I could ... you know ... see her again."

"It didn't occur to you that you could just go back there and have another meal and ask her out?"

"No. ... I suppose that would have been smart but ... you know ..."

"Yes, I know."

"I didn't tell her at first, I thought it might look like, you know ... like ... I was trying to buy her."

"Maurie, that's a great insight."

"Really?"

"Yes, really. So what's she like?"

"She's nice, really nice ... to me and everyone really, she's a really nice person."

Janet, thinking Maurie was on the verge of expressing his deepest thoughts, waited.

"She doesn't mind ... you know."

"Doesn't mind what?"

"That I'm not very smart."

"Oh Maurie, you're a successful farmer, people say you have a talent for selecting the best breeding stock, they say you're ..."

"They laugh at me cause I say stupid things."

"Yes, sometime they do, but mostly it's a mixture of being very fond of you and laughing because sometimes you are very very funny even if you didn't mean to be."

"That's how it is when she laughs except she hugs me and sometimes if I've said something really stupid she tickles me and we ..."

"I'm sure you do, Maurie I'm so pleased, she does sound wonderful."

"Yes. And she's smart too, she has ideas for a restaurant where the service is really fast and people can eat there or take their meal away in a bag ... and"

"There's more?"

"Yes, she wants to serve emu meals on a bun with salad."

"Really?"

Yes, we've built the first one in Kalgoorlie. I've got a picture.
Maurie took a photograph from his pocket and placed it in front
of Janet.

"Maurie, this is wonderful, this is like a ... like a treat that

everyone can afford."

"That's what Ted said, I didn't want to tell him cause I thought
he'd laugh at me but he didn't."

"What did he say?"

"He said it was about time someone did something that
everyone could enjoy."

"Ted said that?"

"Yes, he's different these days ... a bit quieter and a lot ...
nicer."

Madelaine Cox-Carter

Madelaine was the only child of Mildred and John, she had inherited her father's passion for writing and her mother's passion for equality of opportunity. In 1976 she had tearfully laid both her parents to rest. John had developed an untreatable cancer and Mildred lost the will to live after his death and was struck down by a simple case of influenza.

She had adored them both and spent as much time as she could with them in their final weeks and months. John had tried to dictate an opinion piece about the 1975 oil shocks which he wanted titled as 'The Beginning of the End' he provided a vague outline and intended to contrast the fate of the average worker with the fate of the financiers, he died before he could flesh out the detail.

Madelaine had taken his personal papers and notebooks to try and finish the story but there was simply not enough detail to complete the task. While pouring over the neatly labelled boxes she relived many memorable events in Australian life; she remembered the raging and the passion as her father wrote article after article about injustice, corruption and scandal. As she delved further back she recognised the source material for the humorous anecdotes that had filled her childhood, among them a fairly complete telling of the Great Emu War with its colourful cast of characters.

As a rising star in Australian film production she knew she could make it into a feature to rival The Adventures of Barry McKenzie.

She proceeded to write a script.

The End

Gordon Cope

Thanks and Recognition

Benjamin Thorn, the most erudite person I know and my collaborator on the original film script which took the story to the 'happy ending' just beyond the triumph of the registration of the gold claim. Also the most annoyingly thorough and accurate editor on the planet.

Mari Grantun who read and commented and gave endless support and encouragement.

Simon Mellor who provided the front cover and the other illustrations.
He asked how long the book was, I replied it was about 400 pages. He looked staggered and said that in his first book he told the whole story in 28 pages including illustrations. 'What do you do with all the poo from all the animals in the zoo' is bound to become a classic in children's literature.

Garry Slocombe who also read the text and made many helpful comments.

http://www.creativespirits.info/aboriginalculture/history/
aboriginal-history-timeline-1900-1969#ixzz42xIRIoY6
For the many lesser known tales of Aboriginal activity.

WW II Maps of Europe By historicair 22:15, 19 February 2007 (UTC) - US Military Academy, CC BY-SA 3.0,
https://commons.wikimedia.org/w/index.php?curid=1695685

Afterword

The marvellous art of intertwining fact and fiction has sadly become the nuisance of fake news, so I feel compelled to make the following declaration.

Most of the real events are listed below.

There are many actual personages from the period but the characterisations are not necessarily accurate.

Western Australia does have a wheat belt but no adjacent stone country.

The Stirling Ranges are a magnificent national treasure.

There was a plague of emus in 1932.

The army was dispatched to shoot them, they shot relatively few.

The report from the commander is in the Parliamentary Hansard.

There was a successful secession movement.

The referendum result was sent to the Privy Council for legal determination.

The 1933 state election did see all the Ministers and the Premier lose their seats.

There was a farmers strike.

There was a Grain Authority.

There was a Great Depression.

The was a Second World War.

There have subsequently been Western Australian entrepreneurs who were as successful as Robert Robert but certainly not in the period concerned.

The historical events concerning Aboriginal People have been faithfully recorded including the reprehensible actions of the Western Australian State Government and the delivery of the petition to the German Consulate.

The titbits of history and the metaphorical anecdotes like the first cyclotron and the Russian train catastrophe are also accurate.

The author welcomes correspondence via

www.gordoncope.com.au

Gordon

The Great Emu War

Gordon Cope

The Great Emu War

Gordon Cope

Made in the USA
Middletown, DE
03 December 2023

43910784R00196